For the Love
of a Squire

by

Virginie Marconato

For the Love of a Squire

Cover Art by *Lisa Dawn MacDonald*

The Wild Rose Press, Inc.
PO Box 708
Adams Basin, NY 14410-0708
Visit us at www.thewildrosepress.com

Publishing History
First Edition, 2023
Trade Paperback ISBN 978-1-5092-5233-6
Digital ISBN 978-1-5092-5234-3

Published in the United States of America

"What do you want? You clearly came to meet me with a purpose in mind..." she started, her voice slightly hoarse.

Oh, after declaring they did not have anything to tell each other, now she was baiting him because she did not want the interlude to end. Better and better.

"I did, but I'm not sure you will want to hear it, my lady."

"Stop calling me 'my lady'!" Beatrice suddenly snapped. It plunged a dagger in her heart to hear the words in Edward's mouth. So cold, so impersonal.

Remote.

This man had held her in his arms and kissed her with fiery passion. He had made her moan in pleasure. And now he was calling her "my lady" as if she were an old dowager he had no more than a passing acquaintance with! How was she supposed to bear it?

"What would you like me to call you?" Edward asked, a dangerous edge to his voice. It seemed his own temper was fraying.

"You know my name. Use it."

He bared his teeth in a parody of the smile she remembered. "Yes, I do know your name. Perhaps I will use it in front of everyone, in front of your husband. Why not? Since you are ordering me to, I would be a fool not to."

"I didn't order anything."

"You did. As you have every right to. You are a great lady, and I am but a squire. I deserve no less. I expect no less."

Praise for Virginie Marconato

**Other Books by Virginie Marconato
published by The Wild Rose Press, Inc.**

Shadows in the Mist
Dark Highlander

Prologue

England, October 1464

"Do you know that I am dying of desire for you?"

The voice, rich like silk, slid over Beatrice's skin.

She let out a delighted gurgle of laughter and could not bring herself to reprimand Edward for the daring words. By rights he should not entertain such thoughts, never mind utter them out loud, but though she should be incensed, she felt no outrage. She loved to hear how much he desired her, for she desired him just as much.

"You must not speak like this, Edward, it's not right," she said, blushing.

His handsome face darkened, the ever-present pride ready to surge.

"Why should I not?" He drew back from her, the blue in his eyes becoming thundery. "Because you are Sir Hugh's daughter and I am no one? I thought you did not care about such matters. Need I remind you that you were the one who came to me, my lady?"

The use of her title was like a slap in the face. Beatrice could not bear to think she had hurt him. She had not meant it like that at all.

"No, Edward, I told you, I don't care about all that. I thought you would have believed me by now." She nestled back in his arms, and to her relief, he did not push her away. "I said it wasn't right because when you speak

1

like this it makes me desperate for your touch," she whispered, speaking against his neck. "It's not fair."

A grunt left Edward's throat. Beatrice felt the vibration of it against her lips, awakening all the nerve endings in her body.

"Now you are the one who is not being fair," he growled. "You know how much I want you and you speak about being desperate for my touch! What man could hear such a declaration without wanting to have you, I wonder?"

"I know not. I know no other man than you," she answered ingenuously, pressing herself more closely against his flank.

"Well, I'm telling you. I cannot have you looking at me so provocatively and rubbing yourself against me without feeling the need to take you again, lady or no lady."

"Then take me, Edward. I am yours."

He shook his head in regret and purposefully stared at the ceiling. "No. I cannot take you again, not now. It was your first time. You will be sore."

This concern for her well-being made Beatrice all warm inside, but she found herself wishing he would not be so considerate for once. "I am not sore, I swear," she said, trailing a finger on his smooth chest. "I've never felt better."

In truth, and although the fact surprised her, she wasn't lying. Edward had taken her maidenhead with such skill that the pain of it had hardly registered. This first possession had only given her a taste for more. Despite her lack of knowledge on the subject she suspected she had not quite seen the full glory of what lovemaking could be. Far from being sore, she was desperate for him to show her just how glorious the connection between a man and a woman could be.

"I am not sore, Edward," she repeated, reveling in the intimacy of using his name whilst lying in his arms. "Please, love me again."

He turned his head to her. "Or?" he asked, half-amused, half-aroused. "What will you do if I don't?"

"Well, I suppose I will have to go and find another—"

He placed a hand on her mouth, silencing the outrageous boast. "Don't say it," he warned, the fierceness in his voice almost alarming. "I could not bear to hear it."

Beatrice lifted his hand from her mouth and smiled. "Even if you knew it was a lie?" she asked before planting a kiss on his wrist. How could he imagine she would want another man after what they had just done?

"Even so. Not now, not when you so shamelessly forced me to do what I swore I would never do."

"I'm glad one of us was shameless," she said in a breath. "Or we wouldn't be here right now."

This comment did nothing to appease Edward. "Well, we *shouldn't* be here right now, in bed together."

Beatrice knew his sense of honor was stronger than hers, and he was probably right. Their affair would be condemned by all. Not only was she far above him in status but she had been a virgin. In the circumstances, she should never have given herself to him. Still, she could not bring herself to feel guilty. Being in Edward's arms felt right, and that was all that mattered.

"Look at the king, marrying a near commoner for love," she said as inspiration struck. The news of King Edward's shocking mésalliance was all the country could talk about and had inflamed her imagination. If the king of England could brave his counselors and risk public condemnation to follow his heart's desire, why could she, who didn't matter nearly as much, not do the same?

"Our situations are hardly comparable," Edward countered with an irritated movement of the head. He would not be so easily convinced.

"It is. It is time for a self-made man, it is time for new things, for following one's heart. Look at the queen's mother, marrying her first husband's squire for love once she was widowed," Beatrice persisted, warming to her theme.

"She was universally despised for it," Edward reminded her harshly. "And I'm not even a squire, only a stable hand."

"And I am only Sir Hugh's daughter, not a mighty duchess," she replied with a smile.

There would be a way out of this. Suddenly she felt sure of it.

Edward Hardthorne looked at the girl lying against his flank in total abandon, her golden-brown eyes flashing in mischief. Without her headpiece and precious gown, she could have been any of the women who usually shared his bed. Of course that was the exact opposite of who she really was. She was no milkmaid or kitchen scullion—she was Sir Hugh's daughter.

Beatrice de Courcy was utterly out of bounds to a man like him—or should have been.

Only the wily minx had other ideas.

That afternoon she had come to find him in his room and behaved with such audacity that he'd had no choice but to give in to his desire for her. After weeks of fighting it, he had finally surrendered.

Surrender was perhaps not the right word, as she had given him little choice in the matter.

What she had done earlier had robbed him of all powers of thought. It had not taken him long to see that Lady Beatrice was a determined woman, but her daring had literally taken his breath away. He had been so shocked to see the daughter of the lord of the castle kneeling at his feet in her shameless pursuit of him that for a moment he had not thought to stop her. Then he had been too dazzled by the feel of her mouth on him to put an end to the seduction.

Although he was by no means inexperienced, no woman had ever dared to do such a thing to him. That Lady Beatrice should be the first to introduce him to this particular delight, Edward would never have imagined in his wildest dreams.

After a moment of excruciating pleasure, he had given in, knowing she would not stop until she'd had what she wanted from him. Better he taught her what she was desperate for him to teach her than allow himself to use her so selfishly. He would never forget the triumphant gleam in her eyes when he had raised her to her feet and tumbled her onto the bed with a groan.

The same gleam was flashing in her eyes now, making them sparkle with anticipation.

"Please, Edward," she begged, closing her hand around his hard manhood.

Once again he was unable to resist her. If she wanted him, then she would have him. He wanted her too much to think levelly.

He positioned himself above her, careful to rest his weight on his arms.

"It shouldn't hurt this time."

"It hardly did last time," she assured him, ever the bold vixen.

"It should also bring you more satisfaction," he growled, annoyed at his poor performance. Their first lovemaking had been a rushed affair, mind-numbing pleasure crashing through him before he had time to ensure she was fully satisfied. It had been good for her, he knew, but not as good as it could, and *should* be. This time, however, he would have more control, and he would bring her to the heights of passion if it killed him.

"Show me."

"My lady. Your wish is my command."

Beatrice smiled when Edward slid into her heated flesh. It felt right, as if it was meant to be, and she cursed herself for waiting so long before forcing his hand. What had she been thinking! They could have had weeks of this!

Instinctively she wrapped her legs around his muscular back, wanting to meet his thrusts. He groaned in approval. The daring of her actions made her catch her breath. Her behavior was that of the most seasoned harlot, not that of a lady, it was undeniable, but it only added to her pleasure. Soon she felt all the fibers of her body ignite at the same time and rush toward a heated point between her legs. Suddenly made afraid by the strength of the torrent trying to burst out of her, she almost asked Edward to stop. Surely this was not normal? It felt as if she was going to pass out from the intensity of the sensation.

"I…Something is…"

"It's all right," he whispered, closing a hand over her breast. "Let it come."

A long moan escaped Beatrice's lips and she dug her nails into Edward's flanks, keeping him as close to her as possible. A moment later she shattered in a blinding rush of light.

Dear Lord, so *this* was what he meant earlier when she had asked what pleasure should feel like! 'Like an irresistible force catapulting you into oblivion, heating your whole body and turning your skin inside out,' he'd said. Well, he hadn't lied about that.

She lay panting for a while, the bewildering intensity of the experience having taken her breath away.

A moment later Edward came to lie next to her, his own breathing ragged. "Now you have truly experienced pleasure," he murmured in her ear, stroking her hair gently.

She gave a lazy smile, too spent to do more. "Yes. I think I have."

The mind-blowing sensation soon became familiar as, over the next few weeks, she came to find Edward at every opportunity.

They met as often as they could, their bodies catching fire every time they touched. Though she would have loved for him to come and find her first, Beatrice was always the one going to him. He was never so presumptuous as to assume she would welcome his touch. Oh, but welcome it she did! Everywhere she lured him, and every day she would find an opportunity to go to him.

She could not get enough of him, even when there was no time for more than a stolen kiss or a whispered declaration.

It was madness, of course. If her parents found out what she was doing with their stable hand they would...

She shook her head. The proposition was so outrageous she wasn't sure what they would do. One thing was for sure. She would spend the rest of her life paying for it.

Still, she was unable to stop herself. Day after day she came to find Edward. She needed his presence, his touch, like the air she breathed.

One afternoon she came to him running, not ablaze with anticipation but breathless with worry.

"What is it?" he asked, enfolding her into his arms. "What happened?"

"Nothing. Nothing." Beatrice nuzzled against her lover, rubbing her cheek in the crook of his neck, pressing herself against his chest, inhaling his warm, comforting smell, clinging to him like a drowning woman about to be swept away by the current. "I suddenly had a dreadful premonition. What is going to happen to us? What *can* happen?"

"Hush." Beatrice heard the tension in Edward's voice. He wrapped his arms tightly around her and stroked her back, but he did not try to reassure her with empty promises, and he did not tell her that everything would be all right.

Her heart plummeted.

He agreed with her then. Nothing could ever come of this folly.

Though his heart was breaking, Edward stayed silent because he knew Beatrice was right, there was no future for them. The thought had been on his mind constantly for the past month, ever since he had given in to the desire she inspired in him. He had ruined her and he would never be able to set things right. He was a stable hand. He had nothing to offer her except himself.

It was not enough, would never be enough.

Many a time he had tried to put an end to this doomed affair, but Beatrice had ignored his arguments, swept his objections aside. He had prayed for help, but none had come. Eventually he had ceased trying and given himself wholly to his need for her. What he was doing would be universally condemned, but he simply could not leave Beatrice, not while she still wanted him. He belonged to her, heart and soul. The idea of giving her up was enough to tear him in half.

"Would you run away with me?"

The enormity of the words only registered when he heard them spoken out loud. Edward stared at Beatrice in utter bewilderment. Was he mad? Had he just dared ask his lord and master's daughter to run away with him, without even offering her marriage?

"I—"

"Meet me at the oak tonight. We need to talk about this," Edward interrupted. It was not fair to ask her to give an answer on such a momentous decision at a moment's notice. It was too much, too soon, and even more pointedly, he wasn't ready to hear her refusal just yet.

He needed to hold on to the mad possibility that there could be a future for them for a while longer.

"Oh, Edward…"

Beatrice bit her bottom lip and her eyes became huge with intent. Dismayed, Edward understood that she was about to tell him she loved him. She had never said the words out loud, even if he had often sensed she wanted to, even if it had been implied in every gesture.

He, in any case, had never dared to speak about his feelings for her.

"You mustn't think like this, my lady." He stopped

her before she could commit the irreparable. The situation was bad enough as it was. They needed to think rationally. Hugh de Courcy's daughter should not be telling a stable hand that she loved him, and he should not be asking her to abandon everything she was entitled to and run away with him.

"The idea of losing you frightens me more than death," she whispered.

Losing him...

The words sent a chill to his soul. Had he misunderstood the purpose of her visit? Had she come to tell him it was over after all? Had her talk of a premonition been nothing more than a gentle way of preparing him for the inevitable? The idea made his shoulders slump in defeat. If she had decided she ought to put an end to their affair, then he would have no choice but to accept her decision.

"I will see you tonight at the oak," she said when she saw he was frozen in uncertainty.

Then she placed a kiss on his mouth and smiled.

"Tonight, Edward. Make sure you come."

****

"What's this? Lady Beatrice giving assignations to stable lads! Fie, your father would be most displeased. He's been looking for you all morning and all the while you were dallying with servants! Most shocking indeed!"

Beatrice started. While she was pondering on Edward's extraordinary offer, her uncle had sprung out of nowhere and was now blocking her retreat.

"Why is my father looking for me?" she asked, doing her best to appear innocent of any wrongdoing when the heat of Edward's embrace still warmed her body.

Sir Robert seemed to hesitate, then pursed his lips, clearly relishing the idea of imparting the news himself. "He wants to announce your marriage with me."

Beatrice went rigid with shock.

Marriage? To Sir Robert?

"I… We cannot marry! You are my uncle!"

"I was married to your late aunt for two years, so it is not quite the same. We do not share the same blood," he countered with a sideways smile. "We have received a papal dispensation for our union, thanks to your mother's efforts, so there will be no impediment. She is most keen on the match, as am I."

Beatrice's head started to spin. A papal dispensation would have taken weeks to get. If they had it in their possession already, it meant that this marriage had been planned for a while, yet no one had thought to inform her of the fact.

"You are older than my father!" The protest left her mouth before she could think.

"I am thirty-nine. Your father is forty, so no, I am not," Sir Robert said as if this answer should reassure her. It did not.

"Mayhap, but I am only seventeen!"

"And already enough of a slut to let a filthy stable hand paw you!" he hissed, taking her arm roughly. All pretense at bonhomie had vanished in a heartbeat. "I say it's time we got you married, before he ruins you completely."

The slur on her honor was lost as Beatrice realized that, thankfully, he was unaware that her reputation was already compromised. She allowed herself to breathe a little more freely. Perhaps everything would be all right after all. For as soon as she had been threatened with marriage to Sir Robert, she had made up her mind.

She would flee with Edward tonight. His offer, shocking as it may be, could not have come at a better time and gave her the strength to stand up to her uncle.

"Forgive me but I have no wish to marry you!" She snatched her arm away from his grasp, but he planted himself in front of her before she could leave.

"Because of your filthy stable boy, you mean? You will never meet with that dog again, do you hear? If I ever see him anywhere near you, I will kill him," Sir Robert snarled. "You will obey your parents, you will become Lady Devance, and you will have the good grace to like it. Now go and see your father. I should think you have kept him waiting long enough. When you are my wife this will not happen, do you hear? You will never keep me waiting! In all things, you will do my bidding."

Before she could move, he put his hand on her heaving bosom and gave a squeeze. Beatrice stifled a scream of horror.

"Please," she croaked, screwing her eyes shut. In a moment she would be sick.

"Oh, you want more, do you?" he said, deliberately misunderstand her meaning. "Tell me, did you let the pup touch you like I am touching you? Did you like it?" The hand traveled upward to touch the naked skin at her throat.

It took Beatrice all her determination not to kick and shout at him. His hand on her flesh was like a searing burn, but if Edward heard her struggle he would come to her aid, and then she would have to watch as he was executed for killing Sir Robert. No one would listen to her explanations, no one would believe he had only defended her honor. No one would care that they loved each other.

She bit the inside of her mouth so hard she tasted blood.

"Good," Sir Robert said, seeing the effort it cost her not to push him away. "In time you will learn to tolerate me."

"You are mistaken. And I will never love you," she said stiffly, emboldened by the knowledge that she would be long gone in the morning.

A mirthless laugh answered her. "This, my dear, is the least of my problems."

Chapter 1

England, April 1471, six years later

The ground opened under Beatrice's feet.

In front of her, his head bowed in a respectful attitude, was the last man she'd ever expected to see again, even if he was constantly in her thoughts. He was staring straight ahead, making a point of avoiding her gaze. But it was him. There could be no doubt about it. She wavered on her feet.

Edward.

Her Edward.

Despite their cruel separation, she had never stopped thinking of him as hers. Not a day had gone by without her hoping they could be reunited again. And yet now he was here, she wished he had not come, or at least not like this, not in front of her husband.

If I ever see him anywhere near you I will kill him.

Sir Robert's words rang in her mind, and she stole a glance at him to see what his reaction was. He never gave servants more than a passing look, though, so it was just about possible he had not identified Edward as the man he had sworn to kill all those years ago. Indeed, one look was enough to convince her that her husband had not recognized in this proud squire the stable hand who had stolen her heart when she was still a maid in her father's castle.

In truth, it was difficult for her to believe the man in front of them in his refined velvet tunic was the same as the coltish, somewhat unkempt youth who had captured her imagination and made a woman of her. Only someone who had been passionately in love with him would have recognized him at first glance. Edward looked more mature, changed by years of combat training and hardship—and all the more handsome for it.

His gleaming hair, the color of a burst of sunlight, was shorter, not quite to his shoulders. The expression in his cornflower-blue eyes had hardened, and the mouth she had kissed hundreds of times was set in a firm line. In any other man, the effect would have been forbidding. But because he was Edward, it only succeeded in making him more virile and irresistible.

What was he doing here, in her home?

She blinked a few times, wondering for a moment if her mind was not playing tricks with her. For more than six years, her overheated imagination had conjured up his image at every opportunity, clinging to the memory of their time together. Then Edward shook his head in a gesture she would have recognized anywhere, and the last of her doubts vanished.

It was him. He was back to her, but for what purpose she did not know.

She forced herself to ignore the man who would always be the love of her life and turned to the one she had been forced to marry. Sir Robert was unusually affable, talking to a tall man who had identified himself as Sir William Bartlett.

"You are welcome to stay here for as long as you need. If your wife is Lady Margery Raglan, then you are family!" Sir Robert boomed, pleased at the connection.

"I confess that is why we have so opportunely called on your hospitality, my lord. Some men in our company are badly hurt, and we could all do with a rest after a hard battle."

Behind him, a dozen men nodded in approval, each of them bearing some sort of injury. Even Edward's moves seemed less graceful than Beatrice remembered. Her sharp eyes had detected a limp when he walked in but, thankfully, he seemed otherwise unscathed.

Automatically her hand went to her swollen belly, and she felt the child inside her quicken, as if to offer its support.

What must Edward be thinking?

As he took in the scene in front of him, Edward found it almost impossible to school his features into the bland deference he owed their host. Inwardly he was seething with resentment and pondering the wisdom of suggesting Sir Robert Devance's castle for their well-earned rest.

The temptation had been impossible to resist, but he was quickly regretting his decision.

Try as he might, he could not detach his eyes from Beatrice's rounded stomach. Of course he knew she was now married to Sir Robert and had a daughter already, but he hadn't known about this new pregnancy. Seeing the unavoidable proof of another man bedding her was enough to send him mad with powerless fury. All these years spent away from her had not dimmed the feelings he harbored for her.

If only her betrayal had been enough to kill them off once and for all!

But alas, his pathetic heart refused to heed his pride, and although her true nature had been exposed in no uncertain terms, he still thought of her as the only woman he would ever love.

He had been stunned to be told he had to leave her father's castle, but with hindsight perhaps he should have seen it coming. How could he have thought that a man like him meant anything to the daughter of the lord of the manor? Beatrice de Courcy, only child of a wealthy lord, was born for higher things than to be a stable hand's lover.

And indeed, the day after his departure, she had married Sir Robert, her own uncle, as had been arranged all along. It was an alliance which brought her everything she would have had to give up had she run away with him that night. It had been folly for him to even suggest it, and he had never expected her to go through with it, but still it had destroyed him to be rejected without so much as a goodbye, to be shown so unequivocally that he had been nothing but an amusement for her.

As he lay in bed recovering from the beating inflicted on him, he had sworn he would never try to see her again, as it could only add to his humiliation. Yet here he was, a guest in her husband's house, about to accept his hospitality. He would be eating the man's bread, drinking his wine, answering his questions—and all the while he would be lusting after his wife.

For he still desired Beatrice.

No matter how much he was striving not to, how long it had been since their last meeting, how inadvisable and dishonorable it was or how much he kept telling himself he hated her, now that she was in front of him, the reality of his feelings hit him square on the chest.

He did not hate this woman. Far from it.

He ached for her, with every fiber of his being.

****

Toying with her slice of beef, Beatrice was doing her best to listen to Sir William's account of the battle of Barnet without betraying her increasing agitation.

"The king fought like a lion, earning himself a resounding victory at the tip of his sword."

"Warwick is dead, is he not?"

"Yes. Alas, the king had no choice but to kill his once most faithful supporter." Sir William shook his head regretfully. "We all knew it would be a fight to the death this time, and indeed, it was ruthless. I sustained a severe injury on my arm, and there wasn't a single man who walked away from the battlefield without a cut or a missing limb."

The blood oozing onto her trencher made Beatrice's stomach churn. Suddenly she imagined Edward stabbed, pierced by an arrow, or hacked to pieces on a battlefield. In all the years spent trying to imagine his whereabouts, she had never once thought he would find himself in the middle of a fight, since she couldn't have dreamed he would become a squire. But now she was told he could have died ten times over.

She tasted bile in her throat and pushed her food away from her.

Sir William turned to her. "Apologies, my lady. I should have refrained from telling such gruesome stories in front of ladies, especially those nearing their term, as you are."

"Nonsense!" Sir Robert cut in. "If my wife cannot countenance such tales of heroism, then I suggest she leave."

Far from being offended at his blatant rudeness, Beatrice seized on the chance to leave without raising his suspicion. "With your permission, I will retire and leave you to discuss the battle at will."

Her husband waved her away like an irritating fly.

Once out of the great hall, she walked straight to the inner bailey in search of Edward. Sir Robert was busy, so he would not see her in his company. Despite her earlier resolve not to seek Edward out, for his safety, suddenly she could not bear the idea of him leaving the castle without having exchanged a single word with her.

The laughter of inebriated men reached her ears. She spotted a group of them standing by an open fire next to the stables. Unsurprisingly, the first one to draw her attention was Edward. The flames gilded the long, blond hair on his shoulders and made shadows dance on his tunic. He looked almost surreal, like a creature sent from the deepest pits of a fiery world to torment her.

Her breath caught in her throat.

He was really here within the castle walls, breathing the same air as she was, not the lover from her dreams or a ghost from the past, but a man of flesh and bones. If she took but a dozen steps, she would stand in front of him. If she stood on tiptoes, she would reach high enough to kiss his warm neck, if he chose to dip his head at the same moment, their lips would meet.

She shivered at the thought. It was all she had dreamed about for years, but now that kissing him was a physical possibility, she could not deal with it. Not to mention that the consequences of such a rash action were too potentially devastating.

In any case, it would not happen tonight. Right now, the men were urging him to leave the castle walls.

"Let's go and pay our respects to Mistress Annie and her girls," someone suggested. She recognized the castle steward's voice. A coarse man at the best of times, he sounded even worse after a few drinks. "You can tell us what you think. I bet they have more stamina than your pale northern lasses."

Beatrice's face flamed red. He was inviting the men of Sir William's retinue to visit one of the local stew houses. The thought of Edward spending the night in the arms of one of the women working there tore her in half. As soon as he walked into the house they would all pounce on him, unable to believe their luck at the arrival of this choice customer.

Someone made a jest and the men laughed heartily. Sick to her stomach, Beatrice slipped away into the shadows. It had been a mistake to come here.

Edward turned in time to see a silhouette disappear into the darkness. Beatrice? He would not be surprised if she decided to come to find him tonight. She had always been a determined woman, heedless of conventions and propriety. He had found that out to his cost when she had pursued him relentlessly.

But what was she hoping to achieve by coming to him now? What could possibly come of an encounter between them? She had made her choice long ago, marrying her uncle for the prestige the union afforded her rather than following her feelings.

Seeing her dressed in all her finery, pregnant with another man's child, mistress of a well-kept castle and utterly unmoved by his presence, had done what years of rumination had not managed to do. It had made him see that the girl he had once loved was well and truly gone. Beatrice had been a mischievous, headstrong, enchanting little imp, while Lady Devance was a respectable, haughty, married woman who would want nothing more than to forget she had once given herself to a stable hand.

She had not so much as acknowledged his presence when he bowed to her earlier that afternoon. It had stung more than a show of anger would have.

Next to him, the castle steward made a joke that set his teeth on edge, and he found himself wishing Beatrice hadn't come. The discussion was not for a woman's ears, and he didn't want her to think he was as coarse as these men. She thought him well below her dignity already. He did not need to give her more ammunition against him. But then…what should it matter what she thought of him? He should not want to spare her from the men's crudeness or worry what her opinion was!

Irritated by his weakness, he informed the men that he would not join them in their expedition.

"You are one of a kind, Hardthorne," one of Sir William's men told him, wiping his mouth with the back of his hand. "Don't you feel the need to satisfy your urges after a hard battle? I should think we've earned it and more."

"Leave it. It's probably for the best. A strapping lad like him!" another man interposed with a grimace. "He would not give any of us a chance. If he came, the women would flock to him as one and not charge extra for making sure he left barely able to stand!"

"Yeah, and I for one will need more than a quick fumble to be satisfied tonight," an even drunker man said.

"God help the poor girls," Edward muttered under his breath.

He left without another word. His body was taut with need, but only one woman could have satisfied him, a woman he had never had any right to desire.

Married and heavily pregnant, she had never been more out of his reach.

****

Sitting amongst her ladies, Beatrice reclined in the shade. After a sleepless night, she was feeling tired but restless. She would have to find a way to see Edward soon, for she would not survive another moment without speaking to him.

As to what they would tell each other, that was another matter.

How do you open a conversation with a man you haven't seen for nigh on seven years, a man who asked you to run away with him the last time you saw each other? The man who took your maidenhead, the man you have never stopped loving?

The women by her side were sorting out colored threads for a new tapestry. Unable to muster any interest for the project, Beatrice directed her gaze to the fast-flowing river below, and her mind started to drift off, as had become her wont, to the time she had spent with Edward. One day they had gone riding farther away than usual, and he had shown her the valley in the distance.

"My parents live there."

The houses by the river all looked rather run down. Beatrice stared at them in amazement. This was where he had grown up? Never had the difference between them been more vividly illustrated.

"Yes, I know what you're thinking. Please don't say anything," he murmured, and she understood that he regretted showing her who he really was. Not wishing to cause him any further embarrassment, she steered her mare back to the castle without a word.

But she never forgot the little village.

When she had been unable to find Edward anywhere on the morning of her wedding, despair had overwhelmed her, so much so that she had considered going to his parents' house to enquire after him. If she asked around the village, she was bound to find them... In the end she had not had the opportunity to carry out such a daring enterprise. Sir Robert had taken her away as soon as they were married.

She still remembered the wrench of feeling that ripped through her as she rode away from the place where she had been so happy with Edward. For her parents she had not spared one thought. They had sold her to Sir Robert and so were dead to her.

The pain of losing Edward had never lessened.

Her days were a long succession of regrets, but the nights were even worse. Lying in bed, she would torture herself over the memory of his hands running all over her body. Worst of all were the moments Sir Robert came to fulfill his marital duty. Then she would lie still as a corpse, trying to forget the fact that the man laboring over her was not the one she wanted inside her. Not once during their marriage had she met his gaze whilst he possessed her body. He never commented on the fact, satisfied with her passive acceptance.

Every time he left her she curled up in a ball and wept bitter tears.

Beatrice closed her eyes, determined to hide her distress from her ladies. What use would it do to relive such painful moments? After a while, she felt herself slipping into a delicious torpor.

"My, look at that one..." Lady Margaret sounded slightly breathless.

"What about the dark one over there?" Lady Elizabeth answered with a giggle.

"What say you of the big one in the middle? Look at those muscles!"

Beatrice frowned. Muscles? What had that to do with embroidery? She opened her eyes. The ladies had dropped their threads and were engaged in a far more licentious activity, eyeing up a group of men getting ready for a dip in the river below. This was highly improper, but she did not have the heart to put a stop to their peeping. The men paraded in front of them, proud to show off their bodies. Some were tall, others powerfully built. A few had golden skin, one boasted remarkably graceful moves.

Then she saw one man who combined all of these features with arresting good looks and hair as brilliant as the sun.

Edward.

Slowly, he walked out of the water and for a moment Beatrice forgot to breathe.

He stood out from the group of men as surely as if he had been carved by a master sculptor while the others were merely half-hewn blocks of stone. His body was strong, chiseled to perfection yet supple and supremely elegant. He laughed and shook his head, sending a sprinkling of water droplets flying into the air.

Next to her there was a chorus of exclamations.

"Now, that is a man," Lady Margaret said in an awed whisper.

"I'll say!"

Beatrice gulped. Her ladies reveled at the sight of him, but they had no idea how much more there was to Edward than a perfect body.

They didn't know his voice could send shivers to the deepest recesses of a woman's soul. They did not realize the skin on his chest was as smooth as a newborn's cheek, and the muscles under it as taut as a finely strung bow. She knew his body by heart, having caressed, kissed, and licked every inch of it more than once. She knew the way his neck tensed when he was poised over her, the way his back muscles rippled when he moved inside her, how his eyes closed and his mouth opened when he reached his pleasure. She knew the feel and sound of his desire, the smell, the taste of it. She knew everything there was to know about this man, and she would be haunted by the memories of their moments together for as long as she lived.

She swallowed hard, unable to detach her eyes from him.

His voice reached her, faint in the distance. "You don't know what you're talking about!"

The familiarity between him and Sir William made her wonder how a mere squire could be so at ease with his master, but of course Edward was nothing if not engaging. It was impossible to be with him without falling utterly under his charm. The contrast between the way their respective lives had evolved made her chest squeeze in pain. He had gone from stable hand to being a respected squire in the service of an honorable gentleman, while she had been married to a man she hated.

He seemed utterly carefree, while she was drowning in a sea of misery.

"I will retire. I feel a headache coming on." Immediately her ladies made to get up, but she stopped them with a raised hand. "Please stay. Enjoy yourselves.

It's not so often such an opportunity is presented to us."

No one insisted on going with her, and she made her way up the slope alone.

Edward watched Beatrice return slowly to the castle. Although she would be unaware of it, he had been watching her all the time. Even without her great belly he would have recognized her anywhere. Amidst her ladies dressed in a rainbow of colors, she had sparkled like the sun.

Her innate grace alone set her aside from the group. Given the distance, he could not see her pearl-white skin or her rich brown eyes, but they were imprinted in his mind too vividly for him to forget them. He had felt himself grow hard just thinking about the way that flawless skin flushed and those eyes became hazy when pleasure overcame her. Mercifully, his groin was hidden under water and he was soon able to regain mastery over his body.

What about her? What had her reaction been when he had appeared bare-chested from the river? She had told him countless times that she liked his body, but even if she had not, her actions would have made that clear. The memory of the way she had looked at him, and given herself so freely, so shamelessly, left him no peace.

It had been perfection.

At first, he had been daunted to have her in his bed—her, a lady of rank—but every time they'd met she had answered his caresses with a boldness that had taken his breath away. Being with her had felt as natural as breathing. When they made love, she always wrapped her legs around him, drawing him close as if she could not get enough of him. When he undressed in front of her, she always explored his body with her gaze first, then with her mouth, leaving no part untouched.

The way her eyes glowed during their lovemaking, her astonished cries of pleasure, her teasing caresses and whispered words of desire, everything about that woman had made him wild.

She had scratched his back, she had licked his neck. She had kissed him hard, she had sent him utterly mad with longing. No other woman had gone to him with such abandon, with such joy. It was as if they were meant to be together.

Except that it had all been an illusion. They weren't meant to be together at all. They should never even have touched.

Inevitably, one day, she had realized it, and put an end to the madness to follow her true destiny, leaving him to try and deal with the awful loss alone.

There was just one spark of hope, one thing that told him the mighty Lady Devance might not be as indifferent to him as she was striving to be.

Yesterday in the great hall, after they had been dismissed, he had not resisted throwing one last glance in her direction. It had been brief, but for that single heartbeat Beatrice had sent her gaze straight into his and he had known, without a doubt, that not only had she recognized him but she still desired him. There had been no ambiguity in the molten brown eyes. He knew that look too well.

She was dying with the need to have him again.

The thought sent a jolt of desire shooting up his spine and a surge of hurt pride stiffened his resolve.

He was not going to let her get away with it. If she still desired him, he would make sure she felt the sting of unfulfilled need as keenly as he felt it, make sure she knew no rest while he was here. Why should he be the only one to suffer with the wanting of someone he could not have?

He watched her walk up the small hill, knowing this would be a unique opportunity to see her alone—the men were busy washing in the river, her ladies had stayed behind, her husband had gone to the next village.

Pretexting some unfinished task, he rushed back to the castle.

Chapter 2

"How long are you going to pretend you don't know me?"

Although she had been expecting, nay, *hoping* to hear it, the husky voice behind her made Beatrice shiver. After all these years it hadn't changed, and it still had the power to move her in ways she did not comprehend. She was sitting on a bench in a sunny spot hidden from view, almost as if she had contrived a secret assignation with her former lover.

Which, if she were honest with herself, was exactly what she had been doing.

Ever since she had woken that morning, finding a moment alone with Edward had been uppermost in her mind. She had dressed with an attention to detail she could rarely summon these days. Sir Robert, who barely ever looked at her, would never notice that she had chosen her most flattering gown, the gold velvet of which made her hazel eyes appear almost golden themselves, but she hoped Edward might.

She also hoped that looking her best would help her face him with some confidence.

Of course, her belly was huge and cumbersome, but this could not be helped.

When Edward spoke, Beatrice didn't look at him. She didn't even turn her head. Instead, she started plucking at the petals of the daisy she was holding.

He loves me, he loves me not.

"I am not pretending I don't know you. I just don't want anyone to guess how well I do know you," she said nervously. The threat issued by her husband years ago kept playing in her mind. If Sir Robert so much as suspected who his guest's squire really was, he would kill him on the spot. She could not allow this to happen. She could not have his death on her conscience. She had to protect him, even at the cost of her own happiness.

"I see. You are ashamed of this part of your life and you want to forget."

"No, I…" she stammered, pain stabbing at her gut. Was he being deliberately provocative, or was this what he thought? There was bitterness in his voice. Was he lashing out because he was hurt?

"Worry not, my lady. No one will know I once held you in my arms. I won't tell anyone what you did to me to persuade me to take your maidenhead," he growled.

This time Beatrice knew he meant to make her uncomfortable, but the memory of that day only made her body heat up in desire. She shivered from head to toe, remembering the honeyed taste of him under her tongue.

The daisy in her hands was suddenly reduced to shreds.

"Why are you here?" she asked, throwing away what little was left of the flower and finally turning to face Edward. She instantly saw her mistake. He had come to her bare-chested, straight from his swim in the river. Whether it was by design or because he had seized the opportunity to see her while he could, she wasn't sure. Either way it unnerved her.

She lowered her gaze to the ground, fearing she would not be able to resist the temptation to touch him if she saw him in his naked glory.

"You cannot even bear to look at me."

The contempt in his voice lacerated her.

How could he think such a thing? Surely he could see that it was in both their interest not to betray any previous acquaintance.

Not trusting herself to remain calm, Beatrice didn't answer. Edward came to place himself in front of her. With astounding confidence he lifted her chin with a crooked finger and forced her to meet his gaze. Anyone else behaving in such a manner would have been issued a stringent rebuke and their hand would have been slapped away. With Edward, it was all she could do not to take his finger in her mouth and suck at it.

"After all we've been through, you cannot even bear to look at me."

The venom in his voice, combined with the force of his blue stare, made Beatrice waver on her feet. Never had Edward spoken to her so harshly. He seemed to have grown a lot more assertive and confident since their last meeting. Certainly he would never have dared to defy her thus before.

Calling on all her inner strength, she pushed his hand away.

"I *can* look at you. But I am amazed you chose to come to me in such an unseemly state of undress."

"Why? You've seen me wearing much less," he countered with a side smile. "And you didn't seem to mind my state of undress earlier when you looked at me as if you would eat me on the spot. Don't think I missed the longing in your eyes, my lady."

A gasp escaped her lips. He dared to make her ashamed of her behavior when he was the one parading half-naked in front of her!

"Have you recovered from your exertions last night?" Beatrice chose to attack before the fight was lost. It was the only way she would survive the encounter. This new Edward unnerved her.

Last night...

Edward could not help a smile at Beatrice's question. So he had been right—she had come to find him the night before! The mysterious figure in the shadows had been her, and she had not resisted the temptation of seeing him before backing away at the last moment.

"How would you know about this? Unless of course you came to the courtyard to look for me?" he asked, determined to make her squirm.

She bit her lip when she realized her mistake. Apparently she didn't want him to know she was taking an undue interest in him. Too late. He *had* noticed.

He smiled.

"Did you choose a dirty redhead or a dark-haired hag to pleasure you?" she asked, the acid tone only making her discomfiture more obvious.

"My, such language from a lady! And why would you assume the women were all dirty or old?" he asked, at his most provocative. She deserved to worry herself over what he had done—or not done—the previous night and more. He had done the same for almost seven years.

"Are they not? I wouldn't know. You are the one who went to them, not I."

Edward stayed silent for a while, his gaze firmly on hers. As satisfactory as it was to rouse her ire, it was a waste of time. There might never be another opportunity to see her alone, and he did not want to spend it discussing an encounter that had not taken place.

"Is this all you have to tell me after all these years?" he asked bitterly. "You are asking me to describe my evening in a stew house?"

After the way they had parted, he deserved better. But Beatrice didn't seem to think she owed him any explanation, much less any apologies for the way she had treated him, and maybe she did not. He was no one. He could not pretend to anything. Why would she worry herself over a squire?

Still, it hurt.

To add pain to injury, Beatrice had never looked more beautiful than in this instant. If only maternity had spoiled her looks! He might have found it easier to deal with his feelings for her if she had looked different from the girl he remembered, but pregnancy only made her more appealing. Her eyes sparkled with a new intensity, her skin had acquired a healthy glow, and her figure had never been more voluptuous.

She had been beautiful in her youth—she was radiant as a woman.

She had also never worn such refined and costly clothes, which only highlighted the difference in status between them. Although he was not a mere stable hand anymore, the divide between them had never been greater because, as Sir Robert's wife, her consequence was now ten times what it had been as Sir Hugh's daughter.

"I do not see what we could possibly have to discuss," she said with a hauteur he knew she was using as a shield. Try as she may, she could not hide the effect he was having on her and she was trying to put an end to the confrontation because she was finding it too taxing.

The idea pleased him. Hadn't he come precisely with the idea of making her uneasy? It was time to up his game.

"I will not presume to disagree with you, my lady," he purred, moving closer to her. If his words were making her uncomfortable, he would see how she handled the proximity of his near-naked body.

Not well, if the way she flushed was any indication. He smiled, satisfied, when she took a step back.

"What do you want? You clearly came to meet me with a purpose in mind…" she started, her voice slightly hoarse.

Oh, after declaring they did not have anything to tell each other, now she was baiting him because she did not want the interlude to end. Better and better.

"I did, but I'm not sure you will want to hear it, my lady."

"Stop calling me 'my lady'!" Beatrice suddenly snapped. It plunged a dagger in her heart to hear the words in Edward's mouth. So cold, so impersonal.

Remote.

This man had held her in his arms and kissed her with fiery passion. He had made her moan in pleasure. And now he was calling her "my lady" as if she were an old dowager he had no more than a passing acquaintance with! How was she supposed to bear it?

"What would you like me to call you?" Edward asked, a dangerous edge to his voice. It seemed his own temper was fraying.

"You know my name. Use it."

He bared his teeth in a parody of the smile she remembered. "Yes, I do know your name. Perhaps I will use it in front of everyone, in front of your husband. Why not? Since you are ordering me to, I would be a fool not to."

"I didn't order anything."

"You did. As you have every right to. You are a great lady, and I am but a squire. I deserve no less. I expect no less," Edward said bitterly. "I was nothing more than a temporary amusement for you, a way to play the rebel before your marriage."

Is that what he thought? Pain ripped at her insides.

"Oh, why are you doing this to me, Ed…" She stopped, and blushed.

"You can say my name," he coaxed. "You have no reason not to use it."

"I can't," Beatrice breathed. Incredibly, it seemed to her that Edward's velvety voice had reached straight to the place between her legs and wrenched quivers of pleasure from deep within her.

"Why not? You had no hesitation in saying it the day you begged me to take you in the clearing, standing up against a tree." Her legs went liquid at the memory of that moment. "Or when you murmured it in my ear, all hot and sweaty from our lovemaking," he carried on, relentless, leaning in to breathe the words in her ear. "You once screamed it for all to hear, unable to sustain the assault of pleasure. Do you remember how I had to cover your mouth with mine to silence you?"

"Stop it, stop it!" Beatrice cried in desperation. She remembered it only too well. "Please, stop," she finished in a sob.

"Are you ashamed?"

"No. I'm not."

Of course she wasn't.

Beatrice fell rather than sat on the bench, feeling utterly exhausted by this confrontation with a man who had hitherto only had gentle words for her.

Silence stretched between them, interrupted only by the chirping of birds.

"Sir William told us you all fought at Barnet. Were you hurt?" she asked after a while. She already knew he had been—she had seen the stiffness in his walk—but she had no idea what else to say. All she knew was that she did not want to be fighting with him.

He shrugged. "It's nothing. An arrow in the thigh," he said curtly.

"That's hardly nothing!" Beatrice grimaced as she imagined the agony of having a pointy metal head tearing at her flesh.

"It is. Many were not so lucky."

Now that he was closer, she could see the remnants of a bruise on his collarbone and various grazes on his chest. If they had still been lovers she would have kissed each and every single one of them. Instead she averted her gaze.

"So you are a squire now?"

Beatrice hated the strain in her voice as much as the stupid question. Once, conversation had flowed freely between them, and here they were, stilted and embarrassed. Then again, the last time she had seen him bare-chested she had been equally naked and nestled in his arms, not dressed in all her finery and pregnant with another man's child. It was little wonder matters should be tense.

The only things that had not changed were her feelings for him, and his golden beauty. As a youth he had been attractive enough. As a grown man he dazzled by his assurance and strength.

"Did you expect me to remain a stable hand all my

life with no idea of bettering myself?" he asked, his voice little less than a snarl.

"No! Of course not." She was horrified that he should think that, but she knew because of the difference in status between them preserving his pride had always been an issue. To her relief he seemed to understand she had not meant to insult him.

He sighed. "I saved Sir William's life at the battle of Edgecote Moor, almost two years ago." He spoke without emotion, as if the feat was unremarkable. "His previous squire was killed in the melee, and he offered me the position after I took what should have been a lethal blow for him. It was a most generous offer. I have never regretted it. He is a good man."

"Is that how you got your scar?" Beatrice asked. Her fingers were itching to caress the welt on his forearm, the trace of an injury that could easily have killed a man if the blow had fallen on his head.

"Yes."

"What about these?" She indicated a white line on his shoulder and another on his pectoral.

He regarded her curiously, tilting his head. For a moment he was the old Edward, mischievous and full of charm, the man who had held her in his arms and made love to her, not the one who was acting all cold toward her and going out of his way to make her feel uncomfortable.

"You might want to keep this type of questioning to yourself, my lady. You seem very aware of every detail of my physique. Anyone would think you've seen me naked before."

Her cheeks burned. He was right, of course. She was not supposed to know every inch of this man's body! But she did. Her eyes landed on the crook of his neck where once she had dug her nails in the throes of passion. He had borne the trace of it for days.

She reddened further at the memory.

"That's gone," he said, proving that he knew exactly what she was thinking.

Gone. The word in its terrible finality made her heart nearly burst out of her chest.

"Yes, it's all gone," she said in a broken voice.

Just then the child in her belly gave an almighty kick, making her cry out in surprise. For a moment she had quite forgotten she was pregnant. She had been transported back to the past, to the time when she was a girl of seventeen and in love with a kind, handsome man.

She placed a hand on her belly to draw strength from it. Even though she hated its father, she loved her unborn child.

"Is anything the matter?" Edward enquired.

"The baby moved. I'm sorry," Beatrice explained, embarrassed. Why did she have to face him with another man's child in her belly? After six and a half years without each other, they deserved better. "I'm fine," she said awkwardly, aware she sounded—and probably looked—anything but fine.

It was all going horribly wrong. She should be rushing into Edward's arms, not behaving like the lady she did not want to be. Against all odds, they had been given a second chance, and there wouldn't be a third one, she knew it deep in her bones. What was she doing, talking to him about his excursions to the stew house and keeping him at arms' length?

"I'm sorry, I'm so sorry."

A tear fell on her cheek.

Edward tried not to let the sight of Beatrice's distorted face upset him. He had never seen anyone looking so altered, or at least he had never let it affect him so much. Lost to his own pain, he had let his anger get the better of him, and he was not proud of it. He had meant to unsettle her because he had thought that would help soothe his own hurt. Oddly, it had only made it worse.

"I didn't go with the other men last night," he told her suddenly, sending her a searing look.

Beatrice looked at him a long moment. Her eyes were still shiny with unshed tears. "Why are you telling me this?"

"Truthfully, I don't know."

She deserved no such mercy. She deserved to torture herself over the idea that he had spent the night in another woman's arms, just like he was imagining her in her husband's arms night after night. But a pang of guilt had assaulted him at the sight of the anguish he had provoked.

Once, they had known each other inside out. They had guessed each other's feelings. Yet here they were, unable to have a conversation without lashing out at each other. But he felt he should be more gracious in defeat, and not ridicule himself thus.

Besides, Beatrice was with child, and very near her term. This fact alone warranted some restraint on his part.

He took a few steps back and bunched his hands into fists to stop himself from reaching out to her. In spite of everything, he was dying to offer her the comfort she so obviously needed, yet he could not—the danger of discovery was just too great. It wouldn't do for a man to hold the lady of the castle in an intimate embrace, let alone a man in such a state of undress.

But he wanted to wrap his arms around her as he would have if they had still been lovers.

He had not expected this reaction when confronting her. He had been so full of anger and bitterness that he had imagined it would leave no place for tenderness or compassion, but here he was, his resentment fading in light of the urge to make her feel better.

"My lady," he said in a breath.

"Edward, I—" she began, taking a step forward.

He would never know what she meant to tell him, as at that moment a giggle was heard behind the wall. With a start, Beatrice retreated to a more seemly distance. Then her eyes widened in horror, as if she had only just remembered he was bare-chested and they were alone. He nodded and made to leave.

"Don't worry, I will not put you in danger."

After one last scorching look in her direction, he slipped behind a concealing bush.

"Oh, my lady, there you are!"

Beatrice waited until her heartbeat had slowed back to its normal rhythm before turning to address Lady Margaret.

"Yes, I needed some peace and quiet. I'm afraid the baby is getting rather heavy."

Her steady voice took her by surprise. It seemed that years of dissembling in front of Sir Robert were paying off. She was sure no one would suspect that barely a moment ago she had been entertaining lewd thoughts about a half-naked man and considered throwing herself into his arms to ask him to make love to her until she begged for mercy.

"Of course," Lady Margaret said kindly. "Let us get you back to your bed so you can lie down. I will bring you a posset if you wish."

A posset and a rest. Beatrice wanted to scream. She did not want to be treated like an old woman. She wanted to feel alive and desired! She didn't want to go to her room when Edward was here at the castle. She didn't want to lie in bed in the middle of the day unless he was with her, plying her with kisses and telling her she was beautiful.

"Thank you. A posset would be welcome."

With a heavy heart she followed Lady Margaret back to the keep.

****

That night Beatrice lay on her bed rigid with fear.

The chances of her husband coming to her were slim, but she could not rule out the possibility altogether. He had not touched her once during her first pregnancy, deeming it both unclean and dangerous for the baby. Of course, then he had assumed it would be a boy and the safety of his heir had taken priority over everything else, even his urges. When a baby girl had been born, he had waited until after she'd been churched to resume his marital duty.

All in all, and to her profound relief, she had been free from his attentions for almost a year.

With this pregnancy it had been the same. Sir Robert had left her alone as soon as she had announced missing her courses, except on one occasion when, drunk and roused by an argument with his brother, he had stumbled into her bed in the middle of the night.

She gave a shiver of revulsion at the memory. Five months pregnant, she had done her best to shield her baby from the vigorous assault.

She was now eight months gone, much bigger than she had been then. What if he came tonight? Beatrice knew she would not let him approach her. For the first time in their married life she would push him away. She could not envisage being bedded by him, not when Edward had finally come back in her life.

Despite their first heated confrontation, she sensed that this would be a new beginning for her—and that Edward would be an integral part of it.

Chapter 3

A child's wail, the high-pitched sound unmistakable. "But it hurts, Mama!"

"I know, sweetheart, it will do."

The mother's voice, unmistakable too. Beatrice. Edward would have known her anywhere. It seemed that she was at the riverside, hidden behind the hedge, only a few paces from where he had come to a stop. It was as if his feet had led him to her, even when his mind had not known where she was.

He walked toward her before he could talk himself into doing the reasonable thing and leaving.

"I cannot carry you, Alys. You are too heavy," Beatrice was saying in desperation. "You will have to walk."

"I can't! It's too painful."

"Mayhap I can be of assistance?" Edward offered, smiling at the child's willfulness. He would have expected no less from a daughter of Beatrice.

She started when she heard his voice. Crouched by the little girl, she hadn't heard his approach. When she saw him she made to get up, but the bulk of her belly made the movement awkward.

"Allow me."

He held out his hand to her. After a slight hesitation, she took it. For the briefest of moments their gazes locked, and he thought he saw the ghost of their old

43

complicity in her dark irises, but as soon as she was on her feet she removed her hand from his grasp.

"Thank you."

"What's the matter?" he enquired, doing his best to behave with polite detachment, as a squire would with the lady of the castle. There was no one in sight, but the little girl could not be dismissed out of hand. She was watching him intently, and Edward had the feeling she would see through any sign of familiarity between him and her mother.

"Alys walked on a sharp piece of rock while dipping her feet in the river and she cut herself. She cannot walk back all the way to the castle."

"Mama cannot carry me because she is already carrying my little brother, but perhaps you could?" the child told Edward hopefully. "You look strong enough."

He could not help a laugh at the compliment. The girl was pretty as a picture. Fortunately for her, she took after her mother, not her father. With her huge brown eyes that put him in mind of a fawn's, her upturned nose dotted with a few freckles, and her ready smile, he would have known her for Beatrice's daughter anywhere.

"Thank you. I am sure I would be able to carry you if your mama agrees," he said, looking straight at Beatrice. Would she agree? He wasn't sure, even if, undoubtedly, she needed assistance. She might well prefer to avoid his company and send him back to the castle with a message for someone to come and collect them instead.

Could she accept, Beatrice wondered? With Alys injured, she didn't have much choice. Edward was so confident, so powerful. If anyone could help them, he could. She had no doubt he would have carried *her* back to the castle if need be, heavy as she was.

"We would be grateful for your assistance," she murmured.

"Allow me, Lady Alys."

Edward bent down and gathered Alys up in his arms. This was something Beatrice had never thought to see. Edward's beautiful hands, the hands she remembered so vividly, were cradling her daughter, and the little girl had wrapped her arms around his neck easily, as if they had known each other all their lives.

Sir Robert had never held his own daughter thus, which was little wonder, considering he felt no affection for her. Should this second child prove to be another girl, Beatrice felt sure he would show her no more interest. She wrapped her hand over her belly protectively. No matter, she thought fiercely, she would love this child as much as she loved Alys.

The gesture did not escape Edward's notice. "Did you hurt yourself earlier, trying to lift your daughter?" he asked immediately.

"No, no. Everything is fine. Let us go."

"What is your name?" Alys piped, her fluted voice a complete contrast to Edward's masculine rumble.

"Hardthorne."

"No, I mean your real name. I'm sure you do not want me to call you Hardthorne when you are holding me in your arms."

He chuckled at this rebuff worthy of a lady well-versed in the art of courtly love, and even Beatrice could not help a smile. "It's Edward."

"I thank you for helping me and my mama, Edward," Alys said politely.

"It is my pleasure, my lady," he replied, just as

formally.

They walked in silence for a while. After their last encounter, there was still a certain tension in the air, but Beatrice wanted to see Edward's unprompted offer of assistance as promising. Perhaps all was not lost.

Just as she was allowing herself to relax, a wasp came buzzing around. Beatrice instantly froze. As a child, a wasp had flown into her ear and stung her. The pain had been excruciating and she had been petrified of them ever since. Edward swatted it away before she could say anything, the force and precision of his hit sending it a safe distance.

"There, my lady. No need to be afraid. It will not sting you now."

"Thank you, Edward."

She gave him a shaky smile and kept on walking. A moment later, her daughter raised her head and asked with a frown, "Edward, how do you know my mama?"

"Alys, whatever do you mean?" Beatrice cut in sharply. For days she had tried to pretend she didn't know him, and she could not afford to have her efforts ruined now, by her own daughter of all people! "We don't know each other. Surely you know that Edward arrived with Sir William's retinue only the other day."

"But…how does he know you are scared of wasps, then? And you just called him Edward instead of Hardthorne." Alys's eyes, wide with incomprehension, looked back and forth between the two adults.

Beatrice started. She *had* called him Edward. Trust her daughter to be so astute!

"I have a sister who cannot abide wasps," Edward explained when he saw she was too stunned to think of a suitable answer. "I automatically assumed your mama

46

doesn't like them either. Apparently I was right."

"Does your sister have a daughter too?"

"Yes, as a matter of fact she does."

"Where does she live?"

"Alys!" Beatrice snapped, her temper tried beyond endurance by this dangerous line of questioning. "Stop bothering him or he will not want to carry you any longer!"

"Oh, he would never do that, would you, Edward? You know my mama would never manage without you."

Beatrice almost tripped on a root. Edward caught her arm in support but made a point of not looking at her while he did it. Neither of them answered Alys's comment and, mercifully, the little girl let it go. After a while she allowed her head to rest against Edward's shoulder and closed her eyes.

Beatrice swallowed hard, feeling absurdly moved at the sight. Above the child's head Edward met her gaze in a look so bold that it seared her with its intensity. She lowered her head in confusion and then realized she was just as curious as Alys had been about Edward.

She hadn't known he had a sister. What else would she learn about him? Did he have a sweetheart waiting at home? Did he kiss the lucky woman like he had kissed her once, with reverence, or did he allow his wildest impulses to go unchecked? Beatrice had always felt he was reining in his true self with her, as if he did not believe himself worthy of someone like her, and it had hurt. Undoubtedly he behaved more freely with women he did not deem so far above himself. A pang of jealousy invaded her at the thought. The other women in his life had known the true Edward. She had not. He had always withheld a part of himself from her.

Still, she would take what little she could. She would give anything to taste his kisses again, however restrained, even if that was all she could get.

A reluctant laugh escaped her lips. What a ludicrous thing to think! If he kissed her, she would not be able to stop herself from wanting more.

"Why are you laughing?" Edward asked in a low voice. The tone was husky and the question was not one a mere squire would ask a lady.

"It's nothing," Beatrice murmured, wary of what her daughter would think if she heard them. She seemed asleep but it was not certain. The last thing she needed was for Alys to make a comment in front of her father about the level of intimacy between her mother and their handsome guest.

The castle was in view too soon for her liking. She could have walked for miles alone with Edward, even though they had barely exchanged more than a dozen words since Alys had closed her eyes and her condition did not allow her to walk easily. Being reunited with him had done wonders for her well-being. She felt at ease, calmer than she had been for years.

In the courtyard they found Sir Robert by the stables. His expression darkened when he saw them, and he strode over, menace etched in every line of his face.

"Alys, come down," Beatrice whispered urgently, the bubble of peace they'd temporarily enjoyed popping at the ominous sight.

"No! I want to stay with Edward," her daughter said stubbornly, unaware of the danger walking their way.

"Now!" Beatrice all but shouted.

"My lady, we've arrived. You don't need my help anymore."

Picking up Beatrice's desperate tone, Edward placed the girl on the ground and took a step backward. Sir Robert was striding toward his wife and daughter, a thunderous look in his eyes, and Edward thought it better not to draw attention to himself.

"What's this?" Sir Robert snapped, gesturing at the child's bare feet.

"Alys hurt her foot in the river and—"

"The river again!" he roared. "How many times have I told you I did not want my daughter to be raised like a common peasant? From this day hence, there will be no more excursions in the forest, dips in the river, or God knows what else, do you hear?"

"Father, please do not scold Mama. It is not her fault. I asked to go," the little girl said with more aplomb than Edward would have credited a child.

"You will speak when you are spoken to, Alys. Now go back to the nursery," her father instructed curtly. "If your foot hurts, you only have yourself and your mother to blame."

The girl threw one last glance at her mother, who responded with a swift, reassuring smile. Edward was surprised to see the child turn to him next and throw him a grateful look before leaving, proving she was truly Beatrice's daughter. In all the houses he had gone to, the master's children had considered it below their dignity to address a mere squire, no matter how welcome his master was.

Once the child was gone, Sir Robert unleashed his wrath on Beatrice, and Edward had no choice but to clasp his hands behind his back and try to stay calm.

"This will not happen again! Alys is my daughter and a lady." Sir Robert pointed at his wife's swollen belly menacingly. "If this one is my son and heir, he will be raised as befits his rank, not as a farmer's son. Even if it is another girl you will not be allowed to do with her as you have done with Alys, letting her run wild. My children will not shame me thus. Do I make myself clear?"

Astounded at the violence of the attack, Edward risked a glance at Beatrice. She had gone very pale and, knowing just how spirited she was, he expected her to lash back at any moment. He would even enjoy it. Sir Robert deserved nothing less.

"Yes, my lord."

Behind his back, his hands bunched into fists. How could she make such a meek reply after the way her husband had talked to her? He was about to speak when she shot him a warning look. He turned his face away, knowing it was his only chance at control. God help him, there would be no stopping him if Sir Robert carried on with his scolding.

Mercifully, the man seemed to consider that he had made his point and, after one last murderous glance, walked away. As soon as he was out of sight, Beatrice's whole body appeared to sag. Immediately Edward was at her side, offering support.

"My lady, the heat is not recommended for women in your condition, and you look dreadfully pale. Let me escort you back to your rooms. A rest will do you good," he said loudly enough for anyone to hear.

She nodded, understanding she would have no choice but to allow him to lead her back to her bedchamber. "This way."

Edward walked on, trying his best to suppress his fury.

The scene he had just been privy to had had a profound effect on him. Who was this subdued woman?

On the way to Devance Castle, he had prepared himself to face a show of marital harmony. What he had most dreaded to see was Beatrice laughing with her husband, sharing his jokes, and him acting as proud and loving as the man married to her should be. The idea of witnessing gestures of intimacy or affection between them had been enough to turn his stomach. He shouldn't have worried. There was no laughter or intimacy in this marriage, and affection seemed to be the last thing Sir Robert and his wife felt for each other. It should have made things easier to deal with.

Oddly, it made it worse.

Seeing Beatrice criticized and overruled by her husband, ignored, treated no better than a brood mare and a disappointment, was unbearable. Over the years he had tried to tell himself that perhaps the abrupt end to their dalliance had been for the best, that it could not have carried on anyway. He had tried to convince himself that Beatrice was better off where she belonged, with a husband who ensured her rightful place in the world, but he now had to face facts. She was no happier than she had been at her father's. In fact, she was worse off.

This living hell was not what he would have wished on anyone, much less the woman who still, come what may, filled his heart and soul.

His chest constricted in pain when he remembered the girl she had been, so impetuous, so free. No other woman had offered herself to him in the way she had. Her appetite for life and her daring had taken him by surprise.

Once she had even convinced him to make love to her in her own room, in her bed hung with velvet curtains. They had narrowly escaped being caught, but she had not let it deter her. The very next day she had come to find him in the middle of the night, hidden under a hooded cloak. He had tried to push her away, ever conscious of the danger of discovery, but she had won the argument, as she always did. He had been unable to resist her.

And now he saw her belonging to a man who thought nothing of upbraiding her in front of strangers for doing nothing more than allowing her daughter the freedom every child should enjoy. Now that he saw her situation for what it was, his resentment toward Beatrice vanished. All the years he had spent persuading himself that it was over between them disappeared in the blink of an eye. His desire, his need for her, were back with a vengeance.

"Please don't say anything," Beatrice said in a barely audible breath. Evidently his bristling anger was all too visible.

"Why didn't you answer the man?" he hissed, unable to let it lie.

"Why do you think? I just wanted him gone!" she snapped. "There is no reasoning with him when he's in this mood. I have endured the same lecture countless times, and still I take Alys outside whenever I want. I pay no heed to what he says. I just let him think that I do."

This struck Edward as brave, for few people would have dared contravene Sir Robert after such a display of anger. Maybe she had more backbone than he had given her credit for and simply chose her battles. The notion reassured him.

"Why did you take Alys to the river in the first place?" Without condoning Sir Robert's attitude, he had to admit that such occupations were hardly typical of future ladies.

"Did you not go wading in the river as a child, or explore in the forest?" she asked in reply.

He shrugged. "Of course, we all did. We went foraging and fishing and made sure to have a good time of it, but I do not recall any lord's daughter ever joining us."

"That's because they were confined in their castles, locked away in draughty rooms, looking out through the window at the children laughing and shouting, wishing they could be with them, splashing in the water or running in the meadows!"

Something inside him softened. "Is that what you did? Watched the village children in envy from your draughty rooms?"

She made an angry gesture with her hand. "I want my children to be happy while they are young. Is that too much to ask? God knows, they will soon be pawns in their father's ambition and as miserable as I am! So yes, I allow my daughter to wade in the river like a peasant's daughter, because I would rather she was a peasant's daughter, if it makes her happier than being a great lady like I am," Beatrice said as her temper finally broke free. "Alys had such a good time today, and so did I, until *he* spoilt everything, as he always does!"

She pummeled against his chest, all fire restored. But Edward did not feel better for seeing her behave like the girl he remembered. Her reaction was heartbreaking in its violence, betraying years of frustration and hurt.

"Stop," he said softly, taking her wrists in his hands.

"Stop. I understand." She only wanted the best for a child she loved.

Beatrice shook her head, eyes ablaze. "Sir Robert never even thanked you for helping me out there, didn't even acknowledge what you did for his injured child and his pregnant wife. Is that normal behavior? You tell me! Is that the example I would want to show my daughter? No, it is not!"

"Worry not about Lady Alys," he said with a side smile. "She nodded her thanks to me before she left. You have raised her well. She will be as gracious as you are."

Beatrice stilled and looked at Edward in utter incredulity.

"Is that all you can tell me after what happened? That I am *gracious*? Stop being so generous! Why are you not angry with me? You should be! You have every reason to be!" she cried, fighting the urge to lean her forehead against his chest. He was still holding her, her great belly nudging at his trim hips.

"I might be angry with Sir Robert for his treatment of you, but I could never be angry with you, much as I wish I could," he murmured, his mouth at her ear. "And you don't need to thank me for helping you with your daughter. I would do more, if you allowed me."

The meaning of his words was clear. "No, no!" Beatrice cried out in horror, lifting her eyes to him. "You are not to say anything to Sir Robert on my behalf, do you hear me? Never! He cannot find out who you are, he cannot know that we…" She faltered.

Edward took one of the hands he was still holding and brought her fingers to his mouth to place a series of little kisses on the tips. She closed her eyes, so as to enjoy the caress more thoroughly. Oh, how she had missed being touched thus!

"That we…?" he prompted, his voice the seductive purr of a lover, not the respectful tone of a squire.

"Oh, Edward, you know what we did. What good would it do to hear me say it out loud?"

"None," he said slowly, lowering her hand.

They stayed silent for a long moment, hands entwined, gazes locked, bodies closer than what was seemly. Anyone walking in on them would have no doubt about the level of intimacy they shared. Still they could not seem to draw away.

"Why are you here?" Beatrice asked eventually.

"You know why. Sir William wanted the men to rest for a few days before carrying on with the campaign."

"I mean why Devance Castle, of all places?" she insisted. It seemed too much of a coincidence.

"What are you trying to make me say? That I chose the place? That I forced Sir William to stop here? That I did it only with a view of seeing you again?"

Yes, please say it—say you were desperate to see me again.

Beatrice looked at Edward, hope drumming in her chest. Had he manipulated Sir William into claiming hospitality from a distant relative of his wife just so he could get a glimpse of her?

Before he could utter a word, footsteps were heard.

Quick as a warrior draws a sword from its scabbard, Edward released her hands and took a step back. As a result, when Lady Margaret and Lady Elizabeth appeared at the top of the stairs they saw nothing out of order. Sir William's squire was merely taking his leave from their mistress, bowing with all the deference she was due.

"Thank you," Beatrice said coolly. "I will go and lie down now. This heat was getting to me."

With his back to the ladies, Edward branded her with one last look before retreating down the stairs.

"Are you quite well, my lady?" Lady Margaret asked solicitously. "You look flushed."

"No, I'm afraid I am not at all well," Beatrice breathed, watching the tall, graceful figure disappear from view. It was as if Edward had taken all the light with him.

"Can we do anything for you?"

The answer was dreadfully blunt. "No, you can't."

Chapter 4

"You should not be here. It is no place for a lady."

"Nonsense. It's the least I could do." Beatrice smiled encouragingly, but in truth she wasn't sure what she hoped to achieve by coming here. When Ralph tried to sit up, she placed a restraining hand on his shoulder. "You mustn't agitate yourself thus. The physician said you should lie down."

She didn't add that the man had been clear that doing so would not save him, only make his last moments as painless as possible.

"Edward..." Ralph rasped. "I need to see Edward." There was a new urgency in his voice, the desperation of a dying man.

"Who is Edward?" Beatrice asked, heart pumping hard at the absurdity of the question. If there was one man on this earth she knew, it was Edward, but still caution had to prevail. Whatever the circumstances, she could not betray any unseemly knowledge of him.

"Hardthorne, the squire...my...brother...I need..." His voice was failing fast.

"I will go and get him," she soothed, standing up on shaky legs. "Please, in the meantime, do not exert yourself. You must remain calm."

A wan smile answered her rebuff. "My lady, I am dying, so it will make little difference."

There was nothing she could answer to that. "I will

go get this Edward for you."

Beatrice went down the steps as fast as her great belly allowed her and automatically headed toward the courtyard, sensing that Edward would be there. Somehow she always seemed to know where he was, just as she had always known where to find him when he worked at her father's castle.

Indeed, he was exactly where she had imagined him to be, but he was surrounded by a dozen men. Steeling herself, she walked toward the group.

"Which one of you is Sir William's squire?" she asked, careful of addressing no one in particular.

"That would be me, my lady," a deep voice answered, a voice made even huskier by a flare of temper. She had guessed he would be furious at this deliberate slight, but of course she could hardly be seen to know him already.

She met the blue ice in his eyes squarely. "Ralph Emerson is asking for you. I'm afraid we must hurry," she said, doing her best to speak in a natural voice.

The men exchanged worried looks. They knew the gravity of their comrade's injuries and understood what she had not said. The man was dying.

"I'll go," Edward said tersely. The smolder in his eyes vanished, leaving only concern about Ralph's well-being.

"You don't know where his room is. I will show you," she said for the men's benefit. No one would question them leaving together in the circumstances, and she could not countenance letting him go on his own to see his dying friend.

At first Beatrice did her best to match Edward's big strides, but after a while it became too taxing.

"Wait!" she pleaded, out of breath. "I cannot walk as fast as you."

"Of course. Forgive me."

Edward slowed to fall back in stride with her. What was he doing? She was heavy with child, and he was as good as forcing her to break into a run!

Gesturing to her to lead the way, he followed her into a round tower. At the top of the stairs he took her hand.

"My lady. A moment, please."

He wanted to speak, make the most of the private meeting, but he was tongue-tied for once. Beatrice herself seemed unusually subdued. Of its own accord his thumb started to caress the inside of her wrist. He saw her swallow, and he could not blame her. The gesture had made his heartbeat increase too. It seemed he would never be able to be near her without wanting to touch her, wanting much, much more.

"What is it?" she asked in a breath.

Edward shook his head ruefully. They were holding hands and that was daring enough. He could not admit the urge to touch her more intimately made his head spin.

"Why are you the one delivering the message about Ralph?" he asked instead.

"I was with him when he asked for you. It seemed easier that way."

"You were with him?" He was incredulous.

She nodded. "I must warn you, he does not have long to live."

"Yes. I knew that already. His injuries are terrible. He would have better died on the field, for we all knew he would never recover from this." He paused, remembering how Ralph had screamed when they had lifted him up onto the litter. The sound would haunt him for years to come. "Thank you for coming to find me yourself."

She could easily have sent a maid, or not bothered to attend to the injured stranger. To see yet another glimpse of the old Beatrice was a balm to his bruised soul. He gave her hand a light squeeze before letting it go.

"Let's go in," Beatrice whispered. "He was most insistent on seeing you."

They found Ralph writhing on the bed. His mouth was filled with blood and the pillow around his head tainted red.

"Dear God, Ralph!" Edward ran to him while Beatrice recoiled in horror and leaned against the wall.

"My…buried…Isabel…" he said, his voice reduced to a terrifying gurgle.

"I know. I'm here, don't talk. I know. I will make sure you are buried next to her," Edward said in soothing tones. He sat on the bed next to Ralph and looked around for something to wipe the blood off his friend's chin. His gaze met Beatrice's and, though she looked about to fall into a swoon, she nodded and sprang into action.

Willing herself not to be sick, Beatrice took a linen towel from the supply made ready on the chest. Just as she was handing it to Edward, Ralph retched. She screamed and jumped back as if she had been scalded when a few drops of blood landed on her hand. There was a rasp as the dying man tried to take a breath, the noise awful. Edward held his friend in an upright position to help him breathe, but in vain.

A moment later he was still.

Everything went silent. Beatrice watched in pure

horror at the corpse lying in Edward's arms. She had never seen anyone die before, especially not in that horrid manner. Her brain struggled to comprehend the full meaning of what had just happened. Only a moment ago Ralph had been a man with hopes and dreams, with people to love, and now the only thing left of him was this bloody shell.

With a strangled cry, she placed a hand on the wall for support. Edward was at her side in an instant.

"Here, you need to sit down," he said, straightening her. He marched her to a nearby chair and poured a generous measure of wine into a cup. "Drink this. It will help. Don't look at the bed."

The various orders were issued in a dispassionate voice that chilled her to the bone. My God, how many dead men had he seen, to be so composed in front of a corpse? Her hands were shaking in shock, preventing her from taking the drink. He closed her fingers around the cup when she made no move to take it from him.

"Drink," he repeated more gently, sounding more like the old Edward. Beatrice nodded and took a gulp, then another, letting the liquid warm her throat.

"Is he dead?" she asked in a croak. She already knew the answer, but she could not bear the dreadful silence. She had to say something, anything.

Edward nodded, taking the cup from her hands. His gaze flicked to her stomach. "I'm sorry you had to see this, especially now," he said, placing himself so as to obstruct the bed from her view. "Why did you come to see him in the first place?" he asked, cocking his head. He seemed to sense that she needed to talk to stop herself from reliving the event over and over again in her mind.

"Sir William mentioned Ralph's injuries earlier

today, and I thought…I thought I could help." It sounded absurd now. Her presence by his side had made no difference whatsoever. She had barely spoken two words to the man, and he was now dead. "I should have come before, but I didn't think he would die so soon. I should have…"

"It's not your fault," Edward soothed, as if he understood her helplessness. His tone was soft but firm. "You couldn't have saved him. No one could have. We all knew that. But you did him a great favor by making sure he could fulfill his final wish. You came to find me in time and I heard what he wanted. It was the best thing anyone could have done for him."

She nodded slowly, grateful for the reassurance. "He said… Was he your brother?" It seemed incredible to think so, but Ralph had definitely said something about a brother.

"No. I have no brothers, only sisters."

"Was he married? This Isabel he mentioned, was she his wife?"

"No, she was his twin sister. I know he wanted to be buried next to her. We discussed it enough times." Edward's voice had suddenly acquired an edge.

"But you and Ralph must have been close, if he asked for you in preference to anybody else before he died, so I—"

"Why are you asking me all this?" Edward barked before she could finish her sentence. "Why are you suddenly so interested in my whereabouts? You never asked me any of this when we…" He stopped and clenched his jaw.

When we were lovers.

The words hung in the air between them, as

suffocating as smoke. Beatrice stood up, unsure why her questions should have provoked such a reaction in Edward. That he had a temper on him, she knew, but she had never seen him lash out at anyone who did not deserve it, and she hadn't done anything to justify this outburst.

"I am sorry for trying to understand who this man who called you to his deathbed was to you. I thought perhaps you would want to talk about him, that it would help you deal with his horrific death. I see that it was a mistake. Please forgive me," she said rather stiffly. Evidently she had been wrong to suppose they could ever behave as naturally as they had seven years ago. The companionship between them on the walk from the river had been naught but an illusion.

There was little more to be achieved by staying here, save a further widening of the gulf between them.

Feeling slightly nauseous at the notion that they would never be able to recapture what they'd had, Beatrice made to leave, but before she could reach the door she caught a glimpse of her hand. Drops of blood stained her fingers, the scarlet color a vivid contrast to her pale skin. She tried very hard not to panic, but the sight made her shake uncontrollably. A dead man's blood was on her. She gave a cry of disgust and looked at Edward. His hands were stained red, as well.

For a dreadful moment she had an image of how he must have appeared in the middle of the battlefield with an arrow sticking out of his thigh, his blood and that of other men on his hands, his face, his hair. The vision was horrifying.

"No, no," she whimpered, rubbing frantically at her fingers. It only made it worse, smearing her hands with dull red color. "I need to…I can't…"

Her mind, addled by what she had just witnessed, was frozen into inaction, unable to come up with the simple solution to her problem. She flapped her hands aimlessly, not knowing what to do, feeling on the verge of a breakdown. Mercifully, Edward had more presence of mind. He walked her to the basin and plunged her fingers into the water.

"Let me help you."

He put his own hands into the basin and started to wash hers with slow, tender gestures, cleaning each finger in turn, rubbing the inside of her palms gently, stroking the skin of her wrists where her pulse was beating fiercely. Beatrice closed her eyes in confusion. The memory of Ralph's agony sent a shiver of horror down her spine, but Edward's sensual touch had her body dissolving in a pleasure not dissimilar from the quivers she had experienced in his arms.

It had been years since she had been touched thus. Six and half years, to be precise, since Edward had disappeared from her life. Even her ladies' ministrations were not as careful. That their touch was not arousing was perhaps understandable, but she was puzzled to see that Edward was just as efficient and even more gentle. Although his hands were callused from the use of heavy weaponry, the delicacy of his touch was astounding.

His fingers brushed her wedding ring, and she saw him wince at this reminder that she belonged to another man. She swallowed and almost asked him to take it off and throw it away. The heavy metal band had never felt more like a shackle than it did in that moment. The design of it had never appealed to her tastes, but more pointedly, she hated it as the symbol of her union to a man she hated.

Once her hands were clean, Edward took a piece of linen and set about drying them. It felt more like a way of forestalling a momentous conversation because it was obvious that he lingered unnecessarily over the task. Beatrice was equally intimidated. Though the intimacy of the moment was nothing compared to what they had experienced in the past, when they had lain in each other's arms, his caresses were robbing her of all sense.

"Show me your wound," she whispered. "The arrow wound on your thigh." Even if it was true that his limp seemed to have lessened in the last few days, she needed to be reassured. The image of him standing all bloodied was hard to forget.

"Show you my wound? Are you out of your mind?" Edward scoffed, the reaction quite unlike what a man of his condition should have in front of Lady Devance.

"Please. I need to see that it is not…that you are not going to…"

His hands tightened their grip around hers. "I am not going to die. I told you, it's nothing, and nothing like Ralph's injuries, just an arrow. I ripped it out straight away, and the wound is clean." He lifted his eyes to her and she saw that, even if he was refusing to obey, at least he was not making light of her worry. "I swear it. You will have to believe me because I cannot take the risk of showing you. Should anyone walk in whilst we were alone and I had my hose down to my knees, you know what they would think."

Of course. They would imagine she had been pleasuring him. How had she not thought about that? Too preoccupied by the idea of him dying, she had not stopped to imagine what it would look like to an onlooker if he did show her his wound. Her cheeks flamed.

"Oh."

"Precisely," he said with the ghost of a smile. "It's not exactly ladylike behavior. And it would be made much worse by the fact that I am not your husband."

Beatrice felt a shiver of revulsion at the idea of doing such a thing to Sir Robert. What had been a sensual pleasure with Edward would be the most humiliating degradation with him.

"I've never—"

"Please don't say anything." Edward raised a hand. "Please," he repeated almost pleadingly. "I do not want to have to imagine you with him. Ever."

"No, no. But I wouldn't want you to think that I—"

"Believe me, I am trying very hard not to think anything," he said with a ferocity she had rarely heard from him. "You should go now. There is nothing left for you to do here, and you should not be alone with me."

Beatrice knew she should not stay with him. Equally, she knew that once she had left the room she might never find herself alone with him ever again, and she simply could not willingly put an end to the moment.

She lifted her eyes to him beseechingly. The towel had been discarded, but Edward had kept her fingers in his, and she found it impossible to let go.

When Beatrice looked at him with her eyes huge in prayer, heat exploded in Edward's groin. In spite of everything, this woman stirred his blood in a shocking way. Even now, when she was pregnant and so near her term, when she belonged to another man, he wanted her for himself. Even here, in this room where his friend had just died, he wanted to make love to her, bury himself inside her flesh, and forget everything. His desire for her overcame all sense of honor and decency.

A devastating anger at his weakness engulfed him.

"Go!" he repeated in a snarl, letting go of her hands as if the touch burned him. "You have nothing to do here!" At the violence in his tone, Beatrice recoiled. It inflamed him further. "Oh, you are afraid of me now, is that it? You were braver once, my lady. You left me no peace," he jeered, although he could not entirely blame her if she was wary of him. He was afraid of himself right now. The violence of his desire worried him, made him fear he would do something he regretted.

For both their sakes, she had better go.

They were not out in the open, in danger of being seen, no one even knew they were here, no one knew they were together. He could easily place the chair in front of the door and...

No.

He stopped this train of thought before it became too dangerous, before it made him consider doing something he would never have considered doing had the lady in front of him been anyone other than Beatrice.

"I...I am not afraid of you," she stammered, keeping her eyes firmly on him. "Never that."

"Then what are you afraid of?"

Edward knew it had been a mistake to ask the question the moment she bit her bottom lip, the gesture so evocative his blood roared to life. God have mercy, he was going to die of unfulfilled need before the week was out.

"I am afraid of myself, of what I want to do. Right now I want to throw myself in your arms, and I can't even pretend that the shock of Ralph's death is responsible for this unforgivable urge. I want you, Edward. I have never stopped wanting you."

Before he could say anything, she turned and fled.

Chapter 5

Later that day Beatrice watched Edward walk into the great hall, the expression on his face carefully guarded. Not once did he look in her direction or Sir Robert's. He addressed Sir William only and kept his eyes firmly on him.

"I'm afraid Ralph has passed away," he murmured, leaning over to him.

"The Lord have mercy on his soul. He was a good man," Sir William breathed back, though he did not look surprised at this outcome.

"I am sorry," Beatrice told him, clasping her hands together under the table to stop herself from rubbing at them. The man's blood had been on her hands, something she would never forget.

"He expressed the wish to have his body sent back to Cornwall where he wants to be buried," she heard Edward say in his deep, soothing voice.

"Of course. Do you wish to go with him? I know you two were close, what with—"

"With your permission, I would rather stay behind in case we go into battle soon." Although the lie was uttered smoothly, Beatrice had the feeling she was the real reason behind this decision.

As she wasn't quite sure what to make of that observation, she pushed it aside.

"I will go and make the necessary arrangements,"

Sir William announced before taking his leave.

Sir Robert took this opportunity to go about his own business. Beatrice could tell he had absolutely no interest in Ralph's demise. He had carried on eating during the whole conversation, as if the man's death was of no importance. He allowed Sir William to walk away without a word of condolence, and went immediately after, leaving his wife alone with the very man of whom he should have been wary.

Alone with Edward, Beatrice felt her heart pumping hard in her chest. The last time they had been together he had accused her of being afraid of him, and she had admitted to shameful feelings. Possibly for this reason he nodded curtly and made for the door.

"Wait, Edward," she called softly. It would not do for her to be overheard using his name in such a breathless way, but she could not bring herself to call him Hardthorne, not when he was already angry with her.

"My lady?" He turned to her as was proper, but his eyes stayed on the floor.

"You should go to Cornwall to take Ralph's body back," she said. "It's what he would have wanted."

"How could you possibly know what he wanted? You didn't know him," he answered, his voice vibrating with the difficulty of keeping his temper in control. "How familiar are you with these circumstances? Do you often have to deal with people dying of their battle wounds under your roof?" He finally raised his eyes to her to burn her with a searing look.

"No, of course not. I only thought—"

"You thought you would take this opportunity to get rid of me and the danger I represent to your reputation," he declared bluntly. "With me gone, the scandal goes. No one will be able find out what happened between us."

Beatrice blanched under the insult. How could he think she was only using the death of his friend as an opportunity to be rid of him? Did he really believe her to be that shallow and selfish?

"How can you speak thus?" she asked, hurt and disbelief making her voice unsteady.

"Am I not allowed to voice my opinion? Do you intend to dictate how I should speak now? Am I to blindly follow your orders like a menial?" He took a step in her direction, all dark and menacing. "Is that what you mean?"

"Of course it is not! Do not put such words in my mouth!"

They glared at each other, neither prepared to back down. Just then two servants walked in, and started to clear the trestle table. Beatrice nodded to them, then walked to the window, doing her best to appear as if they had not interrupted anything of import.

What was she doing, having an argument with Edward in the middle of the great hall? A private discussion would have been bad enough. But no one should see them together more often than necessary.

Once the two maids had left, Edward came to stand behind her. He remained at a respectable distance, but close enough to be able to speak in a low voice.

"I will arrange everything in accordance to Ralph's wishes, but I mean to stay and go to battle with Sir William if the king summons us. Will you dare order me to do otherwise?"

"You know very well that's not what I meant!" White-hot anger crashed inside Beatrice at this deliberate attempt at misunderstanding. She whipped around. "You have been attributing uncharitable or downright insulting thoughts to me since the moment you arrived. You say all I want to do is get you out of the way because I am wary of the scandal, when all I care about is not losing you again! You dare tell me I am scared of you when you know such a thing is impossible! You criticize me for treating you like a squire in front of everyone when it is the only thing I can do! You *are* a squire and I am not free to behave as I would wish because I am married, I am with child, and I *am* Lady Devance, however much you and I may hate the fact!"

She strode up to him, all prudence forgotten in her indignation. They had never had a moment's disagreement before she got married, and it felt wrong to be hurling accusations at Edward and to have him doubting her. She longed for the time they understood and respected each other.

"Now, unless you want to lose my good opinion, you will start behaving like the Edward I know and loved and stop crediting me with such nonsense!" she said, trembling with anger.

Edward arched an eyebrow at the upbraiding and was momentarily lost for words. Beatrice stood before him, her chest heaving with the heat of the outburst. Eyes flashing and chin held high, she was magnificent.

"Well, you certainly behaved just now like the woman I knew," he murmured to himself.

He was glad to see her allowing her true personality to shine through, something she never did in Sir Robert's presence. Never again did he want to see her spirit crushed, or see her cower in front of a man. He wanted her to be the girl she had been all those years ago, just as she apparently wanted him to be the man he had been then.

Suddenly a grimace twisted her face. She sat down on a chair, her breathing coming in short, ragged bursts. "What is it?" he asked, alarmed.

"Forgive me, I keep getting these twinges. It's nothing to worry about, but they can be quite painful." She gave a wan smile, one hand on her belly.

Edward clasped his hands behind his back, reining in the impulse to go to her. He had no doubt his harsh attitude had been responsible for the sudden spasms.

"Please, it is I who should apologize," he said through gritted teeth. "I am a boor."

Once again he had allowed his temper to get the better of him. But now was not the time to upset her. Only that morning she had seen something her cosseted life had not prepared her for, and he then had added to her distress by snarling at her for doing nothing more than suggest he accompany his friend to his final resting place. No wonder she didn't feel well.

"I'm sorry. You've had a hard enough day, and you should not get agitated so near your term."

Beatrice shook her head slowly. "You're right. But I fear with you around there is little chance of me remaining calm."

A pang of guilt assaulted him, even if she did not seem to mean it as an accusation.

"Do you need to go to your rooms? Shall I fetch one of your ladies?"

"No, you can do…" Beatrice's voice died in her throat when he threw her a meaningful glance. She had been about to say that he could take her there himself, but he could not allow it to happen. It was too dangerous.

If he walked her to her rooms, he would walk in with her, and once he was inside, there would be no stopping them. They would tear at each other's clothes and stumble onto the bed before she'd had time to blink.

It was safer if he stayed well away from her. It had been a narrow escape earlier that day. They would never resist the lure of an empty room a second time. If they could be so bold as to have a private discussion in the great hall where people came in and out, there was no telling what would happen behind closed doors.

"Please, if you would be so kind as to call Lady Margaret," Beatrice said, clasping her fingers together. So she agreed with him…

Edward nodded. "I will go and call her immediately."

He wasn't sure if he should be relieved that his control would not be put to the test or frustrated to be denied the opportunity to kiss her senseless. Relief won when he saw her rub at her fingers. She was still upset by what she had witnessed that morning, and not thinking straight.

It would not do for him to take advantage of her turmoil.

They deserved better. He did not want her to come to him because she was confused or needed reassurance, but in conscience, like the first time, because she wanted *him*, not because she wanted to feel alive or forget the trauma of Ralph's death. Anyone could offer her comfort, and he hoped he was not just anyone.

He had more to give her than reassurance, and he needed to see that she knew it.

After stealing a glance toward the door to make sure no one was coming, he placed his hand on hers to still her nervous rubbing.

"Try to forget about today. I know it won't be easy, but it will achieve nothing to have you lose sleep over it."

Beatrice nodded. But as horrific as the whole thing had been, she already knew that what would keep her up at night was not the memory of Ralph's death but the torturing desire she felt for Edward.

After one last scorching glance, he left.

When Lady Margaret arrived a moment later, Beatrice could not remember why she had summoned her.

****

Chased by the breeze, a few wispy clouds hurried along a pearly gray sky. Beatrice turned her face upward and inhaled the smell of wet earth with delight. Ever since Edward had walked into her great hall five days ago, everything had changed. She felt like an animal coming out of a long slumber, awake once more and ready to live her life to the full.

She had gone for a walk with Sir William and taken Alys along with her, knowing that if their guest was with them her husband would not object to the notion, at least not until they were back. The joy of seeing her daughter run in the meadow to pick flowers more than made up for the scolding she might receive later on from Sir Robert.

"I gather that we are related, albeit in a convoluted sort of way," she said, as she watched the little girl dart from one clump of muscari to the next. "You are married to the daughter of one of Sir Robert's cousins, are you not?"

Sir William beamed at her, the smile of a man in

love. "I have that honor. If I weren't worried about being indelicate, I would say that Lady Margery is the most enchanting woman I have ever met."

"It is not being indelicate for a man to say he favors his wife above other women," Beatrice assured him. "Lady Margery is a lucky woman to be loved thus." Though she worked hard not to let any bitterness taint her comment, she saw that Sir William understood the slight on her husband. There was little chance of him ever speaking of her in such affectionate terms.

"I am glad we chose to rest here after the battle of Barnet," he said, carrying on with the pretense that they were not making any comparison between him and Sir Robert. "You have made us feel most welcome."

The word "battle" struck Beatrice like the arrow that had hit Edward. He had told her he had first crossed paths with Sir William during the battle of Edgecote Moor, and she immediately seized on this opportunity to learn something about his new life.

"We have done no more than our duty. It sometimes seems as if there will be no end to all the fighting, though. Have you taken part in many battles these last few months?" She hoped he would mention Edward of his own accord, for it would not do for her to betray any interest in his squire and ask a direct question.

"A few." The short answer was not encouraging, but she persisted.

"It must be dreadful," she murmured. "So dangerous."

"It is, though of course sometimes it can change one's life for the better." Sir William smiled. "Without a certain battle I would not have met a certain man, and without this man I would never have met my wife."

"How do you mean?" Her heart skipped a beat. He had to be referring to Edward, even if she had no idea how he could possibly owe his meeting with Lady Margery to him.

"My man Hardthorne. You might not remember him." Beatrice barely stopped herself from laughing out loud. Not remember him! If only he knew… She nodded, indicating she knew who he was talking about. "He saved my life during the battle of Edgecote Moor two years ago. My former squire was mortally wounded during the fight, and Hardthorne stepped in front of me to take a blow that should have killed me and could very well have finished him off. As it was, he nearly lost his arm."

"That was very brave of him." Beatrice thought back to the scar she had seen on Edward's forearm and gulped uneasily.

"In view of this, I made him my new squire. He was a low-born man, but I thought such a feat of courage should not go unrewarded."

"Indeed," she agreed, knowing that in the same situation Sir Robert would never have looked at the man twice, never mind thanked him and offered him a position of trust. "And you said you had cause to congratulate yourself on your decision later on?" she prompted.

"I did, a hundredfold, for it was thanks to him that I met Lady Margery a year ago. I now count saving my life as only the second-best turn Hardthorne did for me."

Beatrice smiled at this extravagant comment. Before she could ask how a man like Edward could possibly have contrived a meeting between Sir William Bartlett and Lady Margery Raglan, Alys came running toward them.

"Mama, these are for you!" She handed her a bouquet of cornflowers.

The sight of the vibrant flowers had a spectacular effect on Beatrice. She was instantly taken back to the past—and into Edward's arms.

"Your eyes make me think of cornflowers," she had told him one day, as they lay side by side in his bed.

The blue irises had always put her in mind of the flowers she used to weave into her hair as a child on the rare occasions she had been allowed to roam the meadows outside the castle. Inevitably she would get a scolding from her maid when she had to disentangle the wilted stems from her hair later on, but she was suddenly struck by the symbolism of the image. It was as if Edward had been a part of her, intricately woven into her being, even before his arrival into her life.

"Cornflowers. A common flower, a wild flower, whereas you are like a rose. A delicate, noble flower," he answered bitterly. "How can I begin to compete?"

"I have always had a particular fondness for cornflowers. They are my favorite flower," she mused, ignoring the comment. "I used to put them into my hair when I was younger, to make it less…"

"Less?" he prompted, lifting himself up on one elbow.

"Less ordinary, I suppose. There is nothing beautiful about my hair, it is a perfectly uninteresting shade of brown."

"Uninteresting?" Edward murmured, running his hand through it sensually, making it fall in ripples between his fingers. "It's not uninteresting when it's spread on my pillow." The low drawl made something inside her quiver. "It's softer than a new bird's plumage, shinier than a stallion's coat, and it smells of roses." He buried his nose in the heavy mass and inhaled deeply. "But apart from that, you're right, it is perfectly uninteresting."

Beatrice gave a sigh of pleasure at the heartfelt praise. The man had a way with words. She ran her hand into his golden hair, letting the long locks caress her fingers. "But my hair is nothing compared to yours. It is shinier than the rising sun and softer than my richest gown. Your eyes are of a blue that is almost magical. Mine are just chestnut brown."

"Yes, well, I have a particular fondness for chestnuts, as it happens. They have always been my favorite food. I used to put them in my belly when I was growing up, to make it less…"

"Less?" she giggled, unable to resist his teasing. He was echoing her earlier words exactly.

He laughed. "Less hungry."

"Edward! You are mocking me! It is not kind," she chided, secretly delighted that he was becoming more comfortable in her presence, comfortable enough to be himself and tease her. She hated to see him as uneasy as he often was with her, as if he thought he had to maintain a certain distance between them even while she was in his arms.

"I will mock you if you are going to speak such nonsense. I do not recall chestnuts sparkling as your eyes do, nor do they have golden strands in them. And when you look at me with these amazing eyes of yours, all I want to do is kiss you until you believe that you are the most beautiful woman in the world."

"Then do," she challenged, her heart ready to

explode at the declaration.

The blue in Edward's eyes had gone a shade darker. A moment later, she'd found herself under him, being kissed as if his very life depended on her believing his word.

"The flowers are so blue!" Alys enthused, picking out one stem from the bouquet and holding it close to her face. "Look, Mama!"

"Yes, so blue. Thank you, sweetheart." Beatrice's eyes misted over.

"Why are you crying? I thought cornflowers were your favorite?" Alys was dismayed.

"I'm not crying. It's nothing. Only, I'm afraid I've overtaxed myself somewhat. Perhaps I should sit down for a while." She stole a glance at Sir William. He could not suspect the real reason behind her turmoil, but she felt caught out all the same. If he knew she had just been thinking of the passionate way his squire had made love to her…

"Allow me." He gallantly escorted her to a nearby stump of wood and helped her to sit.

"Thank you."

Just when she had managed to push the mental image of a naked Edward out of her mind, Beatrice saw him walking toward her, looking even more breathtakingly handsome in the flesh than in her memory. The desire she had worked so hard to quell rushed back through her at the way his body moved, with a dazzling a combination of power and grace.

She lowered her eyes before the men could detect the flame ignited within her at the sight of him.

"What is it, Hardthorne?"

"Sir Robert is keen to speak to you, my lord. He was

enquiring earlier about your new suit of armor, but I'm afraid I could not satisfy his curiosity."

"Could you not?" Sir William exclaimed in surprise. "You know more than I do on the subject!"

"I got the impression that he would prefer to talk to a nobleman," Edward answered tactfully. Beatrice could well imagine that her husband would never condescend to discuss anything with a mere squire, but as it suited her to keep Edward as far away from Sir Robert as possible, she was less indignant than she would otherwise have been at the slight. The less time the two men spent together, the better.

"You must hurry back to the castle, Sir William," she said with a smile, jumping on this opportunity to be alone with Edward.

"We will go together as soon as you recover from you indisposition," he answered, as politely as ever. "I cannot leave you and Lady Alys here alone."

"You must go. My husband would not thank me for keeping you when it is clear you are the only one who can answer his questions satisfactorily. I would have thought, like you, that your man would be better placed to do so, but I'm afraid there is no arguing with Lord Devance when the mood takes him to be contrary." Beatrice could not resist showing this small bit of pique toward Sir Robert and had the pleasure of seeing the men exchange a swift glance of agreement. "Besides, it is time for Alys to make her way back. She will be late for her evening meal if she waits for me. Would you be so kind as to take her with you? I'm sure that…"

She glanced at Edward as if to ascertain his name. His blue eyes shot daggers. She repressed a sigh. Did he have to be so touchy all the time?

"Hardthorne, my lady," he said in a grating voice. He was daring her to use his family name for the first time. She did, though it tripped on her tongue.

"I'm sure Hardthorne will be kind enough to escort me back to the castle once I have recovered."

"I am sure he will be," Sir William said with a warning look at his squire. He had not missed the acid tone and was reprimanding him on his coarse manners when addressing a lady. "Are you ready to go, Lady Alys?"

"If Mama is sure she is well…"

"I am, sweetheart. Go. I'll see you later."

Beatrice watched her daughter go with the bouquet of cornflowers in her hand.

"Do you enjoy humiliating me?" Edward's voice was no more than a hiss.

"No, I do not." Beatrice had wanted to be alone with him, but she was quickly regretting it. "Addressing you by your family name is hardly humiliating you. It is the appropriate thing to do. If you weren't so full of yourself, you would see that I can't be seen to pay any particular attention to you."

"Yes, I do see that. You have made it abundantly clear. Heaven forbid that anyone should see the mighty Lady Devance for what she really is."

"What I really am!" Beatrice stood up in outrage, the movement almost as supple as if she weren't eight months pregnant. "Tell me, if you dare! Tell me what I am exactly," she challenged, her voice vibrating with indignation and hurt.

What a comedown! She had gone out of her way to ensure she and Edward could spend a moment together alone, and he was repaying her with yet another of his atrocious accusations. It was not to be borne!

Edward knew he had gone too far when he saw the color on Beatrice's cheeks and the flash in her eyes. Of course he hadn't meant to suggest there was anything less than respectable in her manner toward him, and once again he had allowed his bitterness to speak. What was wrong with him? He seemed to be unable to keep a level head where she was concerned.

Not wanting to inflame her any further, he stayed silent, but she was not so easily appeased.

"Why don't you accuse me of seducing all the men in my father's castle?" she challenged, trembling in fury. "Peter the groom, Richard the farrier's son, or John the spit boy, why not? If I sought to satisfy my urges with you, a mere stable hand, why not with dozens of others of equally low status?"

"Stop twisting my words," Edward snapped, displeased at his lack of control. He should never have thrown such an accusation in her face. It had been both ungracious and unfair, and in truth he was impressed to see that she remembered everyone from her time at her father's castle. She had never considered it below her dignity to speak to everyone, from the gentry visiting to the merest kitchen maid. In fact, it was one of the reasons he had been so drawn to her, and in that respect at least she hadn't changed. He had already had a chance to see that she knew everyone at Devance Castle by name as well.

Oblivious to his musings, Beatrice was working herself into a frenzy. "Can't you see that this is not a game? I do not enjoy having to guard myself constantly in your presence, but I have no choice. If I am not careful, you could get..." She stopped, and suddenly all her righteous energy seem to desert her. Her face fell and she sat back down on the stump.

"I could get what?" Edward asked, alarmed by the sudden pallor in her face.

"You could get killed for what happened between us," she whispered.

"Nonsense. I am not going to get killed, for I do not think you would accuse me of taking you without your consent, would you?"

"Edward!" she cried out, recoiling in shock. "Please tell me you don't believe I could do something like that?"

He berated himself for his choice of words. Somehow it had come out all wrong. He had merely meant to say that he had nothing to fear since he knew for a fact she would never accuse him of such a crime. Guilt gnawed at him. He had ranted against her for ignoring him, thought her cold and distant, and even decided to make her pay for it.

And now he was told that all this time she had been protecting *him* rather that herself and her reputation. God, he really was a fool!

"No, of course I don't believe you could do something like that. Worry not. No one is going to know about us, or put me to death for seducing a willing woman, even one so far above myself," he said gently, kneeling in front of her. "Please do not fret on my account, not in your condition. There are no laws against what we did, even if everyone would see it as wrong."

Beatrice did not appear reassured in the least. "I am not talking about laws and justice. I know you are safe on that front. But you must see that Sir Robert would kill anyone who humiliated him." Edward stayed silent. He could not contradict her there. The man was a violent bully, and testy to boot. "He cannot know who you are and what we did. He mustn't suspect that I..." she faltered.

"That you...?" Edward prompted, heart in his throat.

"Oh, Edward, you know, you must know! What good would it do to hear me say it? I cannot think it, let alone say it out loud!"

"No, you cannot," he said slowly. Dear God, he had been right. She had been about to make an admission married ladies could not make. The other day she had confessed to feeling desire for him. That was momentous enough. But this... "And I am not at liberty to speak either."

He stood up again and waited for Beatrice to compose herself, and for his heartbeat to return to normal. They had almost admitted their love for each other. It was little wonder his heart was thundering in his chest.

Finally, after a moment, he dared look at her.

Some color had returned to her cheeks and she was breathing more easily. He cursed himself for making her so agitated every time they met. She was pregnant and tired, he noticed, taking in the shadows under her eyes. The last thing she needed was for him to make her feel worse. He did not want to see her clutch at her spasming belly again.

"My mother's dead," she said suddenly, her voice expressionless. "I got the letter yesterday."

The change of topic took Edward by surprise. "I'm sorry," he said inadequately.

"Don't be. I'm not sure I am."

This unexpected admission threw him even more. "Why are you telling me this?" he asked after a while, unsure how to proceed.

She sighed. "I know not. Mayhap because you are the only person here who knew her."

"Apart from your…apart from Sir Robert, that is," he amended. The idea that he was her husband was still too raw, and he refused to give him the title.

"Oh, yes, they knew each other well enough," she said with an air that roused his suspicion.

"What do you mean?"

Beatrice moved a stone with the tip of her shoe before answering him, evidently wondering how to word her answer.

"I suspect that my mother was somewhat taken with Sir Robert," she said eventually, her disgust obvious in every syllable. "When her sister, his first wife, died, she was devastated. Naturally at first I assumed she was affected by her sister's death, but I have since come to see that she was in fact more distressed at the idea of seeing Sir Robert disappear out of her life. I am pretty certain that, had she been free to do so, she would have married him herself. As she wasn't, she settled for the next best thing to ensure he would always be around— she married him to me. Certainly she was the one who pushed for the alliance, not my father, as you might have expected."

This was all new to Edward. Indeed, he'd assumed the union had been masterminded by Sir Hugh, not his wife. "Did she tell you as much?"

"No. Sir Robert did, unwittingly, once, when he lashed out at me in a fit of temper, though I don't think he knows quite why my mother was so determined to see this match through."

"What did he tell you?" The word "temper" had

raised the hairs at the back of Edward's neck, and Beatrice's hesitation did nothing to reassure him. Had the man hit her? Fury shot through his veins.

"It was about a year after we got married. I still hadn't fallen with child. He fulminated against my mother for misleading him and saddling him with a useless brood mare."

Beatrice winced at the memory. No matter how many insults her husband had thrown her way over the years, she still felt each of them keenly. Being humiliated was not something you ever got used to.

"He never dared!" Edward spoke through clenched teeth, his voice full of venom. She gave a sad smile.

"He did. You don't know the half of it."

"Then tell me."

"No." She shook her head, fast regretting the comment. If she told Edward any more about the kind of treatment she suffered at her husband's hand, he would never be able to keep his temper in front of him the next time they met. She could not afford to let that happen. She could not put him in danger. Sir Robert must not be given reason to look at him too closely. "I only meant to tell you that my mother married me to this man so he could still be part of her life. She sacrificed me, and it was all in vain since, unlike what she had hoped, we never visited her once in all these years."

It had cost her little to sever the ties with her parents, considering how they had forsaken her, selling her to a monster twice her age.

Edward remained silent, looking at her strangely. He seemed to be mulling over something unpleasant. Beatrice wondered what that might be—and then her eyes widened in horror as realization dawned.

"You…you didn't think I had agreed to the match, did you?" she cried out, every fiber of her being convulsing at the thought.

To her utter dismay, Edward didn't immediately respond.

"I did," he admitted after a pause, planting a dagger in her heart. "He told me you had been betrothed all the while, that you had come to me all the while knowing you would marry him afterward."

As Beatrice's mind was still reeling from the discovery that Edward had thought her complicit in her union with Sir Robert, the meaning of his words did not immediately register, but when they did she stood up in shock.

"He *told* you? When was this?" She had no idea Edward and her husband had ever spoken at the time.

He ignored the question. "He told me you two had been betrothed for weeks, that you only came to me because you wanted to experience some thrill before your marriage."

"And you believed him?" she asked, picking up on his tone. "You believed that I went to you to amuse myself, for some kind of frisson before I began a respectable married life with a man I had chosen for his status?"

She didn't know whether to be appalled or outraged.

Edward made a gesture of frustration. "What else could I think? Why else would a lady like you go to a man like me?"

"Is that all you have to say?" she roared. "After all that happened between us, you thought I just…" She was so incensed she could not finish her sentence. So much for not agitating herself!

"Well, what else was I to believe?" Edward cried out in turn.

Was Beatrice being deliberately provoking? She knew what she had done... Why else would she have sent her future husband to dispose of him once she had understood they could not carry on?

More than six years had passed, but Edward remembered the sting of betrayal as if it were yesterday. By asking Beatrice to run away with him, he had signed the toll on their relationship. She had never intended for him to be anything other than a temporary, if pleasant, distraction, and his shocking offer had made her see that things had gone too far.

He cast his mind back to the fateful night he realized he'd been played for a fool. He had waited a long time for her at the oak, his heart threatening to explode with the hope she would agree to flee with him despite the folly of the enterprise. Every noise had made him turn his head toward the darkness to see if Beatrice had decided to risk it all.

After an excruciatingly long wait, he had heard footsteps, and then a silhouette, tall and dark, markedly different from the one he hoped to see, had emerged from the shadows.

"My lord!" Edward exclaimed, startled at the appearance of Sir Robert.

"You seem surprised, boy. Were you perchance expecting someone else?"

"No, I—"

"Someone more alluring than me, perhaps? Someone you could fondle?" Sir Robert carried on as if he hadn't spoken. Behind him two other men appeared from the bushes, their faces set in a scowl. "Hear me, boy. Lady Beatrice de Courcy will not be coming to you tonight, or indeed any other night. She and I are engaged to be married, have been for the last three months, and you will not be allowed to see, much less touch her, ever again."

Until the day he died Edward would remember the disbelief and the pain he had felt at the words. Beatrice had been betrothed all along! She had come to him, lain in his bed, all the while knowing she was to be married to another, and her own uncle, at that! It could not be. But Sir Robert's next words sounded too true for him to doubt it was anything but the truth.

"My betrothed has a, shall we say, unfortunate contrary disposition and a strong will." This could not be denied. Edward himself had learnt it the hard way. "No doubt she wanted to experience some cheap thrill by letting you paw her with your filthy hands. However, this will now stop. She has seen reason and begged for my forgiveness. In my generosity, I have granted it."

"Where is Lady Beatrice?" Until he heard all this from her own mouth he would not allow himself to despair. "I want to see her."

Sir Robert let out a scornful laugh. "She is too ashamed of her conduct to see you, and I am not inclined to give my agreement. You will never see her again, and you will never speak of this unfortunate lapse to anyone—or I will gut you, do you understand?"

Hurt as he was, Edward's first reaction was one of relief on Beatrice's behalf. Sir Robert seemed to think that nothing more than a few harmless kisses had taken place between him and his betrothed. He could have told the man that he had possessed her countless times, but he refused to humiliate himself further or, more pointedly, to place Beatrice in danger.

"I understand," he answered through gritted teeth.

"Good." Sir Robert gave a sinister smile. "Now, to make sure you do not change your mind and try to see her after all, my friends here are going to escort you out of these premises."

"Edward!" Beatrice cried, bringing him back to the present. He grimaced as he recalled the beating he had suffered at the hands of Sir Robert's "friends." He had been lucky to survive it. "How could you think you meant nothing to me after all we did? I came to you willingly, I gave you my maidenhead!" she reminded him in a furious whisper.

He nodded. He had often wondered about that. Being no untouched virgin on her wedding day was not a position any lady of rank would choose to find herself in. He could easily imagine that a man like Sir Robert would take exception to not being the one to deflower his bride. His reaction would have been terrible.

"How did you manage to talk your way out of that pitfall with Sir Robert?" he asked in an angry snarl. The mere idea of them lying together made him want to howl in rage.

Beatrice's face underwent a transformation. Hate flashed through her eyes and she bared her teeth in a grimace.

"I could not afford to have him know just how far things had gone between us. The idea that we had kissed was enough to make him swear to kill you. Had he known we had lain together, he would have put his threat into execution. So I made sure he never found out I was not a maid. I cut myself on our wedding night to make sure there was some blood on the sheet," she said in a savage voice he had never heard before. "And he was so brusque that I had no difficulty behaving as if the whole thing was an ordeal."

An ordeal...

Edward knew the real loss of her maidenhead had been anything but an ordeal. He still remembered her cry of astonished pleasure when he had entered her flesh for the first time. The idea of Sir Robert possessing her with such a lack of consideration sent his blood boiling.

And, just like that, a veil was removed from his eyes. For the first time he saw clearly what had actually happened.

Beatrice had not chosen to marry her uncle for his fortune or any other reason. She had been forced into this marriage by her mother and suffered appalling treatment at the hands of a man she had hated since her wedding day. She had not sent Sir Robert to dispose of him. She had not used him for cheap thrills.

She had come to him because she wanted him and she still felt for him the love she had felt then.

"I'm sorry you had to go through all this," he said, appalled. She had cut herself, lied about being a virgin, placed herself in danger...just so her new husband would not suspect how far her dalliance with the stable hand had gone.

"So am I. Rest assured that this wedding was none of my doing and that I have regretted it every moment of every day." Beatrice spoke with a depth of bitterness that tugged at his gut. "So to go back to our original discussion—no, I am not sorry my mother is dead, because without her I would have come to find you that day at the oak, and my life would have turned out greatly different!"

Beatrice straightened her back and resisted the urge to cradle her belly as she usually did in moments of distress. By believing her capable of such treachery, Edward had wounded her deeply. They had gone through their share of tribulations together, but she had the impression that the pain of this particular betrayal would never truly heal. How could he ever have thought he meant nothing to her other than an experiment? How could he have believed her capable of such cruelty as to send someone else to tell him she did not want to have anything further to do with him? How could he have had so little faith in her?

Worst of all, how could he have thought her willing to marry a tyrant like Sir Robert just because he was rich?

She had only gone along with the scheme because by then she had been convinced Edward had abandoned her to go back to his parents. In the morning he had been nowhere to be found, and all his belongings had disappeared. She had concluded that he must have heard about her betrothal and, understanding that her marriage would put an end to their dalliance, had simply disappeared before their relationship could be discovered. He had not stayed to talk to her or to make sure she was not being married off by force. He had accepted the change in her circumstances without questioning it.

He had not fought for their love.

She had reasons enough to be angry with him, yet she had not addressed him a single word of reproach since his arrival. And he had the gall to pose as the victim! Now she understood why he had been so bitter, so scathing, the day he had come to see her bare-chested. He thought her a shameless, haughty lady who had taken her pleasure with a menial while it suited her and abandoned him when she thought it was time to become a respectable lady.

Yes, she understood all too well what sort of woman he had thought her to be…and that he had not been prepared to give her the benefit of the doubt.

Oh, the pain of it all!

Edward reached out to her, but she stopped him with a raised hand, unsure of how to surmount her hurt.

"Would you please escort me back to the castle? I'm not sure I want to be with you right now."

Chapter 6

"Why did you give yourself to me?"

Unable to let the matter drop, Edward had come to find Beatrice, despite the danger. Since their discussion that morning he had agonized over it. He needed to know. If she had not been after the frisson of transgressing the rules, then why had she, a lady, sought him out, a mere stable hand?

Beatrice did not betray any surprise at seeing him, a sure indication that she had expected his visit. That didn't mean she would talk to him, however. She was worrying her bottom lip and refusing to meet his eye. Evidently she was still smarting from their earlier confrontation.

"What reason could you have had to do such a thing?" he repeated. He would not leave without an answer. If she had not been after the thrill of transgression, why would Sir Hugh's daughter have taken an interest in a man like him? It did not make sense. "Please tell me. I need to know."

Eventually Beatrice deigned to look at him. "Ah. So you believe now that there was more to it than the wish to feel like a rebel? I am honored."

He sighed. She would not relent until she had made him feel lower than dirt for doubting her. And perhaps it was no more than he deserved.

"I do. But I need to hear your reasons because I

cannot for the life of me understand what Sir Hugh's daughter could possibly see in me. A beautiful woman like you, a learned, refined lady who could have had her pick of men if she wanted to find out what happened between a man and a woman. Why did you choose me, a man who should never even have touched your hand?"

It was hard to expose his most private anguish, but at least his honesty seemed to soften her. Still, she took a moment to answer, as if weighing her words carefully.

"Did you ever push me away when I came to find you at the stables? Do you ever recall telling me you were too busy to see me?" she asked, her voice low. The solar was deserted at the moment, but one could never be too prudent.

"No," he said, puzzled at this enigmatic answer.

"No. You never sent me away. You always found the time to take me into your arms."

"I see." He ran a hand through his hair in dismay. This was not what he had hoped to hear, and he was quickly regretting his question. "So I was always available to service you when you needed it. I guess that puts me in my place."

"No, no, you are misunderstanding me!" Beatrice cried out in earnest, taking a step toward Edward. All attempts at discretion were forgotten in view of the pain she had unwittingly caused him. How could she have expressed herself so clumsily? "That is not what I'm trying to say at all!"

"What *are* you trying to say?" he growled. "You had better find a way of making yourself understood, for at the moment it certainly sounds as if I was nothing more to you than a stud."

"No! Please, Edward. Listen to me. It is not easy for

me to explain."

Beatrice was so keen on having him understand that she took his hand in hers. The way he frowned told her he was taken aback by this spontaneous move. As was she. But as good as it felt to feel the warmth of his skin, it was not prudent to hold him thus when anyone could walk into the room. With regret she let go of his hand.

"Who taught me to jump on my horse?" she asked in a whisper.

"Me. And it took weeks," Edward said with a reluctant smile. "For all your other accomplishments, you were never really a horsewoman, were you?"

"No, I never was," Beatrice agreed, not in the least offended. She had lost count of all the falls she had endured. "Yet you never begrudged me the time or told me off for making mistakes or for not being brave enough."

"So I was a good horse master and you sought to reward me for my services, is that what you're trying to say?" The blue eyes glittered, but the voice was no longer angry. There was a glimpse of the old Edward in his expression. It gave her heart and she allowed herself to answer as she would have seven years ago.

"Yes, that's what it was." Her mouth twisted in mischief. "Fortunately for me the other servants were not as accomplished at their job or I wouldn't have had any time to myself."

Edward arched a brow, just as he would have at the time they were lovers. Her heart lifted. Once again they had managed to get over the hurt and awkwardness. Once again peace was restored. And yet this time she had been so sure she would never get past the pain of his betrayal!

She was starting to believe that nothing could ever come between them.

Time had not diminished their craving for each other. His terrible accusations, the pain of his desertion—nothing seemed to matter when they were together.

"Who believed me the time I said I had seen a fox run into the great hall? You did, when everyone else accused me of telling tall tales. Who held me in his arms when my grandmother died? You. My parents didn't even notice I was heartbroken. You were always there to listen to me, comfort me, or just be with me. My mother never loved me, and my father considered me little more than a disappointment and a nuisance. I never had any brothers or sisters. No one had time for me or wanted to be with me. You did. Or at least…I thought you did."

"I did," Edward immediately countered. "Only I could never understand why you would prefer to spend time with me rather than in more worthy pursuits."

"I cannot think of any worthier pursuit than to be with someone who actually considers me of interest!" Beatrice said hotly, straightening her back. "You cannot understand the terrible loneliness of my position. And I could ask you the same thing. Why did you indulge me? Why did you not send me on my way? You had better things to do than pander to the whims of the spoilt lady of the castle!"

"You were not so spoilt, as I recall. And I would have been a fool to send a beautiful lady on her way, considering what she was prepared to do to me, don't you think?" he whispered conspiratorially. Beatrice's mouth opened in shock. Edward's mood had turned to seduction and her loins had dissolved in a pool of longing. "Don't tell me you've forgotten what pleasure you gave me?"

Oh, no, she hadn't.

"So I was nothing more than a doxy to you," she breathed, deliberately provocative.

"Not so, although you certainly showed some talent for the task."

"That is beyond…"

She wanted to scold him but she could not finish her sentence. Her embarrassment was too acute. Seeing that she could not reprimand him for his bold comment, Edward smiled wolfishly.

"Don't worry, my lady, I am not complaining."

"I…I didn't think you were," she answered wanly.

Edward had always been able to make her feel at a disadvantage. Though she was the lady, and therefore his superior, he somehow seemed to be the one with the upper hand. He had always had a confidence she lacked, a way of finding the chink in her armor, and he instinctively knew how to unsettle her. Like now. His blue eyes were smoldering with satisfaction—and desire. She almost whimpered aloud.

"You still haven't answered my question," she said, forcing herself to be calm. She needed to know what it was about her that had attracted him. "Why did you indulge me?"

Beatrice knew he was only toying with her, that there would be more to it than her willingness to bed him. He could have satisfied his urges with anyone without incurring censure, he could have chosen any of the women in a twenty-mile radius and they would have had him in heartbeat. Yet he had decided to brave punishment and be with her when doing so could only place him in danger.

She waited. Edward's eyes were still ablaze, but his tone became serious once more.

"You made me feel that I could achieve something with my life, that anything was possible, even for someone like me. I wanted you from the moment I saw you, and against all odds, I got you. It made me see that maybe I was worth something, that I could better myself. I learnt to fight when I left your father's castle, something I had never considered doing before, and eventually my skill got me a position as a squire. My parents are proud of my achievements, and they now live in more comfort than I could ever have provided had I stayed a stable hand. None of this would have been possible without you."

She could not countenance his generosity. He made it sound as if his time at her parents' castle had been the life-changing experience every young man was dreaming of. It had been anything but.

"You mean you had no other choice than to try your hand at whatever you could once you had been kicked out of the castle and deprived of your livelihood because of me!" she huffed.

He shrugged. "That is one way of looking at things. But your influence did change my life. You told me one day that the queen of England's mother had chosen a mere squire as her husband when she was a mighty duchess. It gave me food for thought, and the will to try and do something with my life," he clarified, taking her hand in his. "You changed me, for the better. Everything I set out to achieve since I met you I have accomplished. All except one."

Edward averted his eyes, something she had never

seen him do before. Beatrice could not fool herself that she didn't know what that thing he was being denied was. Her. He wanted to have her.

Her throat tightened.

"I wish we could—" she started tentatively, but he stopped her with a raised hand.

"Wish all you want, my lady. We can both see the situation is hopeless."

There was nothing she could answer to that. It *was* hopeless.

"I will leave now. We cannot risk being seen too often together. I do not fear for myself, but I cannot risk putting you in danger," he said fervently, boring a hole into her skull with the force of his stare. "Only know that if it were up to me I would spend my days with you."

"It is the same for me," she whispered, feeling as if she were about to break in two.

He left, taking a piece of her heart with him.

****

The next morning a messenger bearing Sir William's arms rode into the courtyard, his livery covered in dust. Recognizing his friend Martin, Edward immediately went to him in swift, long strides.

"Go and get a drink, I'll get this to Sir William for you."

"Thanks, Hardthorne, I won't say no. I'm exhausted. I've galloped all the way from Bartlett Manor. Lady Margery was most insistent I should not delay for a moment. She wrote as soon as she got Sir William's message."

Tucking the message into his tunic, Edward made his way to the great hall. He knew Sir William would be breaking his fast with Beatrice and Sir Robert, and he could not resist this new opportunity to see her. Each moment counted when the king's summons could arrive any time.

"A message arrived from Lady Margery," he told his master. "I sent Martin to get a drink. He rode hard to get the letter to you as fast as possible."

"My God, the baby!"

In his haste, Sir William almost tore the paper in half. Edward had guessed he would be too eager for news of his wife to mind about who brought the message or remember to dismiss him while he read the letter. Waiting behind his master, he stole a glance at Beatrice who was doing her best to keep eating her slice of venison pie. She had flushed delightfully as soon as he had walked into the room and was in this moment toying with her knife in a rather suggestive if absentminded manner.

Gone was the feigned indifference she had displayed upon his arrival. Anyone looking at her now would conclude that his presence was affecting her. Fortunately, Sir Robert was too busy gorging on his own pie to take any notice of his wife, and Sir William's attention was wholly focused on the letter in his hand. Only Edward saw the way she subconsciously licked her lips when she eventually dared to steal a look at him.

He instantly grew hard.

Cursing inwardly, he clasped his hands in front of him in an unusually formal stance. There was not much choice. Retreating into the background would only draw attention to him and impede his view of Beatrice. He could not detach his gaze from her. She was so beautiful, so desirable! Seated at the table, her belly hidden from view, she did not appear pregnant. For once he could forget she was carrying another man's child for all he could see was her face, framed by a delicate veil, and her hands, small and elegant.

His lips tingled at the sight of hers, his hands itched to touch hers, his breath became as labored as hers.

Beatrice glanced in his direction and flushed when she noticed the way his hands were clasped in front of his groin. So she had guessed the reason behind his sudden change of attitude. He looked at his feet, knowing he would never regain mastery over his body if he carried on looking at her—or she at him.

"The best of news! My wife is safely delivered of a healthy baby!" Sir William exclaimed, raising his glass.

"How wonderful! May we offer our warmest congratulations?" Beatrice said with a smile.

"I thank you, my lady." A shadow flicked across his eyes. "I wish I could have been by her side on this joyous occasion. I wonder… Should I go to her now? But King Edward could call us any time, and I cannot afford to miss the summons."

It suddenly occurred to Beatrice that if Sir William elected to go home today he would take Edward with him. The thought of him departing before she had finished her meal, never to come back, was simply too dire to contemplate. Bile rose in her throat. She was not ready to be parted from him just yet…she would never be ready for it. Nevertheless, she said what she was duty-bound to say.

"I understand your dilemma, Sir William." The smile wavered on her lips. "Go to your wife if you feel you must. It is understandable that you should be eager to see her and the baby as soon as possible."

"Let's not be so hasty. The child will still be there

when you return home in a few weeks," Sir Robert pointed out, wiping his mouth on a napkin with as much grace as a boar wallowing in mud. "If I were you, I would wait to know what the king wants to do before I went anywhere. It should not be long before we find out what his intentions are. Margaret of Anjou is said to have landed on English soil. If this is true, it will not be too long before we are called. He will want to stop her before she rallies more support."

"Yes. Of course. You are right." Sir William nodded, albeit reluctantly.

Relief flooded through Beatrice. It was odd to feel gratitude toward her husband. Nevertheless, she was grateful for his intervention. Edward would not be leaving just yet. She didn't dare to look into his eyes, but she suspected he would be feeling the same relief.

"Wait. You never said if your child was a son..." Sir Robert asked, standing up.

Sir William followed him into the courtyard. "Didn't I? Well, yes, she indeed gifted me with a son."

Outside the sun was shining, having finally burnt off the morning mist. Beatrice shielded her eyes from the brightness and took advantage of the move to eye Edward greedily. Freshly shaven, dressed in a green tunic that seemed molded over his torso, he had never looked better.

"A son and heir, so soon after your wedding—some men have all the luck!" Sir Robert said gratingly, aiming toward the stables where a groom was harnessing a mare he had purchased earlier in the week.

"I am very lucky indeed." Sir William's smile made it clear he felt blessed because he had married the woman he loved, not because she had given him an heir on the first try.

"Lady Beatrice remained barren for more than a year after we got married, despite all my efforts in the marital bed. I did everything I could to get her in pup, but when she finally fell with child, it was only a girl!"

The crude remark landed between them like a stone in a puddle. Edward saw Beatrice grit her teeth at this appalling summary of their married life, and even Sir William seemed somewhat lost for words. As for him, he was feeling murderous and he had the utmost difficulty stopping himself from jumping onto the man and beating him into a pulp.

"Your daughter Alys is a most enchanting girl. You must be very proud of her," Sir William said when the silence became too uncomfortable.

Sir Robert only scoffed. "Let us hope this one is a boy," he said, patting his wife's swollen belly in a gesture that was both proprietary and insulting. His hound would no doubt be stroked with more feeling.

When tears swelled in Beatrice's eyes, Edward turned to help the groom prepare the mare. He did not trust himself not to ram his fist down the man's throat for his heartlessness. But as much as he wanted to defend Beatrice, he did not want to create more problems for her than necessary. He now knew why she was acting so subdued in her husband's presence, and her efforts at protecting him should not be jeopardized by a show of temper that was well within his power to contain.

Should have been within his power to contain, he amended with a shake of the head. But God's bones, he had never met a more aggravating man than that damned Sir Robert.

He tightened the girth of the saddle with a sharp

yank betraying his frustration. The mare instantly neighed in protest. Annoyed at his lack of control, he ran a hand over her neck in apology. How he wished he could do the same to Beatrice, caress her and murmur loving words in her ear, wipe her tears away!

Once he had mastered his flare of temper, Edward turned again and saw her staring into the distance in an obvious effort to keep her distress in check. An irresistible urge to speak overtook him. He would not stir up trouble, but he needed her to know he was on her side, to know he understood what she was going through, to know she was not alone.

"Congratulations, Sir Robert, you have acquired a magnificent animal, if I may be so bold as to say. I have rarely seen the likes of her." He let his hand slide over the slope of the mare's back. "Her proportions are perfect, the grace of her demeanor flawless. She looks full of spirit, too. She will no doubt prove to be a first-rate brood mare for you. What more can a man ask for ? You are a lucky man," he said planting his eyes into Beatrice's.

He saw her take a sharp intake of breath, and he almost winked at her.

Beatrice could not believe Edward's daring. The comments about the mare had truly been meant about her and as a slight on her husband's attitude toward her. This show of support warmed her to the bottom of her soul.

Sir William tilted his head, lost to the double entendre. "You can trust my man's judgment in this. He knows a good mount when he sees one. He could break her for you and it would be a job well done. I have never seen anyone so skilled at it."

Beatrice felt herself going crimson. Break her for

you... The words held a hidden, deeply licentious meaning for her and Edward, a meaning he would not have missed. Indeed, he had broken her in and his skill was second to none.

Fortunately Sir Robert saw nothing amiss in the innocently meant comment.

"I am gratified to hear you approve of her." He patted the mare's flank in much the same way he had patted her stomach earlier. "If you wanted to ride her one day, you can do so with my permission."

"That is very generous of you, my lord. I will be sure to remember it," Edward murmured darkly.

****

The summons they had been waiting for came later that day. King Edward was calling for all his men to join him for a final battle. Once again Edward brought the message to the great hall himself. Beatrice knew he was trying to ensure they saw each other as often as possible, and she was grateful for it, but for once she wished he hadn't come at all, since it was to bring the news of his pending departure.

"The king means to put an end to Margaret of Anjou's Lancastrian pretensions once and for all, capitalizing on his victory at Barnet," Sir William explained for Beatrice's benefit. "I am glad I waited for this opportunity to help him secure the throne. This way I will return to my wife and son in victory."

Beatrice's chest tightened painfully. He seemed to consider that defeat was not an option, but of course it was. And even if the king secured a victory, it still didn't mean that the men fighting for him would benefit from it. An image of Ralph flashed through her mind. He had been on the winning side at the battle of Barnet and yet he had died in unspeakable suffering. Poor Lady Margery might never get to show Sir William his newborn son.

And she herself might never get to see Edward again.

The expression on his face told her he was thinking the same thing. They seemed to be the only two people in the room willing to acknowledge that not everyone would make it back home after the fight. Her nails dug into the palm of her hand.

How would she bear to hear that he had died now that they had found each other again?

"By God, my men and I will join you in this heroic enterprise!" Sir Robert announced, placing his cup on the table with such force that half the ale sloshed out of it.

"You would go to battle?" In her incredulity, Beatrice had spoken out, but she regretted it when he threw her a withering look.

"I would. Why, wife? Do you think I cannot fight as well as the rest of them? Do you think you are married to a coward, perchance?"

"No, of course not," she said swiftly. "Only I was curious as to what would have motivated this decision," she could not help but add. They both knew he had kept himself well out of danger over the last few years, forging up excuse after excuse not to take part in any battles when given the opportunity. For all his cruel behavior toward her, he was indeed a coward when it came to facing real opponents.

"And I, my lady, am curious as to what you think gives you the right to speak to me thus and question my decisions. I was not aware I had to seek your approval in matters of warfare."

Beatrice clenched her fists under the table. "You do not. Indeed you shall do as you deem fit."

"I see we understand each other." After a last venomous look, he returned his attention to Sir William, who looked distinctly ill at ease. As for Edward, she did not dare take one glance at him for fear he would jump at her husband's throat if he saw the slightest sign of discomfort on her part. "I will offer fifteen armed men to King Edward and will follow your retinue. Where are we to regroup?"

"Windsor in the first instance, and then the king will have to rely on his scouts' information to choose the most propitious place for the battle."

"Very well. We will leave on the morrow." Beatrice felt her heart being squeezed in an iron fist at the suddenness of it all. In less than a day, Edward would be gone. But however wretched she felt, she could not allow any emotion to show on her face, for Sir Robert turned his attention back to her immediately. "You will accompany us west to stay at Corlith Manor, wife. It is a residence of mine conveniently situated on the way to Windsor," he explained for Sir William's benefit.

Beatrice looked at her husband in stupefaction. He wanted her to undertake such a journey in her condition? "My lord," she started gingerly, aware he would not countenance another rebuke. "As I am so near my time, I do not think it advisable for me to travel at present, if—"

He cut her short, eyes glittering. "I have heard enough defiance for one day, my lady. It is my wish that my son be born in my childhood home. Of course, given your condition, you will not ride on a horse but in the comfort of your litter," he said magnanimously. "I am not an unreasonable man, and we are not in so much haste, after all."

The faces of those around them showed a consternation that matched her own, and none seemed more thundery than Edward's. He looked on the verge of an outburst. This last provocation could well be his undoing. She shook her head infinitesimally, hoping he would heed her warning and remain silent.

"Perhaps Lady Beatrice should stay here until the baby is born. She is, after all, rather close to her time." As usual, Sir William was the first one daring to speak out, but his protest was waved aside with a peremptory gesture.

"She will accompany us," Sir Robert said with finality. "Corlith is easier to defend than Devance Castle, and I cannot afford to leave her here with a less than adequate guard. It is only a three-day ride away, and she will have nothing to do but rest once she gets there."

It was the first time he had expressed the wish for her to give birth anywhere other than here. Beatrice knew he was making her pay for her earlier defiance, but she did not care. An idea had started to blossom in her head. If she left with the escort, she would spend more time with Edward. An extra three days in his company would be ample reward for a taxing journey.

"Very well, my lord, it will be as you say," she murmured, eyes lowered to hide the gleam in them.

Sir Robert nodded in satisfaction, putting this amenable answer down to his successful handling of her rebellion. Edward was not so easily fooled. He guessed Beatrice was not tamed at all but merely playing a longer game. Would she claim to feel faint at the last moment? Surely even Sir Robert would not make her come if he thought the baby was in any danger. He had no illusion on the level of concern the man had for his wife, but perhaps the idea that his heir could suffer from his obstinacy would make him rethink his decision.

He glanced at her but could not quite interpret the look she threw him.

A moment later, once everyone had gone to oversee the various preparations, he maneuvered to find himself next to Beatrice. There was an uncomfortable niggling at the back of his mind and he needed to reassure himself that she wasn't really considering taking the dangerous journey.

"Tell me you have a plan to avoid joining a retinue of men riding for war tomorrow," he said between his teeth, doing his best to appear calm in case people happened to glance his way.

"I don't," she whispered back.

His heart plummeted. Why was he not surprised? "You cannot go. It's too dangerous."

"My husband clearly disagrees. So I will obey," she answered with a thin smile.

"It is folly and you know it!"

"Edward, please. If I didn't want to go I would find a way not to go." She blushed. "But I do."

He stared at her, horror freezing the blood in his veins when he understood what she meant. "You are doing this to be with me? You are doing this madness for me!"

She nodded, as if it were the most natural thing in the world. "Of course I'm doing it for you. Why else?"

"I cannot let you do it."

"You can and you will," Beatrice answered, displaying the stubbornness he remembered so well. "In any case, I have little choice in the matter. Sir Robert will only bundle me into the litter if I refuse to go."

Edward gritted his teeth. Unfortunately, she might well be right. "You could always pretend to be ill at the last moment, make him believe your travail has begun."

"I could, but I am not going to." Beatrice closed her eyes. "I cannot let you go just yet. I am not ready to watch you leave, not when you are going to face death. I cannot deal with the idea of losing you. I need more time."

"Do you think I feel any different?" he growled, barely resisting the need to draw her into his arms. "But I cannot sacrifice you because of my selfish desire to be with you. You could give birth at any time. It is too dangerous. How would I bear to know you died on the journey because you wanted to be with me?"

There was such urgency in his voice that Beatrice's eyes widened. Then she lowered her gaze to the floor and shook her head.

"I'm sorry. I cannot stay and watch you go if there is something I can do to delay the moment. We are going to be parted soon enough."

Yes, they would.

Despite all his arguments, Edward knew he would give anything to spend more time with Beatrice. The only thing he would not have been prepared to do was put her in danger.

Yet this was precisely what was going to happen.

Chapter 7

They left the next day at dawn, a slow procession aiming toward Windsor. After having spent the morning on the road, they met up with another local lord's retinue, and it was a contingent of some seventy men-at-arms with their various followers that stopped to partake in some refreshments in the middle of the afternoon.

Beatrice had not yet managed to contrive a meeting with Edward, but she resolved not to let the rest of the day go by without seeing him. As they set off he had glared at her, willing her to abandon the enterprise and feign illness while there was still time. She had not. The idea of seeing him ride away from her was enough to make her overcome her dread of the journey ahead.

There was no denying that it would be hard on her. Her belly made every little jolt hard to bear, and it hadn't taken her long to realize that, as incredible as it was, she might have been better on a horse than in a litter that seemed to unseat her every time it went over a hole or bump on the road. But even this physical discomfort was nothing compared to the fear gripping her bones. This was no leisurely expedition. They were an army riding into danger. What if the Lancastrians decided to attack the king's men before they could regroup? She would find herself in the midst of a fight to the death.

Still, there was no use fretting over it now. She would be with the retinue until they reached Corlith

Manor.

All she could do was hope the Lancastrians decided that seventy men-at-arms posed too much of a threat to be ambushed—and grit her teeth every time she was sent flying against the wooden walls of the litter.

For now, at least, they had stopped.

"Strawberries?" Beatrice exclaimed, plunging her nose into the bowl Lady Margaret was handing her. She inhaled the heady smell and groaned. "Where on earth did you get these?"

"Sir William sends them with his compliments. He thought that after the long journey in this heat you might like to partake of something lighter than mutton chops," Lady Margaret told her with a smile.

"Indeed I do." Beatrice glanced at the thick slices of meat cooling in front of her. She hadn't been able to take a single bite. "That is very thoughtful of him. Kindly ask him to come over so I can thank him adequately."

"I know not where he is. His man brought them on his behalf."

Beatrice gave an inward smile. She did not doubt for one moment that Sir William was not responsible for this attention. He might not even be aware he was supposed to have sent the strawberries to her. Edward must have gone into the forest and gathered them himself. A nobleman would never have known where to find the fruit, even supposing he had thought about doing so.

She bit into a juicy berry and closed her eyes in rapture, picturing Edward feeding them to her himself. He had done so once with blackberries from the forest by her father's castle. She still remembered the taste of his kisses after they had eaten the fragrant fruit together.

"If Sir William is unavailable, please ask his squire

to come in his stead," she said. "Hardcross, I think his name is."

"It's Hardthorne," Lady Margaret corrected with sparkling eyes.

"Of course," Beatrice said easily, hiding a pang of jealousy at this reaction. It had not escaped her notice that her lady betrayed an inordinate level of interest in Edward. Not one usually prone to vivacity, Lady Margaret obeyed her orders with a haste confirming her suspicions. Still, it was hard to blame her. You did not meet men like him every day.

A moment later, Edward was by the litter.

"I should thank Sir William for these strawberries, but I do not want to disturb him," she told him levelly, since Lady Margaret was hovering in the background and a few people were within earshot.

"You can thank me instead, my lady," he answered just as matter-of-factly, keeping his gaze fastened on her. "I will make sure he gets the message."

Beatrice had to school her features into impassivity when a gurgle of laughter bubbled within her. They were sharing a secret, just like in the old times, and it felt wonderful.

"Tell him they are delicious. Not quite as indulgent as blackberries, though. I find I have a particular fondness for blackberries."

Edward bowed to hide the fact that his lips were twitching slightly. So Beatrice remembered that day, as he'd hoped she would. His groin stirred in remembrance. They had eaten the fruit off each other's bodies, cleaning the juice with slow, deliberate licks. Never had anything tasted half as delicious as her berry-scented skin.

"I agree, they are delectable. But that particular

pleasure will have to wait." At the word pleasure he saw her eyes flutter. The corner of his mouth lifted infinitesimally. No, he wasn't the only one remembering just how wild their lovemaking had been that day. "It is only spring."

"Of course."

There was nothing more they could say before she dismissed him. Edward willed himself to stay silent when there were so many things he would have liked to tell her. She could not detach her gaze from him—her eyes were impossibly wide, as if she were trying to sear his image into her mind, and he guessed he would appear just as desperate.

"Sir William will want to know how you fared today, my lady," he said before taking his leave. They could not remain staring hungrily at each other in front of everyone for much longer. "He enquired about your wellbeing earlier."

"That is very kind of him. Tell him I am a little weary but otherwise fine."

"I will." Edward was keeping his voice as impassive as hers but his eyes, for her alone, were warm with concern.

"Before you go, if I may." One of Beatrice's ladies, whom he identified as Lady Margaret, cut in as she walked forward. Her cheeks were flushed, and Edward noticed she had difficulty meeting his eye. Wonderful. An admirer was the last thing he needed right now. Or…was it? Perhaps it would help draw people's attention away from him and Beatrice if he was seen with a woman who clearly fawned over him.

"What can I do for you, my lady?" he asked with all the courtesy he was capable of. Then, for good measure, he threw her a smile. The woman instantly went the color of the strawberries he had picked earlier. Perfect.

"I…I heard the men say there was a river nearby."

"Indeed there is."

"I wanted to wash Lady Beatrice's gown. It got soiled earlier on when a jolt sent the contents of her wine cup all over it, but I would be afraid of going on my own for fear of getting lost. If I could trouble you but a moment…"

"It is no trouble," he assured her. In the corner of his eye he saw Beatrice's face become thundery. His mouth twitched. She was furious, but he loved it because it betrayed, more surely than anything else, that she still had feelings for him and nothing could have pleased him more. "Shall we?" he asked, tilting his head in Lady Margaret's direction.

Oh, the wretched man! Never in her life had Beatrice had to work harder at indifference, and she was not entirely sure her voice was steady when she spoke. "There is no need to go just now, Lady Margaret. You should take the opportunity of this stop to have a rest like the rest of us."

"But I—"

"The river is not far, and it will take but a moment," Edward cut in smoothly. "But it is indeed safer if she doesn't go alone around these unknown parts."

"Then I thank you," Beatrice said as graciously as she could.

Calmly, as if he had not suspected her turmoil, he turned to her lady and flashed her a smile that would have reduced any woman to a puddle of need. "I await your pleasure."

Beatrice clenched her jaw in a desperate attempt to

stay composed. Why was Edward smiling at Lady Margaret thus? In a moment he would offer her his arm! Jealousy gnawed at her insides. Why could she not be the one to go somewhere alone with Edward?

"Make haste, Lady Margaret," she said with some asperity. "This heat is unbearable. I am eager to get changed."

"I apologize. I thought you had no need for the gown straight away. Evidently I was mistaken," Edward said with a humility aimed at hiding the mischief sparkling in his eyes. "We shall return presently."

They departed together and Beatrice felt her heart break a little.

In another day, two at the most, Edward would leave her for good, to go into battle. Now she knew he was in Sir William Bartlett's employ, she would at least be able to keep herself informed of his fate, but it would be a poor substitute for his presence by her side. She did not know how she would bear his absence this time. The need she had for him went far beyond mere physical desire—it was even more intense than it had been at her father's castle, and it frightened her.

When Lady Margaret returned a while later, Beatrice had gone back into the litter and was feigning sleep. She did not want to see her lady's eyes alight with the pleasure of having spent a moment in Edward's company or hear her enthuse about how helpful he had been.

They set off immediately after. Having eaten and drunk their fill, the men were eager to push on. In the litter, the heat was stifling, and Beatrice soon began to feel nauseous. The morning had been bad enough, but the long journey was starting to take its toll. Try as she might she just could not find a comfortable position, and she suspected her whole body would be covered in bruises by the time she reached Corlith.

Toward the evening they arrived at a river, only to discover the bridge was too frail to allow the passage of their large retinue.

The nearest crossing point was some miles upstream. As they had stopped already, the men decided to camp out here. The scouts sent to investigate quickly found a suitable spot in a nearby field. Sir Robert ruled that Beatrice would sleep in the litter, for want of a better alternative.

She didn't protest, knowing she would only be ignored if she did. Even she could see there were no other options. Night was falling fast and they had not seen a village for miles. She went to stretch her legs, taking deep breaths of the cool evening air in the hope of steadying her churning stomach. It had been an exhausting day, but she feared she would not be able to sleep.

"Let me get you settled somewhere under the trees. You will be more comfortable than in the hot, cramped litter," Edward's soft whisper suddenly reached her. Kneeling on the ground, he was busy cleaning Sir William's saddle. She stared ahead of her, ignoring him. In the fading light she was sure no one looking at them would suspect they were actually talking to each other.

"No," she said under her breath. If he took it upon himself to provide her with a sleeping place it would be too conspicuous.

"I could have a word with Sir William," he insisted, keeping his back turned to her. "He could—"

"No," she repeated, her body tensing up in protest.

After the trying day, she was feeling dizzy, and all of a sudden she wavered on her feet. Instantly Edward was up, offering her his arm.

"Look at you—you're exhausted. You need to lie down and get some proper sleep. You nearly fell over." This last was spoken louder to justify his forwardness.

"Please take me back to my litter as arranged and call Lady Margaret to attend to me." Beatrice made a point of wording her answer in such a way that he could not ignore her mind was made up. She didn't meet his eye, but she knew he would be bristling with anger at her refusal to accept his help. Nonetheless, he had no other choice but to obey her instructions without any comment, as any squire should.

Once at the litter, Beatrice felt a tug on her arm. The meaning was clear. Edward was begging her not to go in, urging her to relent. She could not. To have him help her so deliberately go against her husband's instructions would raise too many comments. Even if Sir Robert didn't notice anything was amiss, someone was bound to report on the squire's unseemly interest in his wife. Already she could not believe the lingering looks between them had gone undetected. She should not tempt fate any more than they had.

She tried to disengage her hand from Edward's hold, but he didn't let her. Short of snatching it away there was nothing she could do. Of course doing so was out of the question. They were surrounded by people. She looked at him beseechingly but he did not budge.

"Please," she whispered under her breath. "Edward, let me go."

His jaw was set in granite, his eyes glittered in disapproval. In this instant no one would have suspected him of harboring unseemly feelings for the lady of the castle. If she hadn't known better she would have thought he hated her. As she did know him, she understood that what he really hated was his powerlessness. He was on the verge of an outburst. She could not let it happen, not in front of everyone.

"I thank you for your help, Hardthorne. You can go back to the other servants. I need to be alone now," she said, mustering all her inner strength to sound like the haughty lady she had never been in front of him. She needed him to go away before he did something that betrayed his inner feelings.

She succeeded only too well in her mission. The look of pain in his eyes pierced her own heart. He looked like a man mortally wounded. Before she could utter one word of apology he stopped her with a lethal stare.

"I will do as you wish and go back to where I belong."

Slowly the grip on her hand loosened, and a moment later she was free. Towering over her with a look of thunder on his face, Edward glared at her until she lowered her eyes in shame. Her heart was thudding unbearably fast in her chest. He made a curt bow and strode away from her, ripping her chest in half as he did. She guessed he would go into the forest to reflect that for the first time she had acted as if he was not worthy to kiss the ground she walked on.

Beatrice willed her feet up the steps of the litter and fell down onto the seat just as her legs gave way from under her.

Unsurprisingly, she spent a sleepless night, but the pains in her stomach were nothing compared to the remorse racking through her. Her wretchedness was so acute that for a moment she considered going out into the night in search of Edward to apologize for her rudeness, to beg him to forgive her. She quickly came to her senses. Such a rash plan would never work. She had no idea where he would be. In the darkness she would get lost, and what explanation could she give for such a foolhardy escapade if anyone saw her?

In the morning, he didn't come to see her, and she didn't see him anywhere. A terrible thought assailed her. Had he left, unable to deal with the situation between them?

"Have there been any desertions in the night?" she asked Lady Margaret when she came to bring her some food. "I know some men would try anything to avoid going into battle." She knew no such thing, but her lady didn't seem overly surprised by her question, evidently agreeing that it was a possibility.

"No, as far as I know all the men are still here," she replied with a frown.

"That is good to know." Beatrice gritted her teeth, only partially relieved. If Edward had not fled, then he was avoiding her. It was just as bad.

"You must have something to eat, my lady," Lady Margaret entreated her.

Looking at the slices of ham she'd brought her, Beatrice shook her head. Her stomach was still queasy from the trying day yesterday. "I'm not hungry," she muttered, thinking that the only thing she would have considered eating right now were some refreshing strawberries. But none would come today, not while Edward was furious with her.

They set off soon after, making the long detour to the next crossing point on the river. It was even hotter than it had been the day before, and by the time the sun reached its zenith Beatrice could not ignore that something was seriously wrong. Cramps had started to assault her, but Sir Robert didn't come to enquire after her welfare once. Sir William did when the retinue stopped to allow the horses a drink later in the afternoon, but she did not dare tell him anything.

In the end, she didn't need to. He took one look at her grimacing face and understood what she had not said.

"Please let me speak to your husband, my lady. This is not right. We should take you to a place where you could have a proper rest before we carry on. A little delay cannot hurt."

She desperately wanted to agree, but she shook her head. "We are not so far from Corlith now. I am sure I will be all right once I've had something to drink."

Both Lady Margaret and Sir William pursed their lips, but Beatrice did not let their reaction worry her because, at that precise moment, what awfully resembled a contraction ripped through her. She waved them both away and dug her nails into her palm, whimpering in fright at the realization.

Her travail had begun.

****

She should have been out by now.

Edward kept his eye on the litter, hoping to see Beatrice come out. Everyone else was in the meadow, taking in the cool evening air, but she was nowhere to be seen. A moment passed, and then Lady Margaret came out from the drawn curtains, her face a mask of worry, and hastened to where Sir Robert's men were erecting his tent for the night.

He didn't need anymore to know something was

wrong.

Muttering a series of curses under his breath, Edward approached the litter in a purposeful stride. He was still seething at Beatrice's treatment of him the night before, but he could not ignore his instinct. Every fiber of his body was telling him to go to her and see that she was all right.

Knowing he was in plain sight of many, he approached the groom tending to the horses and tapped him on the shoulder.

"Go and get a drink. I'll take care of them."

The man didn't need to be asked twice. With a grateful nod he hurried toward the rest of the men.

Edward forced himself to remove the harnesses and bring water to the horses before he approached the litter.

"My lady, we have stopped for the night. Would you like to take the air?" he asked in an impersonal tone.

When a muffled cry of pain answered the question, he almost ripped the litter curtain open. No wonder Beatrice was not feeling well. In her state, being jolted for two days in this accursed vehicle would be tantamount to torture. Unable to wait another moment, he lifted the curtain. Inside, the heat was unbearable. He let out a curse when he saw her lying on the seat, her face contorted in a mask of pain, her hands clutching at her belly, her hair matted with sweat.

His whole body went cold at the sight. "Beatrice." It was only a whisper. He doubted she would have heard him use her name, such an intimate, forbidden thing to so. "Speak to me. What's wrong?" he asked, although he had already guessed that it would be the baby.

She opened her eyes and tried to sit up. "I have had these pains all day, and it's getting worse...I think the baby is coming."

"It's too early!" He was aghast.

"Not by much, a little over three weeks, I think, but it's…" She stopped and inhaled sharply. "Oh, but it is coming, I know it is!"

"You cannot stay here. We need to get you somewhere you can get help." He looked around and saw nothing but fields and trees. "We passed a village and a manor house not so long ago," he said suddenly. "I will go and make some enquiries."

"No, Edward, don't leave me, I'm scared." She took his hand and tried to draw him closer to her. "My baby… It needs help!"

"I know, and so do you. I cannot stay, but I will send your lady. You won't be on your own, I promise." Just then he saw Lady Margaret hurrying back. He took his hand out of Beatrice's grasp and retreated to a more seemly distance. "Lady Beatrice fears she has gone into labor. Do whatever you can to help her," he instructed the woman curtly.

The look of terror on her face told him she would be of no use in the event of a birth. More likely she would faint before Beatrice had even lifted her gown. If anyone was going to help her, it was him. He was loath to leave her in this state, but he had no choice.

He stepped down from the litter and broke into a run.

****

Beatrice lay in a comfortable bed, unable to believe she was not going to give birth under the stars. She and Lady Margaret had been led to a manor house where a room waited for them. She hadn't asked how this miracle had come to be, so relieved had she been to get out of the litter, where she had thought she was about to die.

Her problems were not quite over, though. She still had to give birth unassisted to a baby that was too early. By her side Lady Margaret was wiping her brow and muttering useless encouragements.

"We will need water, clean linen, and a knife," Beatrice instructed her between gasps. The pains had changed slightly and, remembering the day Alys had been born, she was now sure the baby was indeed coming. "You will have to help me."

"I can't!" Lady Margaret recoiled in terror.

"There is no one else. You will have to." She panted as another contraction seized her.

"I have never—"

A knock on the door interrupted the protest, and a young woman came into the room, her composure and smiling face an incongruous if highly welcome sight.

"Well, what do have we here?"

"Who are you?" Beatrice gasped, although the sheer relief of seeing someone looking more competent than Lady Margaret made her body relax somewhat.

"Joan Winters. I'm a midwife. Your husband knocked on my door as if his own life depended on my coming, rather than yours and that of the babe's." Mistress Joan chuckled as she approached the bed. "He thundered into the village earlier, bellowing that he needed a midwife, and I swear he would have raised the hounds of hell themselves had I not swiftly answered."

"My husband?" Beatrice was incredulous. She knew Lady Margaret had gone to tell Sir Robert about the situation, but from what she had said, he had not been overly worried. Mayhap he had changed his mind when he realized that his stubbornness might cost him his precious heir. "He wants to ensure that we have a son this time, you see, and—"

Another contraction tore through her, cutting her explanation short.

"What man doesn't?" Clearly accustomed to such an attitude, Mistress Joan was unimpressed. "It's only natural. But I have seen enough anxious fathers in my time to tell you that as long as you make it in one piece he will forget all about his precious heir if the babe turns out to be a girl."

Beatrice gave a mirthless laugh but did not waste her breath contradicting the kind woman.

"The baby is a month early, mayhap slightly less," she informed the midwife, banishing all thoughts of Sir Robert from her mind. Something more important was at stake.

"It should be fine. You look strong enough, and we are in the warm months," Mistress Joan said with a brisk shrug. Her confidence was reassuring. "Now, let us get this baby out of you, shall we?"

After what felt like days of excruciating labor, Beatrice was handed her newborn daughter and started to weep. Such was her relief that she could not bring herself to worry about her husband's reaction when he learnt he had fathered another girl. The baby was small but perfect and, more importantly, alive. Earlier that day she would not have bet on this happy outcome.

Having examined the little girl, Mistress Joan declared herself satisfied.

"She will need feeding, though," she said. "And the sooner the better. I imagine that given the circumstances of the birth, arrangements have not been made to find a wet nurse?"

"No. But I will feed her myself if you will be kind

enough to show me how. I am her mother, after all," Beatrice answered roundly. Mistress Joan's eyes crinkled with approval at this unusual decision from a lady of rank.

"It's easy enough." She settled the baby and encouraged her to suckle on her mother's nipple. It didn't take the little girl long to understand what was required of her and latch on. "Here. How does it feel?"

"Unbelievable." Beatrice beamed, watching her daughter snuggled up against her. Sir Robert had not deemed it appropriate for her to feed Alys, and she had always regretted it. Had she suspected how wonderful it would feel, she would have faced his wrath and done it anyway.

"Good. Then all there is for me to do now is to bring the news to the proud father and take him out of his misery. I could hear his pacing outside the door all night. This is not something I have had to handle before, I must confess." Mistress Joan chuckled. "Why, I even considered asking him to come in and help, just to stop his distractive prowling! I tried telling him your screams would only upset him, but he refused to budge. Men are usually uninterested about such matters, but he would not go to bed until he knew you were safely delivered."

"Are you sure?" Beatrice asked, as suspicion invaded her once more.

Whilst her attention had been focused on managing the labor pains she had not given much thought to the midwife's tale, but now it seemed highly unlikely that Sir Robert would have roused a sleepy village for her sake. Even more extraordinary was the idea of him forgoing his sleep to pace outside her door all night with her screams for sole company.

Only one man she knew would do that.

Before she could ask her if the man who had come was the most handsome one she had ever laid eyes on, the midwife stroked the baby's cheek.

"She really is a beauty. Let us hope she has your husband's blue eyes."

"My husband has brown eyes, like me," Beatrice breathed, as her suspicions were confirmed. "*Edward* went to find you," she said to herself.

The two women looked at each other for a fleeting moment.

"I see." Mistress Joan quickly recovered but her eyes sparkled with a new intent. "Well, in any case, I should go and tell him that his girl has come to no harm."

"The baby is not his!" Beatrice said immediately, knowing that was the only conclusion Mistress Joan could have drawn from the series of events. But she could not have her insinuating to Sir Robert that the baby was not his child. As much as she wished he wasn't the father, he was, and she could not afford to have him doubt his paternity. Things were bad enough already.

The midwife tilted her head. "I did not mean the baby. But this Edward will need to be told that *you* are all right. I fully expect him to burst into the room any moment if I don't go to him now."

Chapter 8

"He will not come to me when he finds out this is another girl. He did not come when Alys was born," Beatrice told Edward with a sad smile.

He had risked it all to come to see her, and though they both knew it was pure madness, she did not have the will to send him away. The birth had drained her, and having him with her when she was feeling so vulnerable had made her heart explode with an excess of joy, gratitude, and desire all combined.

"He would not be that callous, surely?"

She snorted. How could he even ask the question. Had he not met the man? "He wants his son and heir. Nothing else would interest him."

"I don't care if he wants the next king of England! You are safe and the baby lives! After all the hardship he put you through, he should be thankful for this at least!" Away from prying eyes Edward was not even trying to control his temper. Beatrice found a smile at this heated reaction, which was so much like the Edward she remembered. "Why are you smiling?" he asked, shaking his head in irritation. "God knows there is little to smile about."

"The midwife said that you would not care about the sex of the child," she could not help but say.

"Damn right I don't!" he roared, resuming his restless prowling. "But...why on earth would she say such a thing?"

"Because she thought you were the father."

The look he threw her was so intense Beatrice had to avert her gaze. Oh, if only this baby had been his, not Sir Robert's! The mere thought of carrying Edward's child made her insides twist in longing.

"Thank you for getting Mistress Joan to attend to me," she said, her voice shaky with emotion. "Why did you do it? I thought you were mad with me for the way I treated you, as you had every right to be."

The blue eyes sent sparks. "I *was* mad with you, I'm not going to deny it. Does that mean I should have let you go through this ordeal on your own? Does that mean I should have let you or your baby die and have your deaths on my conscience for the rest of my days? Once upon a time, you would not have asked me that question. I thought you knew me better than that."

Beatrice's face fell and Edward berated himself for hurting her with his comments. But really, did she think him capable of ignoring the danger and pain she'd been in, all because of a disagreement between them?

"I did. I do. I'm sorry. I'm exhausted, I'm not sure what to feel, or how to explain it. You don't know what I've been through these last few years. If I hadn't had my Alys, I think I would have…" She stopped and wiped a tear from her cheeks, looking more miserable than he had ever seen her. "Countless times I wished I could see you again, and now that you're finally here, I cannot deal with it. I don't know how to behave. I seem to hurt you every time I open my mouth. Forgive me? I really don't mean to."

This earnest admission was enough to appease him. He could never stay angry with Beatrice for long, and she seemed genuinely contrite and confused. It was little wonder, given what she'd had to endure in the last few days. What was he doing snarling at her? It was just as she'd said, now that they were actually reunited, he did not know how to behave. He could not be the lover anymore, and he did not know how—much less *want*—to be anything else.

"I understand," he said softly. "Please don't cry. I do not deserve it."

"I'm sorry for how I acted yesterday. I had no right to speak to you that way," she said hurriedly. "I do not think you do not belong with me, I…I only wanted to keep you out of danger."

"I know you did, but you have to stop thinking about me, protecting me, and focus on yourself instead." Edward gave a sigh and sat next to her on the bed. "You could have died tonight. I told you it was dangerous to travel so near your term." The mere idea that she could be dead right now was enough to make his gut clench in cold dread.

"I know. This is all a mess!"

It was. A terrible, terrible mess.

"I've missed you," Edward whispered, unable to keep the fact to himself any longer. He should not speak thus to another man's wife, but he had missed her, every moment of every day, even when he was telling himself he hated her, and he needed her to know it. "I've missed you terribly, Beatrice."

Her eyes widened at the intimate use of her name. He had not called her Beatrice since his return, only that time in the litter, but he knew that, lost to the pain of her labor she had not heard him. For a while she just looked at him and then her face crumpled.

"Oh, Edward, I've missed you too!" she cried out. "So much. I've been in hell without you!"

A tear fell on the back of her hand.

Before Beatrice could move, Edward had taken her hand in his and, keeping his eyes firmly fastened on hers, he licked off the salty drop from her skin. The feel of his warm, silky tongue on her flesh sent a jolt of undiluted desire coursing down her veins. She whimpered as an image of Edward's head nestled between her thighs crashed through her mind. He had once kissed her soft center just before entering her. The memory of that brief, scandalous kiss made her croak out loud. He had never dared to renew the experience, but she had never forgotten the feel of it.

It had blown her mind away.

She saw in Edward's eyes that he was thinking of the same thing. She swallowed and the tears she had tried to keep at bay began flowing freely. There would be no containing them any longer.

"Forgive me, forgive me," he said, raining kisses on the hand he was still holding. "You have just been through an ordeal. I have no right making you feel sad. You should be resting. You are exhausted."

He stood, but she tightened her fingers around his in a desperate grip and forced him back down onto the bed.

"No!" Beatrice almost screamed. "Don't leave me, not yet, not like this!" Edward would be gone in the morning along with the retinue of men. She did not see how she could bear the separation. "I need you. Stay here, please stay with me a while. I…"

She looked around helplessly. What could she say? Nothing. What did she have to offer him? Nothing. A teary woman who had just given birth to another man's child, whose body was bloodied, sweaty and torn, had little to entice him. Besides, what purpose would it serve for him to remain any longer? It made no sense to delay his departure or to pretend anything could happen between them.

Yet for a moment Edward had looked at her as if she were a woman he was free to love, as if they could get past the lady-and-squire relationship, as if a future was possible for them.

"I cannot stay, you know that," he said softly. "I had to see that you were all right, but it was selfish of me. I should not have come at all. Forgive me."

After one least kiss on the tip of her fingers he left the room.

At the sound of the door closing, something died inside of Beatrice, and she knew that this time she would never get over the heartbreak.

****

Sir Robert came to see her in the morning, taking Beatrice by surprise. She had not expected his visit, nor did she feel particularly honored by it.

"We are leaving presently," he informed her in a cold voice. "We cannot delay anymore."

The comment stung. The fact that she had given birth in what could only have been called abject conditions was obviously considered an inconvenience to him rather than an ordeal for her. The inconvenience might possibly have been overlooked if the baby had been a boy but was certainly not forgiven for a mere girl.

Beatrice's heart seized in her chest. So this was it. The men were leaving. More to the point, *Edward* was leaving. She did not care about the others, least of all her husband. He could have elected to go to the farthest corners of the kingdom and remain there until his death as far as she was concerned.

"Thorpe will stay with you to ensure your safety," Sir Robert added, pointing to a young man waiting by the door. He looked barely past his teens, and half frightened to death by the prospect.

She merely nodded. So much for Corlith Manor being easier to defend than Devance Castle! That her husband was prepared to leave her in an unknown place with only one untried man in attendance was all the proof she needed to be shown that he had meant to take her along on this journey with the sole purpose of inconveniencing her, not of ensuring her safety.

Beatrice gave a sigh. She hadn't said a word since Sir Robert had entered the room, but he didn't seem to expect any comment from her. The only part of her he was interested in was her womb, and in his mind it had failed him yet again. There was nothing she could or wanted to say. He walked over to the cot where the baby was sleeping and watched her for a while.

"I trust next time you will not disappoint me, my lady, and will present me with an heir at last," he said, unable to repress a movement of impatience.

The full horror of what he said hit Beatrice like a blow to the skull. He was already thinking of resuming his visits to her bed and fathering another child on her. She remained silent for fear she would retch if she opened her mouth.

"I will see you at Devance Castle when we return from battle. There is little cause for you to go to Corlith Manor now. I bid you good day."

With those words he left.

Alone at last, Beatrice took her daughter in her arms

and looked at her until her eyes ached. The lack of sleep, the throbbing pain between her legs, the misery of her situation almost defeated her. Edward was about to leave, and she did not even have Alys to comfort her. Then the baby gave a yawn, and her heart filled with undiluted love. How odd that she should love so much someone who had been imposed upon her by a man she hated! She could not help but wonder what she would feel holding in her arms Edward's child instead of Sir Robert's, a child whose father she actually loved.

Well, she would never get to know the answer to that question now, would she?

After her wedding, she had thought for a few weeks she was carrying Edward's baby. Her monthly courses had stopped, giving her cause to believe he had got her with child. After months of vain hope, however, she had been forced to conclude that she wasn't pregnant. Her stomach had stayed desperately flat and there had been no other symptoms. A wise woman consulted in secret had dashed her final hopes. Sometimes a woman's courses dried without her being with child, most notably in situations of intense mental strain. Could she think of a recent event that could have induced such a state?

Thinking of her forced union to Sir Robert, Beatrice had laughed and laughed until her sides hurt, fearing for a moment that she was truly losing her mind.

So no, she had not borne Edward a child. There had been nothing to show for their few weeks of happiness. Perhaps she should have been relieved it was the case, as Sir Robert's reaction to even the slightest suspicion of it would have been terrible. He seemed to believe that she and the stable lad, as he always referred to him, had done nothing more than kiss, and she was keen to maintain that impression.

Still she had mourned for the child she had thought to carry, for what would never be.

For months she had pretended that her courses came and went regularly. The lie both avoided an unnecessary, unpleasant confrontation with Sir Robert and afforded her a week's respite from his attentions every month. She cut herself to stain some cloth in case the servants reported to him. The pain was a small price to pay, and he never noticed the faint scars on the soles of her feet.

The first year of her marriage had been dire, the worst of all.

Edward had disappeared from her life so completely, so unbearably. The man who had once been at the center of her world had vanished without a trace. Nothing at Devance Castle reminded her of him, and she could not go back to the meadow where they had made love under the stars one night or haunt the place where they had shared their first kiss. No one even knew who he was, even if she could have talked about him. She could only dream about their time together.

She hadn't kept any trinkets from him or thought to cut a lock of his hair. He had never written her any letters or given her anything except happiness and dizzying pleasure. He was gone irremediably and the loss had made her hollow inside. Each passing day had only made that hole bigger.

Then one day, for no reason, her courses had returned, and six months later she had felt Alys kick in her womb, filling some of the void left by Edward's absence. Now at least she had someone to love.

But it wasn't the same. As much as she loved her daughter, it just wasn't the same.

Settling the baby at her breast, Beatrice fell into a doze. When she woke, everything was eerily quiet and the sun was high in the sky. Her heart nearly stopped at the realization.

Edward was gone.

While she slept, he had left, never to return again.

****

The men were ready, waiting for Sir Robert's orders to march on.

Edward looked at Sir William, who shook his head. He had exposed his plan to him a moment ago, only to be met with a staunch refusal. Knowing his master would not change his mind, he did the only thing he could do. Lifting the sleeve of his tunic, he bared the scar he had sustained in saving his liege's life in battle. Sir William would understand that he was calling on this debt of honor at last. He was telling him that with or without his help he was going to stay behind.

If he wasn't allowed to remain, then he would desert.

Edward knew he had won the argument when Sir William ran a hand through his hair and gave a sigh of surrender. The look in his eyes clearly said he didn't think it a good idea but still, at last, he resolved to help him.

"Sir Robert, allow me to repay your generous hospitality and that of Lady Beatrice by leaving my squire behind to look after her and the baby, since they are to remain behind. That way my conscience will be clear whilst going into battle."

Sir Robert's eyebrows arched at the offer. "I thank you, but I have already arranged for one of my men to stay here with them."

"I do not doubt it, but between you and me, Hardthorne is much more suited to such menial tasks than following me into battle. He is not as brave as your men would be when facing a charging enemy." Sir William made a grimace of regret. "We would miss him less in the melee than we would one of your seasoned soldiers, and Thorpe looks like a man better employed at war than looking after a woman and her baby."

This was such an outrageous lie that Edward thought for a moment his master did not truly intend to help him. Surely his description of Thorpe would raise Sir Robert's suspicion. The lad had barely left his mother's skirts and was as far removed from being a seasoned soldier as could be conceived. But against all odds, Sir Robert gave a snort of agreement and Edward allowed himself to breathe. Trust Sir William to know that shameless flattery would work. The slight on his own courage he ignored. It was just a way of making him pay for his defiance, and he did not care. As long as he was allowed to remain behind with Beatrice and ensure her safety, he could be accused of cowardice and much more besides. Sir William knew the truth, and it was all that mattered.

"Very well. If you are sure you will not miss your man, then let us not delay any further." Sir Robert waved his hand dismissively. It was clear he was uninterested in who would stay behind to safeguard his wife and daughter, as long as it wasn't him. "God knows we hadn't planned for this contretemps."

Without further ado, he strode over to the waiting men.

As soon as he was gone, Sir William rounded on Edward.

"You—"

"I'm staying," he said calmly, raising a hand to forestall any protest. "I cannot have Lady Devance on her own when she has just given birth and armies of soldiers are passing by. She needs someone to ensure no harm comes to her or the baby."

"I daresay, but it doesn't have to be you!"

"It does. This Thorpe cannot be trusted to protect her, for one, and you know it. For another…" He stopped and looked at his master as he had never done before, as you would look at a friend. "Tell me, if it were Lady Margery, what would you do?"

"It is hardly the same! She is my wife, I love her, so of course I would want to stay with her!" Sir William exclaimed heatedly.

"What if she weren't your wife, what if she were married to someone else? Would you stop loving her then?"

A tense silence followed the words. The two men stared at each other.

"God forgive me, I think I wouldn't," Sir William said in a breath, paling as if afraid to understand what Edward was telling him.

"And if this husband of hers treated her like an object, if he considered her as nothing more than a brood mare for his heir and a failure at that, if he forced her to go on an excruciating travel when she was about to give birth, and then left her behind without any care for her wellbeing or safety, wouldn't you do everything in your power to stay with her? To protect her?"

There was another pause whilst Sir William digested the words.

"Edward, this is dangerous. You cannot think like this," he said hurriedly, gripping his squire's arm. "No good can ever come out of it. You've fallen for a woman who cannot be yours."

"Yes, I have. Seven years ago."

Sir William's eyes widened at this extraordinary declaration. "How do you mean?"

Edward sighed, wondering how to word his explanation. He wanted to be honest, but he did not want to lose the esteem of a good man.

"You always praise the courage that made me save your life at the battle of Edgecote Moor, but it was nothing. I had nothing to lose then, for I had lost the will to live." He gritted his teeth as he thought back to the dark moments he had gone through. "Well, now I am reunited with Lady Beatrice, and that will to live is back with a vengeance. I am grateful you are allowing me to stay behind with her. I did not wish to abandon you during the night, when I returned to her, for I would have done so, with or without your blessing, and it would have been a poor return for what you did for me."

"You had better assure me that the lady's honor will not be compromised by the whole affair," Sir William warned.

Edward was loath to lie to his master. "I cannot do that," he said slowly. "If it were only my heart in danger of being broken I might find the strength to fight my need for her, but...I believe Lady Beatrice returns my feelings."

The words hung between them for a while.

"Tell me all," Sir William ordered darkly.

And so Edward told him about how they had met, doing his best to place the blame for the dalliance on himself rather than Beatrice. He kept to himself her shameless pursuit of him and their numerous encounters, focusing instead on the fact that he had never stopped loving her since he had been a simple stable hand in her father's employ.

He could tell that Sir William guessed he was hiding the extent of their relationship, but it did not matter. The light in his eyes was compassionate rather than censorial, and he trusted his master absolutely. Their secret was safe, guaranteed both by Sir William's scrupulous honor and his intense dislike of Sir Robert.

"I'm guessing we did not go to Devance Castle because my wife is a relative of Sir Robert's after all," Sir William said wryly.

"Of course we did." When his master's eyes narrowed, Edward had no choice but to tell him the truth. "At least, that is what allowed us to claim hospitality so easily."

"I am starting to wonder if you did not strike me yourself during the battle at Barnet, just to make sure we had a reason to call at Devance Castle." Edward smiled at the jest and knew that whatever happened next, at least he had not lost his master's esteem. "You need to be careful, though. I know Sir Robert doesn't show his wife half the interest he should, but he might notice that you do. One glance at you when you talk about her would convince anyone that you are in love with her."

Yes, Edward could well imagine…

"I thank you for the advice, but mercifully we will be alone, or as near as. There is little danger of word ever getting back to him."

"My friend, I am not sure what you are trying to achieve." This time there was pity in Sir William's voice. Edward shook his head ruefully.

"Neither am I. I only know that I have no choice."

Chapter 9

Bridget.

The name came to Beatrice's mind unbidden. She would name her baby daughter after her beloved grandmother. The two women had always shared a special bond. Beatrice remembered her as the only human being who, with the exception of Edward, had ever taken an interest in her.

One day her grandmother had revealed to her that she had married Beatrice's grandfather out of duty when her affection had been engaged elsewhere. There was nothing odd in this, of course. Women in general, and in the de Courcy family in particular, were expected to marry for advancement, not love, but her grandmother's admission had been a revelation. It had felt as if the older woman had told her that she should follow her heart should she fall for another man than the husband her parents had selected for her.

It was a startlingly radical piece of advice, in keeping with the old woman's unique personality. Of course she might have been less encouraging had she seen her granddaughter fall in love with a mere stable hand. No doubt her own flame had been someone suitable for a lady of rank, even if he wasn't the man her father had in mind for her. Beatrice would never know.

More than ever she wished her grandmother were by her side now. She would introduce her to her new great-granddaughter, and she would ask her opinion of Edward. What did she think of him? Was there any hope for them?

He had once asked her to forgo everything to be with him. Would she have hesitated, had he already been a squire at the time? If she had not been so foolishly cautious and had accepted his offer to flee immediately, he would have whisked her away before Sir Robert could marry her. Hindsight was a painful gift, for it showed you what you should have done but only when it was too late. Had she been told on that fateful night that by hesitating she would lose Edward forever and end up being married to Sir Robert, she would have left the castle on the instant, taking none of her possessions with her.

Beatrice was suddenly convinced that Edward would have found favor with her grandmother, especially if she had witnessed Sir Robert's callousness toward her. A very perceptive woman, she would have concluded that no one could have found contentment, much less happiness, with such a husband, however well born he might be. She would have given Edward her full approval had Beatrice dared to ask for it.

In any case, it was too late. Her grandmother was dead, and Edward was gone. He might well die in battle before the week was out.

Beatrice wiped the tears from her cheeks and resolved to sleep a while. She might not feel so wretched once she'd had some rest, she told herself, knowing that her despair had nothing to do with exhaustion.

As soon as she woke, Lady Margaret came to find her.

"Lady Alstridge expressed the wish to see you."

"Please ask her to come in."

Beatrice stood in welcome. To Lady Margaret's shock, she had insisted that she be allowed to get up from time to time. The midwife, unaccustomed to ladies keeping to their beds for days on end after giving birth, had readily agreed. As long as she didn't overtax herself she would feel better for behaving normally, Mistress Joan had ruled.

"I am forever indebted to you for allowing me shelter yesterday," Beatrice told Lady Alstridge when she entered. The woman had welcomed her under her roof without hesitation, and this generosity had possibly saved both her life and that of her daughter.

"Nonsense," the elderly lady said roundly. "I have given birth six times myself, and I wouldn't wish a labor in a ditch on my worst enemy. It is hard enough in the comfort of your own bed."

Through her wretchedness Beatrice found a smile. "Indeed." Once again she felt a rush of gratitude to Edward for procuring her a safe haven in which to give birth.

"You are welcome to stay here for as long as you need. I spoke to Mistress Joan earlier, and I understand you will not be fit to travel immediately."

"No, I will not be able to get back to Devance Castle for at least a week." Beatrice knew the lady was tactfully referring to the tearing she had suffered during her travail. The sting was less pronounced today, but the wound was still sore, and the midwife wanted to keep an eye on it. "But we can always go somewhere else if our presence here is an inconvenience. You have done more than enough for us."

"I will not hear of you leaving this room before you are fully recovered," Lady Alstridge said with decision.

"I would not want to have to answer for my refusal to that formidable squire of yours, should anything happen to you. He would no doubt demand my head for it. He was rather intimidating when he came knocking at the door, you know." She let out a small laugh.

"Yes, I'm afraid he can be rather intimidating when he puts his mind to it," Beatrice agreed, picturing Edward's fury if she suffered any discomfort that could have been avoided. Then she remembered he was gone and would never even get to hear about it. She bit the inside of her mouth to stop her distress from showing.

"I'll say! Intimidating is one word for him, but I can think of a few others. I could not resist him anymore than I could have resisted my own son. He was most eloquent in his plea. And of course, he is breathtakingly handsome, which never hurt a man pleading his cause." The lady winked and suddenly appeared ten years younger. "But that won't have escaped your notice, my dear."

Beatrice felt herself go crimson. The woman didn't know the half of it. Mercifully, Lady Alstridge didn't dwell on her praise of Edward.

"In any case, you will be doing me a favor if you stay here a while longer. I am to visit my sister in London and will be gone for a few weeks. It would put my mind at ease to know that the house is not empty while all these soldiers are on the loose. It will be protected with you and your man around."

Beatrice squeezed the lady's hand gratefully. "I thank you for this most generous offer. I am sure my husband will compensate you for your trouble," she said, privately knowing that he would do no such thing if left to his own device. She would see to it herself. "And don't worry about your house. I'm sure Thorpe can indeed be relied upon to keep it safe."

"Oh, this reminds me, he was waiting outside to deliver a message from your husband. Shall I let him in?"

Beatrice did her best not to let her hatred show at the mention of Sir Robert or her surprise at the fact that he had asked Thorpe to deliver a message. He had left only that morning, and his displeasure had been evident. What could he possibly have to tell her? Nevertheless, she did her best not to allow the lady to see the animosity she bore her husband. She had always been careful not to let it show, fearing that once her true feelings were allowed free rein, she would never be able to control them again.

"Please ask him to come in."

Once Lady Alstridge had gone, Beatrice walked to the window. In the distance, the road to Windsor was empty. She tried to picture Edward on horseback, resplendent in his velvet tunic, riding his bay horse next to Sir William. Was he thinking about her, or was his mind already on the battle ahead?

She wondered how she would survive the next few days. Awake at night feeding her baby, she would imagine him on the battlefield, lying in the mud, mortally wounded. Perhaps he would contrive a way to send her a letter while there was no chance of her husband seeing it, but even if he did she would not be able to reply.

How could it all have ended thus? He had come back to her only to be brutally taken away again.

Footsteps made her straighten her back. She didn't turn to welcome Thorpe, giving herself a moment to compose herself. He would not be able to guess what was making her so despondent, and she was loath to have him imagine that the departure of Sir Robert for war was responsible for her distress.

"My poor man, I wager you thought this expedition would cover you with glory and prestige, and now you are staying behind, saddled with a woman and her newborn baby. You must feel sadly misused."

"I might do, with another woman." Beatrice turned quickly at the deep voice answering her question. "But I can hardly complain about staying behind when I was the one asking for it. I guess glory and prestige will have to wait."

"Edward! You!"

With a cry Beatrice ran to him—but half way across the room she stopped and faltered. Edward closed the gap between them in two strides and received her in his arms. He could not resist the urge to do so. In the privacy of the room, no one would know what they did.

For a while he cradled her, saying nothing, allowing her softness to warm him, pretending he had every right to hold her thus. Then Beatrice let out a breathy moan that shot straight to his groin. Before he knew it his hold around her tightened and he let out a feral, possessive growl.

They drew apart, suddenly self-conscious.

"What are you doing here? Where is Thorpe? I thought…"

"You thought I had gone without even saying good bye," he finished in her stead.

"Yes," Beatrice admitted in a small voice, as if fearing he would hold the thought against her. He did not, knowing she could hardly be blamed for assuming as much when he hadn't warned her of his intentions. "How on earth did you contrive this?"

Edward hesitated. "Sir William helped me." He

would not tell Beatrice the whole truth, that her husband's total disregard in her fate had played a large part in the success of his plan. A more considerate man would never have allowed a complete stranger to take care of his wife and newborn child, preferring to leave with them a man—or three—he knew and trusted.

"So Sir William knows about us?" He was gratified to hear only curiosity in her question, not dismay. She wasn't appalled at having their past exposed, or ashamed by it. She was merely wondering how he had managed to find a way to stay with her.

"He knows enough to have allowed me to stay behind."

Beatrice gave a sigh and allowed her head to rest on his shoulder again. Edward's body, starved by lack of her warmth for so long, gave a jolt of recognition. His heart, which had missed her like a flower would miss the sun, started to beat in wild abandon. He could so easily lose himself in this embrace...

"I regret that I cannot express my gratitude to Sir William." She talked with her mouth pressed against his pectoral, as if she wanted to get inside of him, burrow in so they would never be parted. It was a feeling he could all too readily understand.

He wanted to do the same.

"You can thank me instead," he murmured, allowing himself to place a kiss on her hair. "It was my idea, after all."

"Thank you. For this *and* the strawberries. I know they were your idea as well."

She laughed, and he took a step backward, suddenly afraid of being on his own with her. There was nothing to stop them if they wanted to kiss, or more, no one to report to Sir Robert. The freedom was dizzying. Intoxicating.

Dangerous.

"What are we to do now?" Beatrice asked in a whisper, proving she was as daunted as he was by the possibilities available to them. She didn't try to get back into his arms, instead staying at a respectable distance.

"What *can* we do?" he answered with a shake of the head. "We are not at liberty to decide anything, any more than we were seven years ago."

He went to the window, turning his back to her as he stared at the road ahead just as she had done earlier. He thought back to Sir William's question. What *was* he hoping to achieve? He wasn't sure, but for better or for worse he was here now, with a thudding heart and a throbbing to match in his lower body.

Dear God, this would never end well…

"Do you know that for years I hated you?" he said abruptly. Perhaps recalling how he had kept that hate burning for so long would help douse the desire in his loins.

"You…*hated* me?" Beatrice's voice was no more than an appalled whisper.

He sighed. Did he have to be so blunt?

He turned to face her. "It was the only way I could stay sane. I told myself you had used me for your pleasure and then asked your chosen husband to get rid of me once you had tired of me, that I had been nothing but an embarrassing dalliance in your mind, a mistake, something to be ashamed of and best forgotten."

Every word pierced Beatrice's heart with the precision of a well-aimed dagger. It was unbearable to hear Sir Robert being called her chosen husband and

Edward a mistake, even if she understood why he would think that.

"And I hated you as well, hated you for abandoning me when I needed you the most," she said, panting in an excess of emotion. "I told myself I hated you for amusing yourself with me and then leaving me behind so easily. I knew it wasn't fair but...I resented you for letting me go to Sir Robert, for not fighting for me, for not caring about what would happen to me, for disappearing so completely out my life when you were constantly in my mind."

"I never abandoned you," he said in a breath.

"No. I know that now. But I kept thinking that if I had never known you I would have been better able to cope with the misery of my marriage."

Beatrice shook her head sadly. Indeed, if she hadn't known the pleasure you could get from lying in a man's arms, she might not have seen that what her husband was doing to her was nothing less than rape, she might have assumed it was what marital duty was supposed to be like. Certainly her own mother had told her on her wedding night that she should just learn to accept a man's attentions, however distasteful or painful they might be.

Beatrice had almost screamed back that she knew for a fact that with the right man lovemaking was not a chore to be endured but a pleasure to be savored and that such a thing would never happen with Sir Robert.

"If I had never met you, I would have carried on as before, not happily but at least oblivious to other, delightful possibilities. You made me see there was more to life than what I had been shown, and once I knew this I could not go back."

She and Edward just stared at each other. No, fate had not been kind to them.

"I'm sorry."

She shook her head. "It's all in the past. You are here now, and you are not going to be killed in battle. That is all that matters," she said with fervor. Compared to the pain of losing him, anything could be borne. "We will have a few weeks alone together."

Precious days snatched from fate's cruel plans, and nowhere near enough.

Edward nodded slowly, understanding all she was not saying. "I will go and get settled."

Once he was gone, Beatrice fell onto her bed and stared at the ceiling, marveling at the way Edward's return had transformed her from a wretched shell of a woman to one full of hope and joy.

Only he could have had that effect on her.

Dependable, efficient, thoughtful Edward. He had tempted her appetite during the journey, and seen to her comfort every step of the way. He had saved her from a dangerous labor on the road and provided her with a safe bed and a midwife, thereby saving her baby's life and possibly hers. He had risked Sir William's disapproval to ensure her safety, he had made her feel loved and cherished.

What had she ever done for him in return?

She had put his life in danger, humiliated him, made him feel lower than a servant when she had not simply ignored him...

She cuddled her little girl in her arms and fell into a deep musing. They would be spending the next few weeks here alone, or near enough. She would have to make amends for her hurtful behavior and seize this opportunity with both hands. If she didn't, she would spend the rest of her life regretting it. If she didn't at least try to live for few days as a happy woman, she would be unworthy of everything Edward had done for her.

****

"Would you be godfather to little Bridget?"

Beatrice looked at Edward nervously, knowing that he would balk at the idea. He regarded her in silence for a long moment, but then he shook his head.

"I cannot."

"She is so small, so fragile… We have to baptize her in case she…" She stopped before she said out loud that her baby might not live more than a few days. It seemed as if this would be tempting fate. "Lady Margaret and Mistress Joan have agreed to be godmothers. But I also need a man, a man I trust."

Tradition dictated that the mother should not be present at the christening, and she could not bear to let her little girl out of her sight. Although this birth had not gone according to plan, she knew the priest would not countenance her presence at the ceremony until she had been properly churched in six weeks' time. At least if Edward was with Bridget her mind would be at ease.

"Your husband will not accept me, a mere squire, as godfather to his child, be she a girl," Edward countered. "He will want a more prestigious—"

"My husband…" Beatrice cut in with a voice full of venom. "My *husband* will do what I deem necessary in this instance. Bridget has to be baptized. I am not risking her immortal soul for a man who will never show any interest in her. If he wanted her to have more prestigious godparents, then he should have left instructions regarding the matter. In any case, as you say, she is only a girl, not his precious heir, so I am sure he will quickly forget the affront. Say you will do it, Edward!" she cried in anguish.

"Are you commanding me to do it?" he asked, his voice thundery.

"No, I am asking you a favor!" she answered, exasperated at his stubbornness. "Will you stop trying to make me sound like a haughty lady? I thought you would have started believing by now that I of all people can treat you as an equal!"

Far from being chastened, Edward bristled at the rebuke. "An equal! Would you speak in such a tone to me if you thought I was your equal? Would you ignore me in front of other people if I was your equal? I think not."

"I have no choice! I don't ignore you, but I do not want people to know that I know you, much less *how* I have come to know you!"

"Yes. I think you have made that abundantly clear."

"Yes, but you don't know why!"

"Then tell me," he ordered, regarding her stonily, daring her to refuse. Never had he behaved so peremptorily with her before, and Beatrice knew she would not be able to talk her way out of an explanation this time.

"It is Sir Robert…I do not want him to know you for the stable hand who worked at my father's castle."

"Why not?" he asked more gently, when he saw she was at least being honest. "Are you ashamed?"

"No! Never. I will never be ashamed of what happened between us," she answered fiercely. "But Sir Robert swore to kill you if he ever saw you again. That day, the day we were supposed to meet at the oak, he heard us agreeing to meet, and he confronted me."

"Yes, I had already guessed that much. But why did you not come yourself?"

"I could not. My parents told me that day they had given their consent to my marriage to Sir Robert." Beatrice grimaced, remembered her despair at the unexpected news. "I could not escape for a moment that night, because they had organized a big banquet in my honor, with everyone waiting to congratulate me, trapping me. It was torture. I came to find you as soon as I could, in the morning, but you were gone."

Beatrice tried hard not to sound accusatory as she now knew he had been sent away by Sir Robert, not gone of his own accord, but she could not quite hide the hurt Edward's desertion had caused her. For years she had thought he had given up on their love without a fight, that he had not even waited to hear her explanation before leaving.

"I looked everywhere, refusing to believe you would merely have left and gone back to your parents' village without a word, but evidently you had, for you were nowhere to be found."

"Is this what your husband told you?" Edward was incredulous. "That I had gone back to my parents' village?"

"Why, yes. Isn't it what happened?" The incredulity in Beatrice's voice matched his.

"No, not quite," he answered gratingly. "He came to find me at the oak instead of you."

"What?" Beatrice cried out. "Is that what you meant when you said he had spoken to you?" She had never stopped to wonder when or where this encounter had happened, but of course Sir Robert would have known where to find him since he'd overheard them.

Lady Beatrice giving assignations to stable lads.

Oh, Lord.

"Yes, he came to find me, and he wasn't alone. At the time, I didn't know he was betrothed to you, of course. I only knew him as your uncle." He spat out the word. "He quickly corrected that impression. He told me that you two were to marry, that you had come to your senses and never wanted to see me again. Obviously I refused to leave without seeing you one last time."

"And then what happened?" Beatrice sensed that Edward had cut his explanation short to protect her sensibilities. But she needed to know. "What did he do to you? Tell me!" she insisted when he stayed silent.

"He had his henchmen beat me up," Edward answered reluctantly. "When I woke, I was alone in the forest, far from the castle. They must have taken me there while I was unconscious. So you see, I am not too surprised that Sir Robert hasn't recognized me all this time. It was dark for the first part of our encounter and later on I was beaten out of all recognition."

Beatrice wrapped her arms around her midriff in an effort to stop herself from collapsing from the inside. She could almost feel every hit Edward had suffered at the hands of the two thugs. It was all her fault! The man who was married to her, who had fathered her daughters, had beaten up Edward and left him for dead simply for daring to touch her!

She had almost cost him his life—and could still cause his death if they were discovered together.

"I never knew he came to find you that night, I swear, much less what he did to you." She spoke in a halting voice, willing him to believe her. "I didn't send him in my stead, and I didn't ask him to dispose of you. I thought you had concluded I didn't want to be with you and fled in disappointment when I didn't come to meet you or that you had come to hear about my engagement and decided to leave instead of compromising me."

"That is not why I went away, but certainly why I never came back to find you," Edward answered, not doubting for one moment Beatrice was telling the truth. She sounded too raw and looked too shocked at hearing what had happened that night. "I was not afraid of what Sir Robert would do to me, but for all my resentment I could not bear putting you in a difficult position."

That and the fact that he hadn't wanted to show her the extent of his injuries, of course. For days he had looked a fright, with his face cut and bruised. He'd also had a broken ankle that made it hard to walk.

"I was so distraught at your disappearance that I considered going to your parents' house to ask about you." Beatrice shook her head. "You showed me where it was once, remember?"

Yes, he had, but he had never entertained the thought that she would consider being seen in such a place.

"You would have gone to the village?"

Edward knew he sounded huskier than normal, but the declaration had moved him deeply. This lady would have gone after him, risked her reputation, exposed her deepest secrets to poor peasants just to know what had become of him. He could all too well imagine his parents' bewilderment if she had claimed to be looking for their son.

"Yes, I would have," she said with conviction. "But I forced myself not to because doing so would inevitably raise Sir Robert's suspicion. He had sworn to kill you should we see each other again, so I could not risk letting him know what you meant to me. He was, and still is, under the impression we had merely kissed a few times, and I thought not seeking you was your best protection against his wrath. If I had gone to find you, he would have understood that we had shared much more than that."

So much misunderstanding, so many secrets between them, so much time lost! Edward was sick at the thought.

"It's all forgotten now," he said softly. Now they knew where they stood, it was all that mattered. "You now know I never abandoned you willingly, and I can see that you were trapped by a vicious man and doing your best to protect me."

"Yes, you didn't forsake me and I did not betray you."

They looked at each other in silence for a while before the baby started to squirm. Immediately Beatrice went to the cot and took her in her arms. Together they presented such a lovely picture that he cleared his throat.

"You still haven't answered me," she told him, raising her chin. "Will you be Bridget's godfather?"

"Is Mistress Joan worried about her health?" He frowned in concern.

"No, not particularly," Beatrice admitted, rocking the babe from side to side. "But she is so small. She was early, and babies are so vulnerable, even when they appear healthy." Her voice was unsteady, as if the idea of losing her child was enough to make her weak at the knee. He understood the sentiment all too well.

"Yes," he whispered to himself. Life was a fragile

thing, indeed.

"So will you do it?"

"Does it mean so much to you? You could ask one of the local lords. I am sure I could find someone for you."

"No. I want you." The words resonated in the air between them, heavy with meaning. "I want you, Edward, and no one else," she repeated, withstanding his piercing stare. They both knew she wasn't talking about the christening anymore. She was acknowledging out loud what she had felt for years. His heart tripped in his chest. Oh, the joy of hearing such words, even if they were veiled, even if he had no right to them!

"Then I will be godfather to little Bridget," Edward said, purposefully bringing the discussion back to the baby for fear he would do something foolish if he allowed himself to dwell on what she had just said.

Beatrice nodded, as if nothing of importance had been revealed.

"Thank you. I will see the priest about it immediately."

Chapter 10

"Lady Beatrice has asked to see you." Mistress Joan walked into the hall where Edward was breaking his fast. He immediately stood, prompting her to add. "She is feeding her child at the moment."

"Then I will wait a while."

Mistress Joan tilted her head. "Aye, 'tis perhaps better, though I wager she would receive you all the same."

There was a glint of compassion in her eye when he had expected censure. He had the feeling Mistress Joan had seen beyond the lady-and-squire relationship and could not disapprove of it because she had seen how miserable Beatrice was with her husband.

"You do know I would never do anything that would compromise my lady's honor?" he asked, choosing to be frank with her. This was not the exact truth. He had already taken every liberty with Beatrice, and he feared he might do so again at the earliest opportunity, but he could hardly admit to that.

Besides, he preferred to think he would be able to resist the temptation.

"I do know it," Mistress Joan said roundly. "And more's the pity for her. But if you wanted to compromise *my* honor, you wouldn't hear any complaints, I can assure you."

Edward had to laugh even if he suspected the

woman was not entirely speaking in jest. He had already seen that the looks she gave him were far from innocent. He knew these looks well—he had seen them from admiring women more often than he cared to remember. If he wanted to take her to bed he would not be rebuked.

"Thank you. I am sure I should be tempted to take you at your word," he said with a tilt of the head.

"But you are not," she clarified, stepping closer to him. "More's the pity for me." Regret tainted her voice and desire made her eyes bright. Edward did not see what he could say or do to sweeten his refusal, but in truth he felt no inclination to do what she appeared desperate for him to do.

She seemed to understand his helplessness and, after one last wink in his direction, she disappeared.

As soon as she was gone Edward's thoughts turned back to Beatrice, still waiting for him. He would take a cup of small ale to her. She always seemed to be thirsty these days, courtesy of breastfeeding Bridget. He turned to pour the drink—and stopped with his hand in midair.

Beatrice was standing in the doorway, and her face bore the hallmarks of a blazing fury.

"I was just about to come upstairs," he said in a voice aimed at diffusing her anger. Unsurprisingly, it failed.

"Did you stay behind to protect me and my baby, or with the less chivalrous aim of bedding the midwife?" she asked acidly, clasping her hands in front of her in an obvious effort at calmness.

Beatrice hated the fact that she could not control her rage. She should behave with cold dignity, but the sight of Mistress Joan going doe-eyed in front of Edward had been enough to make her livid with jealousy. It should

161

not affect her so. She should not get herself into such a state for a mere squire's flirtation. Except that the man towering over her, his face set in disapproval wasn't a mere squire!

It was Edward, *her* Edward.

She had foolishly thought they still belonged to each other, yet the very next day she found him flirting with the midwife! There had been no room for misinterpretation. Mistress Joan had clearly been trying to entice him to her bed. That she was a young, pretty woman only added to Beatrice's dismay. If Edward wanted her, there was nothing to stop him from having her. They were both free and, more importantly, she wasn't so far above him that he would feel he had to keep his desire on a tight leash like he did with her.

Edward pursed his lips. "So you heard the exchange between me and Mistress Joan." He said "heard" but his cold smile meant "spied on." She gulped when she saw he was angry himself. A storm was brewing in his eyes, but she wasn't going to back down despite the warning.

"Yes, I did, if you must know. I had sent her to get you, but she was clearly waylaid and I was starting to wonder what was taking you so long. Now I understand."

He was not chastened in the least. "If you heard our conversation, then you heard me refusing her advances," he said tersely.

She had, but Beatrice was not prepared be reasonable, she had been too hurt by the scene. "What I heard was you telling her you should take her at her word. What I saw was that you were in no hurry to come to me, although that is officially why you stayed behind instead of going to war and doing your duty to the king like a man."

The last word died on her lips when Edward's countenance changed under the insult. He became a different man, hard and dangerous.

"Like a man, you say! Am I not man enough for you, my lady?" he asked in a snarl, eyes flashing. "Do you need some kind of proof of my virility, is that it?"

Beatrice's heart threatened to stop beating. Edward was walking slowly toward her, blocking her retreat, edging her into a corner, forcing her into the confrontation she had so foolishly provoked but was now desperate to avoid. She would never get past him, not now.

He had never seemed so tall, so masculine, so intimidating.

So furious with her.

"What do you want me to do to prove I am indeed a man?" he hissed. "Does anything come to mind?"

Even though he was angry the words made her insides go liquid with desire rather than fear. She swallowed hard. "Edward, don't," she said in a breath, aware she had gone too far. She should never have questioned his bravery, especially not when he had stayed behind only to be with her. "I'm—"

"You're what?" he asked at his most deadly just when her back came into contact with the wall behind her. She was trapped.

"I'm sorry," she finished in a whisper.

"Oh, you are *sorry* now. But sorry for what? For accusing me of cowardice or of lechery? For trying to hurt me deliberately? For questioning my honor? For speaking to me as if I am no more than a servant? For forbidding me to bed a willing woman?" He placed one hand on the wall behind her. Against her cheek she felt

163

the heat of his forearm. It was so close she could have kissed it if she had dared to turn her head. "So tell me, my lady, what exactly are you sorry for? I would like to know."

The intensity of his gaze drilled a hole in her head. Beatrice felt her legs turn to water.

"Edward, please!"

He shook his head, refusing to relent. "I don't understand. First you insult me, and then you apologize. Now you are begging me. You need to make up your mind. What do you want from me?" He leaned in fractionally, stopping just before their bodies touched. "What do you want from me that would not compromise your honor and make me traitor to your husband?"

"Nothing," she said in a sob. "There's nothing."

"Yet you would deny me the opportunity to spend the night with a woman who is available and willing? You heard her. She wants me," he challenged, speaking as boldly as he had ever spoken to her. "She would have me anytime."

"I have no right to stop you from going to another woman, I know," she whispered, fighting the urge to inch forward and nestle into his arms. She did not want to argue with him. She did not want him to look at her with such anger in his eyes. This was not how she wanted to spend their few weeks together.

"You heard my conversation with Mistress Joan," he carried on, relentless. "You heard I was not tempted, yet you threw accusations at me. You saw me refuse her offer, yet you chose to ignore it." Suddenly the intent in his eyes changed and his voice became softer, closer to the sensual purr that could make her insides dissolve with longing. "Hear me out, Beatrice. I am not tempted by her or anyone else. There is only one person in the world I want, the only one I cannot have."

Beatrice could feel her legs starting to shake, her breathing getting faster. He was too close, too seductive. She could not cope. She had not felt desire for a man in more than six years and now she was drunk with it. Since Edward had arrived back in her life she had wanted him with every fiber of her body.

She was tired of fighting it, and too weak to try.

"This woman…" she started, urging him to speak what was on his mind.

"This woman has no right to demand my fidelity because she has a husband herself," Edward breathed, turning his head to speak the words straight in her ear. The simple gesture was so erotic Beatrice's eyes closed of their own accord. "She cannot pretend to give me what I want, but still I cannot let her go. I am not free from her. What can I do? What am I to do? I cannot touch her. She can never belong to me."

The note of pain in his voice was Beatrice's undoing. She pressed her cheek against the velvet of his tunic and gave a sob at the familiar smell of him, so heady, so comforting.

"What if she told you she wants nothing but to belong to you, that she is dying with need of you? What if she begged you to touch her even if you think you have no right to? What if she told you she has only ever felt alive when you were holding her in your arms? Would you forgive her for her hurtful words toward you?" She raised her chin up to him. "Would you kiss her and put an end to the torturing desire she feels for you?"

"I would," he growled, placing his other hand on the wall behind her, trapping her. "If I was sure she would not regret it afterward. She is a lady. I am not a lord."

"The only thing she could regret is missing this opportunity," she said edging forward, pressing her hips against his in invitation. "Please, Edward, kiss me."

Still he did not move. In that moment she hated the fact that she wasn't a farmer's daughter or a simple maid. She hated that he felt below her, unworthy of her, that he was stopping himself from treating her like a woman just because she was a lady.

Of course she could have kissed him first. She could have taken the initiative, like she had all those years ago, but today she needed to see that his desire for her overcame everything else because, now that she was married, she was jeopardizing everything for him. That her husband was not the man she wanted did not change facts. She was supposed to be faithful to him, and he would be within his rights to punish her if he found out about this.

But she cared not. For a kiss from Edward she would have braved the Devil himself.

Edward was in hell—or paradise. He wasn't quite sure which. Beatrice was inches away from him, trapped between his arms, ready to surrender, her eyes were hazy with longing, her mouth open, awaiting his kiss. Every muscle ached with the need to have her.

Could he dare to kiss her? Oddly he felt more intimidated by her as a grown man than he had as a youth. Of course then, if she had been a lady, at least she had been free. She was a married woman now, and a mother. Even if she clearly still wanted him, the prospect was daunting for a man of honor such as he liked to think himself.

Never had she been more desirable yet more

unattainable. He thought he would never gather the courage to kiss her despite his unequivocal desire to do so, but then she let out a long moan and he decided to kiss her because the alternative—walking away from her—was unthinkable. The hands on the wall moved to embrace her, one cradling her nape, the other one wrapping around her waist. He groaned and came closer, trapping her between the wall and his own throbbing body.

There was a brief pause before he dipped his head. Their lips touching was like the spark igniting saltpeter. His whole body burst into flames, and there were no more hesitations. He crushed his mouth onto hers and kissed her with all the force of his passion, all restraint forgotten.

He closed his eyes in rapture.

This was not one of the tentative kisses he remembered from when he had been unable to get past the notion that she was so far above him. This was a kiss from a grown man confident in his skill, hungry for her. The thought that after so long she still desired him so passionately set fire to his soul as well as his body.

Beatrice kissed him back with a fierceness verging on despair, clinging to his neck, pressing herself closer to him. Edward responded by nudging his hardness against her thigh.

She gasped when she felt how ready he was and the noise recalled him to his senses. Dear God, what was wrong with him? Lost to his need, he was crushing her, grinding her delicate back against the stone wall! He pulled back, but immediately she protested and drew him back to her, clutching at his tunic.

"No," she screamed, the sound of someone driven to

the edge of madness. "Don't go!"

"Oh, I'm not going anywhere," he growled.

He kissed her again, careful this time not to press her too tightly to the wall. She was grinding her hips against him, her fingers entangled in his hair. The message was clear.

She wanted more of him, just as he wanted more of her.

He went to lift the hem of her gown, remembering how she had loved being taken standing up, that day in the woods. Perhaps she would like it just as much now. In any case, his desire was so impervious that it would not allow him to wait until they had reached a bed. It did not matter that they were in full view of anyone walking into the room—in that moment nothing counted but Beatrice and his need to possess her.

Edward placed his lips on her neck and nuzzled at her flesh, letting the smell and taste of her wash over his senses. He stroked her inner thigh slowly, marveling at the softness of her skin, but when he reached the top of her leg she gave a strangled cry and squeezed her thighs together. Never before had she refused him any caresses, however daring. He froze, understanding she had changed her mind. She had wanted to be kissed, but she would not allow anything more to happen.

He let out a grunt of frustration, his body painfully hard with arousal.

"Edward, I'm sorry," she cried out in anguish. "But I can't…"

It took Edward all his inner strength to step away from her. "Of course. I understand. I cannot ask this of you," he said in a growl. He didn't want to sound so gruff, but he could not hide the effort it was costing him to be understanding. "You are married now, and you owe your loyalty to—"

"What? No, never! I don't owe him anything, not after the way he has treated me, and what he did to you!" she snarled and there could be no doubt that she meant it absolutely. The tension in his chest eased.

"Then what is it?" he asked more gently, stroking her cheek. It was obvious it was costing her as much to step away from him as it cost him. "Are you afraid someone might see us?" In truth they should not have been so remiss as to kiss in such a public place, never mind to start making love in such a reckless manner. "I could go and bolt the door."

"No, it's not that," she whispered. "Though I am amazed it did not even cross my mind."

She averted her eyes, as if astounded to have forgotten herself to the point of risking being seen in such a compromising position together. He could understand the sentiment all too readily. He would never have thought himself capable of behaving so recklessly and take a married woman. But this married woman would make him lose his mind.

"Then what is it? Please tell me."

"During labor I... It's been only a few days since Bridget was born, and Mistress Joan told me that I had been... It was a difficult birth and, well..." She was struggling to explain herself, flushing in embarrassment. "I'm sorry... but I'm worried it's going to hurt."

Edward was stunned. Of course, she'd just had a baby. How could he have been so oblivious as to forget something like that? It was far too soon to be making love!

"My God, I'm so sorry." He had never felt so

ashamed of himself. Lost in his desire for her, he had forgotten everything. How could he have even supposed she would be ready for a man right now?

"Do you think—" she started tentatively. He cut her question short with a kiss.

"No," he said decisively. He would not attempt it, even if she begged him on her knees He would rather cut off his own arm than cause her any hurt or discomfort. "Listen to me. It's not going to hurt because nothing is going to happen. Forgive me, my lady, please. For a moment I forgot everything."

"I will if you stop calling me 'my lady.' I cannot be 'my lady' to you, not now, not after…" Beatrice shook her head, her voice trailing. Not after the desperate kiss they'd shared. "I'm the one who is sorry. I shouldn't have made you kiss me when I knew I could not—"

He silenced her with another kiss. "Oh, Beatrice, you did not *make* me kiss you. I kissed you because after so many years of torture I could not wait another moment to taste your lips." He brushed her swollen mouth with the tip of his fingers, causing them both to sigh with irrepressible longing. "But much as I want to, I will not take you to bed. Not today, not until you are ready."

Edward gritted his teeth. His body was throbbing with need, urging him to reconsider the foolish promise. In truth he should promise not to touch her again. Her body would eventually recover, but she would still be married.

"Thank you." He saw the way Beatrice held herself, careful not to touch him. She obviously didn't want to add to his discomfort, and he loved her for the thoughtfulness, but he took her in his arms all the same. He needed to hold her, and to hell with his pulsing body.

To his relief, she melted against him.

"Don't thank me," he whispered in her ear. "I should have been more considerate."

"I'm glad you weren't. I wanted to kiss you."

Edward held Beatrice for a long moment, allowing his heartbeat to slow down. It would be a while before his desire subsided, but the punishment would be fully deserved. He had been so intent on making her pay for her provocative words, so focused on his own feelings and desire that he had forgotten about her. What had he been thinking, making love to a woman who had given birth less than a week ago? It was unforgivable.

Then Beatrice looked at him with wide eyes and he saw that she didn't think him unforgivably inconsiderate. She seemed to believe that she was the one at fault.

"Will you ever forgive me for what I told you earlier?" Beatrice spoke against Edward's chest to hide her flaming cheeks. "Of course you are not a coward, and you do not need to prove anything to me or anyone. I am so sorry. I only said that because I was angry."

"Hush. I know. I was angry too."

"I wanted to hurt you. I could not stand seeing you with Mistress Joan. I envied her."

He gave an incredulous laugh. "You have no reason to envy her. She is nothing compared to you."

No, maybe not in status, but she was Edward's equal, and in this instance it was all that mattered.

"I don't mean it like this," she said ruefully. "You can be yourself with her. You are not afraid to act instinctively. With me you always stay in control. You never step out of line. I understand why you would feel this is necessary, but I wish you could get past it. I wish you could just be a man in front of a woman you desired, not a squire in front of a lady married to someone else," she said after a slight hesitation. Would he understand what she meant, or would he take umbrage?

"Maybe one day I will." Edward plunged his blue gaze into hers. Something shifted inside Beatrice at the promise. Oh, if only he would! If only one day they could be together with no shadow hanging over them!

"I will wait for that day," she breathed.

Edward's wistful smile told her it might take longer than she'd like.

"Will you do something for me in the meantime?" he asked, taking both her hands in his, suddenly serious. "Will you let me sleep in your bed tonight?"

The request left Beatrice speechless. "But I won't be able to give you what you want…"

"Will you let me hold you?"

"Yes." She flushed like a shy maiden.

"Then you will give me exactly what I want."

As promised, Edward came to find her that night, once everyone was asleep. Beatrice had just placed Bridget back into her cot when she heard him slip into the room. She lifted the blanket to let him into the bed as naturally as if they had been married for twenty years, and he settled down next to her. In the moonlight they looked at each other for a long time, drinking in each other in silence, barely touching, not uttering a word.

They never even kissed.

Then he wrapped his arms around her and drew her close. The intimacy of lying in each other's arms was somehow more meaningful than the fiery embrace of the afternoon.

"Thank you for allowing me to come here," Edward said, stroking her cheek softly.

"I think I was about to ask for the same thing," Beatrice mused out loud. "But I only realized it when you spoke."

That night Beatrice slept in Edward's arms for the first time, and she knew she did not want it to be the last.

****

Her head propped in her hand, Beatrice watched Edward sleep. Never had she seen anyone more mouth-wateringly beautiful.

"Good morning. Did you not sleep?" he asked when he finally opened his eyes.

"Not much," she admitted with a smile. "I had to feed Bridget, don't forget, while you slept on, oblivious to anything around you."

Of course this was only part of the explanation for the lack of sleep…

Most of her night had been spent watching Edward and marveling at her luck to be back in his bed. His even breathing had made his chest rise and fall in a steady, soothing rhythm, but she had been too fascinated to fall asleep herself. Her fingers had itched to trace the contours of his face or stroke the taut stomach that had always particularly appealed to her. When he had turned his back to her, she had almost placed a kiss on the muscular shoulders blades after watching them ripple with the movement.

Everything about him was so powerfully masculine. So arousing.

Eventually he had lain flat on his back once more and she had not resisted the temptation to touch him. Her hand had landed on his pectoral, right above where his heart was. The move hadn't woken him, but automatically his fingers had crept up to entwine

173

themselves with hers. Beatrice had stopped breathing for a moment at the sheer happiness of feeling his hand wrapped around hers. After that it had taken her but a moment to fall asleep.

Edward watched Beatrice's face flushed with the pleasure of waking up by his side.

Although he had known it would only make it more difficult to keep his urges in check, he had agreed to her demand that he sleep bare chested. He had kept his breeches on, though, and of course he had not expected Beatrice herself to sleep naked. Thank God she hadn't, for the sight of her glorious body would have been too much to bear. The glimpses of it under the thin, revealing chemise were enough to set fire to his blood.

It had taken him a while to fall asleep, but he had kept his eyes firmly closed, fearing that if he saw her looking at him he would break his promise to wait until she was ready to take her into his arms. Judging from the little sighs and moans that had escaped her lips at regular intervals, he'd guessed she was looking at him, fighting the urge to touch him. The thought of her hands running over his skin had made him harden painfully. The surge of desire had been so intense he had turned his back to her to hide it from her.

Once he had regained control of his body, he had flipped over onto his back once more.

Immediately he had felt her hand land on his chest, light as a butterfly. Unable to stop himself, he had wrapped his fingers around hers. The contact, intimate and natural, had moved something inside of him. Her hand was so small, so soft and warm, so unequivocally feminine and delicate!

Once he had Beatrice nestled against his flank, he'd

been able to fall asleep.

When he had woken at dawn, their fingers had still been entwined.

"This is the first time we have woken together," Beatrice observed in a lazy voice. "I hope it won't be the last. I want to make the most of our time here. We have already lost a week."

"You are not suggesting that I sleep in here with you every night?" he asked, placing a kiss on the back of her hand, then nipping her at wrist gently. He could have devoured her whole.

"I am. And you kissing me like this is hardly going to make me change my mind."

"What if I didn't want to?" he teased.

"I could always try to persuade you." She nuzzled her head in the crook of his neck and kissed his throat.

Edward steeled himself to withstand the assault. He was already hard from waking up next to her, and the sensual caress was not helping. Beatrice seemed utterly unaware of the torture it was for him to feel her soft, yielding body against his.

"What are you going to tell Lady Margaret?" he asked, desperate to focus on something other than her tempting body and her maddening kisses. He would have to stop her if she kissed him anywhere below the neck, as he would never be strong enough to withstand the sweet agony for too long. "Won't she get suspicious if she sees me coming out of your rooms in the morning?"

"She might in other circumstances. Fortunately, as my husband foolishly agreed to leave you behind to ensure no harm would come to us, I can use this as an alibi." Beatrice smiled. Indeed Sir Robert had introduced the fox into the coop himself. "I am growing increasingly fearful for our safety, having heard of hordes of soldiers roaming the land."

"Are you, my lady?" he raised an eyebrow teasingly.

"I am, Hardthorne," she replied formally, taking him up on the pretense that she was merely Lady Devance asking for the squire's protection, not Beatrice trying to entice Edward into her bed. "It is my wish that you should stay within calling distance at all times. And so you will sleep in the antechamber to watch over me and Bridget. No one will know you actually spend the time with me in bed," she whispered in his ear, reverting back to an intimate tone of voice.

The provocative words were maddeningly arousing, as was the fire burning in her eyes. Edward gave a mental curse. His desire, momentarily distracted, awoke with a vengeance. In bed with the woman he desired above all others, he was struggling to keep his urges in check.

The baby started to cry, providing a welcome distraction. He immediately got up, eager to put some distance between Beatrice and himself.

"Could you bring her to me?" she asked, settling herself for a feed.

"Of course."

Beatrice was surprised to see Edward jump to answer the baby's cry so promptly. Then she saw him hesitate before picking up the little girl. Her chest tightened. Maybe she had misunderstood his eagerness to leave the bed. Maybe he hadn't got up to attend to Bridget after all.

"Do you mind holding her?" she asked, knowing he would find it difficult to deal with the notion that another man had fathered this child of hers.

"No, no."

He bent over the cot to take the baby into his arms. She instantly quietened, comforted by the warm embrace.

An irrepressible rush of love flooded Beatrice's heart at the sight of Bridget's downy cheek pressed against Edward's chest on the exact place she had put her hand during the night. His muscular arm was the perfect cradle for her, and there was something intensely moving about the picture they made together.

Edward was looking at Bridget with an odd expression on his face. "She's perfect, so beautiful," he said in a soft voice. "My baby…"

Beatrice wondered for a moment if she had heard correctly. His baby? Oh, if only she were, she thought with a smile.

Then he lifted his blue eyes, and the smile froze on her lips. Her face grew ashen, and her whole body dissolved in shock. It was as if her bones had gone liquid and her flesh had melted away at the same time.

"You mean…" The enormity of what she was about to say made her sit her upright. "You cannot mean that you have baby of your own?" Her head started to spin. "And a *wife*?" she finished, choking on the word.

"It's not what you think." He met her gaze steadily but the light in his eyes only confirmed her suspicions—that and the fact that he had not immediately denied it.

"My God, you do have a wife!" she screamed. He gave a sigh and Beatrice's insides crumbled to dust. "You came to my bed, you slept with me, you kissed me, you would have made love to me, when all the while you have someone else waiting for you at home, a wife and baby?"

She didn't know if she was incredulous, outraged,

or hurt beyond repair.

Silence stretched in the room, heavy as peat smoke.

"I want you to go," she said, sounding like a ghost of her usual self.

"Will you at least listen to me?" Edward was struggling to master his own temper.

"I don't think so. Please give me my daughter," she breathed, unable to look at him in his golden beauty, this beauty who belonged to someone else. He was a husband, a father! She could not stand to be with him another instant. "I want you to leave."

Far from obeying her request Edward stared at her with blazing eyes.

"Why are you accusing me? Aren't *you* married? Haven't you got two children of your own?" His anger was unleashed in a torrent of recrimination such as she had never imagined she would hear from his mouth. "Didn't you let me sleep in your bed despite all this? Didn't you dare me to kiss you? Didn't you want me last night? As desperately as I wanted you? Wouldn't you have let me take you had you not been wary of the pain? We both know you stopped me not because you felt any loyalty to your husband or because you did not want to be taken against the wall like a common slut but because you were afraid of being hurt. So don't play the hypocrite with me now!"

He had never dared speak to her like this before, so honestly, so scathingly. Beatrice realized with no small measure of irony that she had finally got her wish granted. At last Edward was addressing her as if there were no difference of rank between them, but instead of whispering love words in her ear, he was hitting her with harsh recriminations.

The pain was unbearable.

Beatrice turned her head away under the onslaught, but Edward was not finished. Now he had begun, it seemed he could not stop. She had started this and would have to deal with the consequences.

"What did you think? That I would lie in a hole for years, never touching another woman? That I would pine away for you until the day I die? Well, I'm sorry to disappoint you. I did sleep with other women, women who were not so far above myself, unlike you, who wanted me like Mistress Joan wants me," he said, pouring years of disillusion and frustration onto her. "I did try to have a life without you."

But he hadn't been able to. From the moment he had set eyes on her, no one had ever been able to compete with Beatrice.

Edward thought back to the time he had bedded Maude, the kitchen maid at Sir Hugh's castle. Although she had never known it, he had only gone to her because of Beatrice. His senses had been put to the torture by their passionate kissing and his body had been on fire, demanding release. He had done the only thing he could have done to stop himself from dishonoring his master's daughter, by leaving abruptly—and rushing to another woman.

Even seven years later he was not proud of it. Thrusting deep inside Maude's warm flesh, he had closed his eyes and imagined her to be Beatrice, the woman he really wanted. When Maude had cried out her pleasure, he had buried his head into the crook of her neck to stop himself from shouting out Beatrice's name.

He had been so ashamed of his behavior that he had avoided Maude for weeks afterward.

Later, in every woman he had bedded he had tried to find something of Beatrice.

It had never worked. He would always withhold a part of himself with them. He had never allowed any of them to pleasure him with their mouths. A few had tried, but he had always stopped them. The thought of Beatrice loving him had made it impossible to bear the idea. This was a memory between him and her alone. He could not refrain his urges, but he could at least preserve this.

For a while, after his departure from Beatrice's father's castle, Edward had tried to go without women, and he might have made it had it not been for the constant solicitations. Whether he wanted it or not, he attracted women, and after a while he had stopped fighting the demands of his body. Being faithful to Beatrice had brought him no satisfaction and he could not realistically spend his whole life living like a monk. It would make no difference if he remained celibate or not.

So he had started to bed other women, never seeking them out but never pushing them away either. The pleasure of these brief encounters had never come close to what he had experienced in Beatrice's arms.

When Isabel had fallen with child, he had done his duty and married her. He had made her his wife, but she could just as easily have been his previous conquest or the next. Isabel had loved him, though, and he had tried to tell himself that he might come to love her eventually. Unsurprisingly, it had never happened. He had cared for her, and he had been looking forward to having a baby, but he had never had for her the depth of feeling he'd felt for Beatrice.

Beatrice, who was looking at him right now with eyes full of unshed tears.

"No, I did not think you would remain celibate," she whispered. "Only I thought you would have told me you had rebuilt a life and had a family before you made me think that you still..." She stopped, looking utterly wretched.

"Made you think that I still love you?" he finished in an impossibly bitter tone.

"Yes."

Their anger spent, they stayed silent, eyeing each other, full to the brim with resentment and regret over what might have been, what could never be.

"Please give me my daughter. She will be hungry," Beatrice pleaded, desperate to put an end to the torture. This was just an excuse. Bridget was quietly lying in Edward's arms, not in the least fractious. Despite their heated argument, he was cradling her as delicately as he had done earlier. The child was still as a statue, looking up at him with a mesmerized expression. Beatrice could only imagine how safe Bridget must be feeling in the cocoon of his arms. The two of them looked like they belonged together.

But they didn't. They never would.

Soon Edward would leave and go back to be with his own family. That was why he looked so comfortable with a baby in his arms—because he had done this all before, with another woman's baby, a woman he had promised his love and protection to... A woman he had kissed and held in his arms... A woman he made love to, night after night.

A woman who had a claim on him, who was free to be with him.

Beatrice swallowed a sob. All these years when she'd had to endure Sir Robert in her bed, another woman had lain next to Edward. When her husband had treated her no better than a brood mare and a whore, a stranger had enjoyed Edward's exquisite caresses, had shivered under his touch, had cried out with the pleasure he gave her. Another woman had made a life with him, had borne him a child. The pain of the betrayal was unbelievable, dizzying.

Silently she held out her arms to ask for her baby back, unable to bear Edward's presence in her room any longer.

Without a word, he handed the little girl over, and their fingers touched briefly. Beatrice kept her eyes on her daughter's face for fear that one glance at Edward would make her crumble in despair. Only a moment ago she had woken up in his arms and thought they had found each other again. They had done no such thing.

She had just found out how irreconcilable the divide between them was.

They were both married to other people. They each had another life. Neither had the power to influence fate or the means to change the past.

As she settled the child on her breast, Edward shrugged on his shirt and tunic. Then he left the room, still not having uttered a single word.

Tears streaming down her face, Beatrice tried not to imagine Edward's wife feeding a golden-haired baby while he watched over them in pride and love.

He had a baby, a *wife*.

How had she not seen it coming? How had she assumed that a man like him would remain unattached? All these years she had tortured herself imagining him in the arms of countless lovers, but it had never occurred to her that he would in fact have committed himself to one woman. The pain of it was even worse. She might have been able to compete with anonymous conquests, but she would never do so with a wife he was devoted to.

Who was this lucky woman?

She thought back to the scene she had witnessed between Edward and Mistress Joan the day before. She had berated him for his behavior, when all the while he had probably refused the midwife's advances out of loyalty to his wife, not out of consideration for her. And she had been naïve enough to think his feelings toward her were unchanged! What a fool she was.

But what about their passionate kiss?

Say what he would, Edward *had* let her think he still had feelings for her. She had not imagined the passion in his touch. Had she not stopped him, he would have taken her. There was no doubt about it. He had been so fired up he would have had her there and then, against the wall. So what? Yes, he still desired her—she had seen it in his eyes, she had felt the proof of it hard against her body—but it was not quite the same. Beatrice was not so innocent as to ignore that a man could take a woman without feeling any love for her, the fact that men went to Mistress Annie and her girls made that clear.

Men had urges, and Edward had been away from home for weeks, perhaps months. It would make sense for him to want to indulge his senses after such a long period of enforced celibacy, and who better to do it with than his old flame? It would be an interesting challenge for him. Now that she was not pregnant anymore and her husband was away, he was free to have her. He'd counted on the fact that she would not push him away, for when had she ever done such a thing?

She wiped a tear from her eyes at her stupidity. After

183

spending the night next to him, she had truly thought they could start something, with nothing changed between them.

She could not have been more wrong. Everything *was* irremediably changed, and they were not about to start anything.

Rather, it was all over.

That night she slept alone. She had barely seen Edward during the day. She knew he would not have abandoned his post—her safety and that of Bridget would still be uppermost in his mind—but he purposefully kept out of the way, making a point of avoiding her.

Tired and sick to her soul, she retired to bed without eating.

The following day the midwife came to visit her, which did little to ease her pain. It only reminded her that the woman had tried to entice Edward into her bed. For a moment, Beatrice toyed with the idea of telling her that he was married and out of bounds.

She stayed silent, knowing this petty revenge would not make her feel better, and let Mistress Joan examine her.

"Be careful, my lady," the woman warned, once she had declared that her injuries were healing as they should. "There are reports of soldiers passing through the countryside on their way back home, drunk on victory or, worse, embittered by defeat. They created havoc in our village last night."

"So the battle is over, then?" Beatrice realized that since Edward had not gone into danger she had not given the battle any thought, even though her own husband had taken part in the fighting.

"Apparently so, since the men are now at a loose end. I am not unduly worried for you, though. I wager your man can be trusted to guarantee your safety."

"Yes, he can," she answered tersely, disliking the glint in Mistress Joan's eye. A moment later she dismissed her with a bluntness she had never before shown anyone in her life.

Chapter 11

"I'll tell you what's the most difficult for a man in my situation. The lack of women. When you have to travel as fast as I do, there aren't many opportunities for dalliances, if you get my meaning. But now that I've been to Lady Margery and then come here to you, I can rest awhile, and I wouldn't mind giving the midwife a moment of my precious time." The man winked, then seemed to think it more appropriate to ask permission first. "You wouldn't mind, would you? She's a tasty piece."

Edward shrugged. The man clearly thought he was whiling away the tedium of his assignment in the arms of Mistress Joan, and it was a reasonable assumption, he had to admit.

"If she will have you, then go ahead," he told the messenger, his attention wholly on the letter he had just delivered. "It is none of my concern what you do with her." It might even make him feel less guilty about refusing her advances.

"She's outside in the courtyard playing with the baby. I'll go over now. Come with me. You can say Lady Devance asked for her child and take it away, because we certainly won't be needing it for what I have in mind!"

He laughed at his own wit and stepped outside. Edward followed, tucking the letter into his tunic.

"Forget it," he growled, as his eyes landed on the woman seated with Bridget in the shade of a tree.

"Oh, come, my friend," the man said, slapping him on the shoulder. "You can have her back in your bed tonight and no harm done. I guarantee I'll be gone by then."

"I said forget it," Edward repeated, catching his wrist in a restraining grip. "That's not the midwife. That's Lady Devance herself."

The man rubbed at his wrist. "No! What is she doing here, dressed like a commoner and playing with her baby?" Edward didn't answer, but it was true that in this moment Beatrice looked nothing like the great lady she was. Her plain clothes and simple hairpiece made her look like exactly like Mistress Joan. The fact that she had chosen to spend time with her baby alone would have made the messenger mistake her for the midwife. "Why, I thought she was your doxy!"

"Well, she's not, so I would go without for a little longer if I were you," Edward hissed, as the irony of the situation pierced at his heart. The man was not to know it, but Beatrice herself, not the midwife, was the woman who was warming his bed. Or at least would have been in other circumstances.

"Aye, I suppose I will have to go without." The man sighed and kicked a stone with the tip of his boot. "Pity you warned me. I would have gone there and tried my luck, and who knows, maybe for a change the mighty lady would have liked a bit of r—"

The man never got to finish his sentence. "Enough! You will go back to Sir William before I lose my temper, and you will show the lady the respect she deserves. Do I make myself clear? There will be no more talk about showing her a bit of rough and no more thinking about it!"

"As you say."

Beatrice lifted her head at the sound of Edward's raised voice. He was over by the stables, holding a man by the throat, keeping him pinned against the wall. Her heart missed a beat. Were they under threat? She hastily gathered her baby in her arms and made for the safety of the house, but before she could enter the great hall she saw the man retreat toward the gate and Edward run his hand through his hair in a gesture betraying frustration rather than menace. He looked like a man sorry to have lost his temper, not one who had just fought off a dangerous opponent.

She went to him, intent on finding out what had happened.

"Who was that man?" she asked, holding Bridget close to her chest.

"No one. A messenger from Sir William." Beatrice mused on the fact that while her own husband still hadn't thought it necessary to apprise her of his whereabouts, Sir William was sending his squire news of their progress.

"What's wrong? Is the news bad?" she asked when she saw that Edward was still looking tense.

"No. Why would you think that?"

She raised an incredulous eyebrow. "Perhaps because for a moment it looked as if you were going to murder the man on the spot?"

"Leave it. It's nothing." The tone left her no choice other than to obey. She kept her peace, and he showed her the message. "King Edward has won a resounding victory. The fighting was hard but Edward of Lancaster is now dead, his army has fled, and Margaret of Anjou is captured. This time it might be truly over."

Beatrice noted that Edward didn't mention anything about her husband. For a moment the hope that he had been killed in battle swelled in her chest. If her husband was dead, then she would finally be free from his tyranny… The thought must have registered on her face, for Edward folded up the message with decision.

"No one we know was seriously hurt," he said, placing the message back in his tunic.

She lowered her head in shame. What was she thinking! No matter what she thought of Sir Robert, she should not have wished for his death in such horrid circumstances. Besides, even if she had been a widow, the situation would still have been far from ideal. She might have been free, but Edward still had a family waiting for him.

When the baby started to fuss, Beatrice patted her back and started to walk. Edward fell into step with her. It felt as if they were both ready to move forward after the heated argument of the other day. Of course the fact remained that he was out of bounds in ways he had never been before, but Beatrice knew she could not spend another day without speaking to him.

There was just one thing she needed to do before they could resume a normal relationship.

"I owe you an apology," she whispered, staring straight ahead of her. "I had no right speaking to you as I did the other day. The shock got to me. I'm sorry," she said after a slight hesitation. She sensed Edward's surprise at hearing her apologize to him. It was not something she found easy to do, and he knew it.

"Don't be. I said some hurtful things too, a lot worse

than you did, in fact." He sounded truly repentant.

"I was jealous, I will confess. I could not bear the idea of you being married, and still cannot," she said, coloring a little at the admission. Then she pushed the image of his wife out of her mind to concentrate on his child. "Is your baby a boy or a girl?"

For a while no answer came. Then Edward spoke in a voice that raised the hairs at the back of her neck. "I don't know. I never met it."

She stopped walking and turned to look at him. "You mean that, like Sir William, you left before it was born?"

As she spoke the words, Beatrice knew the explanation would be a lot more tragic than this. Edward's eyes were veiled with sorrow.

"I mean that I will never meet it. My wife is dead and the baby died with her."

She gasped and automatically tightened her hold on her daughter. "What happened?" she asked after what seemed an eternity.

Edward made a gesture betraying the absurdity of the situation. "The sweating sickness. Isabel was eight months gone when she died." He trailed a finger on Bridget's cheek, the gesture wistful. "The baby would be just over a year old now. A boy or a girl…I will never know."

"I'm so sorry."

"I sometimes think I do not deserve a family." He planted his gaze in hers. "Isabel was never the woman I loved. I think she knew it, but she never complained."

Beatrice's heart skipped a beat. This time she could not mistake his meaning. *She* was the woman he loved. "I wager you were a good husband to her nonetheless," she said awkwardly.

There was no answer. Beatrice could see Edward was feeling guilty for not having been able to return his wife's love, and nothing she could say would make him feel better. They walked in silence for a while, reaching a little garden where a fountain was bubbling in the distance. The soothing sound of the water helped to restore the mood between them after such a tense conversation.

"Do you remember when you asked me if Ralph was my brother?" Edward asked suddenly.

"Yes. Vividly." Beatrice was still smarting at the rebuff she had earned with her questioning. "You railed against me, saying I had never taken an interest in your family before."

"Well, you hadn't," he argued with a smile that defused her anger. He was right, and for once she was not going to argue, not when they had only just put their disagreement behind.

"No. I admit that every time we met I was more interested in you." This answer lit a light in Edward's eyes as he remembered what form her interest had taken. He sent her a scorching look that reddened her to the roots of her hair. "Please. Don't look at me like this, Edward," she murmured.

"I wasn't aware I was looking at you in any particular way," he said, lifting an eyebrow.

"Well, you are." The wolfish smile she got in return told her he had been all too aware of what he was doing. Edward had always known how to arouse her with a single glance or make her swoon with a few chosen words.

"I say you are too easily provoked, my lady," he

purred, leaning closer.

Beatrice knew it was not the case. No one else could have made her bones liquefy with no more than a smile. Only one man could have that effect on her. "I am not. But you are too skilled at this."

"I will do my best to control myself."

"Don't. I would not have you behave any other way."

"Very well, then I will look at you as I wish." The incendiary look he threw her made her gasp out loud.

"Please. This is not right. I have my baby in my arms!" she said in mock outrage. "I cannot be thinking about…that…with Bridget so close to me!"

"She won't know. And it is not my fault I think of…*that* when I look at you. You have never looked more beautiful than you do now, in your simple dress. Velvet never really became you." He winked and then became serious again. "Anyway, Ralph was not my brother but my brother-in-law. Isabel was his twin sister."

Beatrice tried to remember Ralph's features so she could get a sense of what Edward's wife might have looked like, but she could not recall a single thing. All she could think of was his blood-soaked chin and shirt. Automatically she rubbed her fingers against her gown and shook her head to chase the dreadful memory away.

"That's why he wanted to see you before he died," she said quietly. The poor man had not said "brother." He had simply not had the strength to finish the word "brother-in-law."

"Yes. Isabel and he were very close and had always said they wanted to be buried together. I guess he wanted to make sure his instructions were carried out."

"Your wife didn't ask to get buried next to you…?" She stopped, finding it too painful to imagine Edward married to another woman, even if she was now dead.

"No. At least she never said any different. Then again, I don't think she imagined she would be dead before the age of twenty-five."

"Of course not. I'm sorry," she repeated inadequately.

The irony of the situation was not lost on Beatrice. A moment ago she had hoped her husband had died in battle, making her a widow before remembering that, as Edward was married, it would make little difference. Now she was told Edward was free after all, but she had learned Sir Robert was still alive.

Nothing had changed. They still could not be together.

Just then Lady Margaret came running to them. "My lady!"

"What is it?"

"The cook has just told me the village is being invaded by hordes of soldiers returning from battle, drunk on their victory. A few women were assaulted last night. Please come back inside! You could be seen from the road, and in your present attire the men might think you no more than a commoner and—"

"Calm yourself," Beatrice exhorted her. "Mistress Joan already told me about the soldiers the other day, but we are quite safe here, unlike the poor village girls."

Edward moved forward, a tower of strength between the two women. "I fear that Lady Margaret is right, my lady. The country is not safe at present. I am under strict orders to ensure your safety. I am sure your husband would want you safe, whatever it takes. With your permission, I will sleep in the antechamber tonight and make sure no one troubles you."

Beatrice knew he was telling her he had forgiven her. Her heart leapt at the idea of sleeping in his arms again.

"Yes, I think it is probably for the best. I am sure that knowing you are looking after his wife so well would set Sir Robert's mind at rest," she told Edward, meeting his blue eyes squarely. The glint in them made her shiver.

"Then I will go and make the necessary arrangements."

He bowed and walked back to the house whilst the two ladies looked on, a look of wistful longing etched on both their faces.

****

The next few days were spent in a daze of happiness. Edward slept with Beatrice in his arms every night and he rarely left her side during the day, ostensibly to ensure she and Bridget would come to no harm. One morning a party of soldiers was seen passing in front of the manor house. They never entered the gate, but it helped to give weight to the pretense that he was following her so closely merely because he was obeying Sir Robert's orders.

Then one day a messenger came with a letter from Sir Robert. Remembering what had happened the last time a messenger had come to the manor, Edward decided he was not even going to let Beatrice see the man, and he brought the letter to her himself. He found her in the garden by the fountain, a spot that had become a favorite with her.

"A message from your husband, my lady."

"I'm alone, Edward," she told him with a tilt of the head, by which she meant he could stop calling her "my lady." He knew just how much she hated it, and in truth, he hated it also. "Why couldn't you send the man to me? There is no need to contrive private meetings now, when we are almost always together."

"I know, but one can never be too careful," he replied cautiously, handing her the letter. "This man is in Sir Robert's employ. I would hate for him to report that he found you dressed in the sort of clothes that would never pass your husband's approval."

"I see. You are very protective of me, are you not?" she teased, unaware of his other reason for doing so.

"It is for the best, believe me," he replied, recalling the way Sir William's messenger had ogled her, believing her to be the midwife. For days now she had dressed in plain clothes, enjoying the liberty if afforded her. Of course it did not take away any of her beauty but undeniably, it made her appear more like a commoner than was advisable. He did not want to put her in a position of having to refuse a man's advances, and he wasn't sure he could vouch for his reaction if anyone attempted anything.

Beatrice read the message and lifted glittering eyes to him.

"What makes you smile so?" he asked, loving the joy on her face. God, she was beautiful!

"Now that the battle is over, Sir Robert is going to stay in Wales for a couple of weeks to sort out various affairs," she informed him in a breathless whisper. "He will not be back to Devance Castle before the end of the month, which means we are in no hurry to leave." The prospect only made her smile grow wider. "Sir William will travel north with him. He will go to his wife and child and join him again before they leave for Devance Castle. You are to await his arrival there. Oh, Edward, this is the best of news!"

In her joy Beatrice wanted to fall into Edward's arms and kiss him. The impulse was hard to suppress. She almost gave in to temptation, but she knew it would not be fair to him. She was still wary of lovemaking, even if she could feel her injuries healing nicely, so she had avoided kissing him since that day in the hall, conscious that once the spark was ignited it would be almost impossible for them to stop before things got out of hands. As he did not want to hurt her, it would only make things difficult for them both.

He saw her hesitation and smiled ruefully. So he was fighting a desire to kiss her as well…

"Soon, Edward," she promised, lowering her eyes. He didn't answer, but it was clear that his longing for her was equally strong.

One particularly pleasant afternoon they went for a walk alone with Bridget. Edward carried the baby all the way and talked about everything and anything, as he would to someone who was not out of his reach. Beatrice had never spent a more perfect day. She wondered if people seeing them from a distance would guess the real relationship between them. They probably looked like a young family enjoying a stroll together, her simple gown and their obvious companionship only adding to the illusion.

When Bridget needed feeding, they sat by the river, then settled her on a blanket between them while she slept. Watching the ripples of silvery water dancing in the sunlight, Beatrice wondered how it was that just being in Edward's company made her so intensely happy.

It was as if she had found a part of her she didn't know was missing.

But why him, of all men? Even if her attraction could be explained by the fact that he was sinfully handsome and treated her like no one else ever had, she knew it was something else, something that passed her understanding.

Just as she was musing about what made this man so irresistible to her, she noticed he was watching her just as curiously.

"Your eyes, or rather the look in them, was what first made me look at you differently and see past the fact that you were the daughter of Sir Hugh," Edward said, proving his thoughts had followed a similar pattern to hers. "There was this intensity in your gaze that made me think we shared a secret, even if we had never met before. No one had ever looked at me quite like that before. You did not see me as a servant or an inferior, or even a friend, an equal, or a lover. You looked at me as if we belonged to each other, as if we already shared a past together."

"I suppose I had dreamt about you so often that, in a way, we did." Beatrice blushed. She had never told him what she had been doing to him in those dreams, and she would not tell him now. That was a secret for her alone.

For days after she'd had her first dream about Edward, disturbed by the very erotic nature of it she could not meet his eyes, but equally, she had been unable to keep out of his way.

One day while he was saddling her father's gray horse she had watched from the side, for fear that her confusion should be detected if she stood too close to him.

In the end she had chosen the wrong place to be.

After helping her father into the saddle, Edward walked over to her. Dazed, she watched him stop in front of her, the hint of a smile etched on his lips.

"My lady." It was the first time he addressed her directly. She'd heard his deep, seductive voice before, of course, but when he spoke to her, with his blue eyes planted straight into hers, that voice seemed to have acquired a new intensity.

"Y…Yes?" she stammered.

"Pardon me but I have to get your father's riding whip. It's right behind you."

He flashed her a brilliant smile, revealing even white teeth. Something uncoiled inside of Beatrice, something she had never felt before. It was unsettling, disturbing.

Delicious.

It made her imagination run riot. She imagined Edward's mouth following a path over her flesh, his lips kissing every part of her body, his tongue licking its way to her most secret part, his eyes lighting up in desire as he took her in his arms to make love to her.

He watched her without moving, but after a while the smile widened. "Pardon me, my lady but… You are still blocking the way. I cannot get the whip."

"Of course. I'm so sorry." Beatrice scuttled to the other end of the room, her cheeks red with confusion. Fortunately, there was no way for him to know what she had been imagining. What an idiot he must think her! The first time they spoke, and she was acting like a simpleton.

Edward gave her a surreptitious glance as he walked

back past her, whip in hand. Absurdly she thought he would look better atop the mighty horse than her father ever had. He had the physique of a warrior, broad and muscular yet supple and lean, whereas her father's stout figure looked less than imposing. She tried to picture Edward in the saddle, whip in hand, booted and spurred, dressed like a nobleman, and bit her lip when an unmistakable wave of desire invaded her.

She rushed outside to meet her father, who was now ready to leave.

"Make sure you finish that Latin translation today," he instructed her before leaving, as uninterested as ever. "You have been uncommonly distracted these last few days."

There was no denying it, her mind had been on other matters, but it must have been bad for him to notice it. He never noticed anything she did.

"Yes, Father," she said meekly.

Once he had trotted off, Beatrice stole one last glance at Edward behind her. He was regarding her with an odd expression on his face. The cornflower blue eyes were glinting, but there was no way of guessing what he was thinking. He could have been amused at her inability to behave like a lady or irritated that her clumsiness had made her father wait unduly. Without another word, she fled to the security of the castle, unnerved by the idea that this stable hand had guessed he was haunting her every dream.

From that day onward, Beatrice actively spied on Edward. Every chance she got she walked over to the stables just to get a glimpse of him. She had asked her father to buy her a new horse on the pretext that she wanted to learn to jump. He had not questioned this whim, although a more perceptive father would have been surprised by the demand. Beatrice had never been a horse lover. Of course she could ride adequately, as every lady of rank could, but no more.

The mare served as her excuse for daily visits to the stables. She pretended to care for the animal, but all the while her eyes were firmly stuck on the blond youth who appealed to her a little more every day. Everything he did fascinated her. There was an innate sensuality in his gestures, and she never tired of hearing him speak to Peter the groom.

Her fingers weaved through the mare's mane, and she imagined she was running her hand through his silky blond hair. When she stroked the animal's rump she wondered what it would be like to caress his muscular chest. Without knowing quite why, she knew it would feel soft under her touch, yet taut and powerful.

Having run out of things to do, loath to leave, she decided to feed her horse an apple. Just as the soft muzzle brushed her palm, her gaze met Edward's across the room. The effect on her body was as odd as it was spectacular. It felt as if *he* were kissing her hand, not the mare. Desire shot through her veins and she let out a small cry.

"My lady, did she bite you?" Edward was at her side in an instant, concern etched on his face. He took her hand in his, the first time he had ever touched her skin on skin. He straightened her fingers to check her palm for an injury that didn't exist. "You need to be careful. She has a temper on her, that mare of yours," he warned.

He didn't let go of her hand immediately, even though he must have seen there was no harm done.

"I know," she replied in a voice so hoarse it sounded

like someone else's. "I want…" She stopped. The words had come of their own accord, but she could not finish the sentence.

I want you.

"I want to give her another apple," she said instead.

There was the tiniest caress on her wrist, so brief she could have imagined it. "You are spoiling her, I'm afraid. Once she knows what she can get out of you, she will leave you no peace."

"I will have to take the risk. I cannot help myself."

His eyes flashed. "Can you not? Mayhap you should try, for this is a dangerous thing."

Beatrice fled in fright because she was suddenly certain her life had taken a turn that could only land her in trouble. This was more than a simple infatuation based on Edward's good looks—it was a full-blown fascination in danger of becoming something else again, something much more potent.

After a sleepless night spent fighting her need for the man, trying to ignore what her mind, her body, and her heart all were telling her, she returned to the stables. Nothing would keep her away from Edward now. She was already in too deep. At least the night's musings had made that clear.

"I think I was hurt yesterday after all." Staring straight into his blue eyes, she handed him her hand. Edward took it slowly. "I wondered if you could do something about it. I was up all night trying to think what I should do, but I could not think of an answer. I thought you might be able to help me."

Her boldness astounded her, but Edward only stared back at her, his own eyes ablaze. "I suppose there is one thing I could do. But it—"

"Whatever it is, just do it," she instructed him, cutting his explanation short once she was certain he had understood the real meaning behind her words. "I trust you."

He led her to a secluded spot behind the stables, away from Peter's inquisitive gaze. Beatrice's heart pounded unbearably hard in her chest, and for a moment she wondered if she had not bitten off more than she could chew. As much as she had dreamed of the moment, now it had come she could not help a sense of trepidation. Alone with a man who was, after all, little more than a stranger, she was suddenly intimidated. That she desired that man did not make the prospect less daunting.

Unsurprisingly, Beatrice had never kissed anyone before. She had never even been in a position to be kissed. All the men she had been alone with were members of her family, not strapping young men who looked ready to tumble her to the floor. She swallowed hard. Now that Edward was finally about to take her into his arms, all she could think of was how impossibly virile he was.

It didn't take Beatrice long, however, to understand that he would never kiss her, despite his clear intention to do so, if she didn't lift her mouth to him first. Virile he might be, but she was Sir Hugh's daughter. He would never be so presumptuous. All her doubts went out the window. If she wanted to kiss him, giving him no choice was her only option.

As soon as their lips touched she knew she had taken the right decision. The kiss made her melt with an emotion she didn't know could exist. Whatever happened next, she would never regret this moment of pure, undiluted joy. She wrapped her arms around Edward and closed her eyes in rapture. They kissed as if their life were about to end, as if they feared they would never be allowed another moment together.

Quickly, too quickly, Edward pulled away. "My lady… No. This is wrong."

"I know, it's wrong," she panted, pressing herself against his chest, her lips tingling with the passion of their kiss. It was a delicious sensation, intoxicating. "It's wrong, but it feels so right. Kiss me again."

He did.

In the next few days they met in secret and shared increasingly heated kisses, but each time Edward pushed her away before she was ready leave to the warmth of his embrace. At first she had taken it as a sign of a lack of interest in her, but she had quickly come to see that he was in fact exerting iron control for her sake. He didn't want to compromise her honor, and she was starting to understand that he was right to fear such a thing. Shocking as the idea was, she had no intention of stopping at a few kisses. She wanted to give herself to him fully.

One evening he pushed her forcibly away from him, breaking up an embrace that was becoming too daring.

"No, my lady," he said, removing his hand from her breast as if her flesh had suddenly become boiling hot. "Please go before I shame us both by doing something I have no right to do." His face was a mask of painful restraint. When she did not move, he ran away, staggering like a drunken man.

That day Beatrice understood that, far from lacking interest in her, Edward was frightened by the force of his desire and did not want to take any more liberties with her. Respectful of her honor, he would never take the final, irretrievable step. Though she admired his scruples, she could not be as reasonable as he was.

She desperately wanted him, and she would make sure to get what she wanted, what they both wanted. If he did not readily surrender, then she would have no choice but to force his hand, just as she had for their first kiss.

The following day, heart in her throat at her own daring, she set a trap for him. She was nervous, but her mind was made up. She would tell Edward she wanted him to do what he thought he had no right to do. His reaction took her aback by its violence, though. Confident in their desire for each other, she had not for one moment imagined he would not go along with her plan.

"I want you to make love to me, Edward," she whispered, bringing her lips to his ear. As usual, they had kissed with a fierceness bordering on madness. Beatrice sensed he was about to push her away, but the pulsing in her body would not allow her to walk away from him this time. "I want you to be the first man to possess me."

A delicious heat invaded her body at the provocative words. Beatrice had never thought she would be in a position to decide which man would take her maidenhead. She had always assumed it would be her husband on their wedding night, a husband she hadn't chosen, a local lord she barely knew. The prospect was not an enticing one, to say the least, but here was the chance to follow her own desire for once. She would give herself to a man she actually wanted, a man who fired up her blood, not a stranger who would bed her to seal an alliance concluded for his own advancement.

She squeezed herself closer against Edward and felt the hardness between his legs. A whimper escaped her lips. She knew what it meant. He wanted to make love as much as she did. He was about to finally make her his.

She moaned in anticipation and closed her eyes.

When he didn't move, she opened them again. The look on Edward's face froze her on the spot.

"My lady, if you have an ounce of pity for me, you will let me go," he groaned, wrenching himself from her arms. Far from looking delighted, he had the face of a man about to withstand the cruelest torture.

"But I thought...I thought you would be pleased," she finished lamely.

Edward let out a muffled curse. "*Pleased*? Do you have any idea what you are asking me to do? You will be ruined." He yanked at his hair, the gesture betraying both anger and frustration. "You are Sir Hugh's daughter, not a kitchen maid I can tumble at will. You do not belong to a man like me."

Beatrice would not listen to this. "I do not *belong* to anyone, and I am old enough to know my own mind. I am here because, say what you will, you want me and I want you. Being Sir Hugh's daughter only means that my life is not my own. Well, I think I should at least have a say in what is done to my body. If I choose to be with a man like you, it is my..." Then she stopped as the meaning of his words hit her. "Kitchen maid? Who? It's Maude—you've had Maude, haven't you?"

The pain of the discovery was searing. Edward did not deny it, he only looked at her with his amazing blue eyes. Of course, deep down, she knew he would be an experienced lover. A man like him, aged nineteen, could hardly be expected to be a virgin, but she had never stopped to put a face to his various conquests. Maude! Beatrice already knew she would never be able to look at the woman again without wanting to hit her.

"What has she got that I haven't?" she demanded, flaring in temper. "Tell me." Suddenly she was acting like the lady he was in awe of, nothing like the lover who had shamefully melted under his kisses.

The question wrenched an incredulous laugh out of him. "Nothing, she's got nothing that you haven't got, my lady," he replied, putting the emphasis on her title. Beatrice was the one with a title and fortune, unlike Maude, who was toiling away in the kitchens just to keep starvation at bay. He meant that she was the lucky one of the two.

Right now it didn't feel so, though.

"Oh but she *has* something I haven't got because she has you," she cried in despair.

"She doesn't have me. It happened only once, and it won't happen again."

The flippant answer was a knife to Beatrice's guts. Edward was all but telling her he could have any woman he wanted, that he never fought the attraction he felt to them. And yet he was refusing her when she had bared her soul to him. He was turning her down when she had found the courage to acknowledge her feelings for him and tell him of her heart's desire. He was pulling back when she had finally resolved to take the most momentous step in her life.

He was right on one thing—she would be ruined if she was found in his arms.

Still the notion was not enough to stop her. Beatrice had never wanted for anything in her life. Everything was provided for her, even before she had expressed the need for it. All her wishes were pre-empted. She had never been denied anything because she was entitled to everything. Edward was both the first thing she truly desired and the one she could not have. She could not command him to love her. The shocking thought crossed her mind that perhaps she could order him to make love to her, but that was not what she wanted.

She wanted him to come to her because he could not stop himself, because he wanted her as desperately as she wanted him, not because he dared not refuse for fear of retaliation. She did not want him to feel she was using him.

"My lady, you must see I cannot presume to ask you to give yourself to me," he said, revealing vivid agony. This admission made her forget all about Maude and the others. She could tell that his longing for her surpassed everything he had ever felt for anyone else.

Desire flared anew, burning everything in its path, every doubt, every last vestige of her anger, and the potential danger of discovery.

"No, I do see that. But you are not asking anything. I come to you freely," she replied, levelling her eyes with his. "Just tell me this. If I weren't Lady Beatrice, only Beatrice, would you want me? Would you take me like you took Maude?"

He had groaned, giving her the answer she had hoped to hear. It had been enough, and a heartbeat later she had knelt in front of him.

Cheeks flushed as her memories of their early days wended through her mind, Beatrice looked at Edward and saw that, mercifully, he was oblivious to the direction her thoughts had taken. He had no idea she had been reliving their first time together. A fish leapt out of the water and fell back into the river with a splash. Bridget gurgled.

In that moment everything was perfect.

"When I looked at you, I didn't see the mighty Lady Beatrice, only my soulmate," Edward said quietly. "With anyone else, the idea would have felt preposterous, but with you it was as if it was meant to be. Of course it's easy for me to say, because why would I not fall in love with you? You are a dream for a man like me. The opposite is rather less understandable."

A smile curled Beatrice's lip as she took in the magnificence on display in front of her. Indeed, there was no accounting for the appeal Edward could have exerted on her! True, she was a lady, but she was a woman first and foremost, and she defied anyone to feel immune to his charm. Yet his undeniable beauty could only explain part of the attraction she felt.

"It was the same for me. I felt like I belonged to you from the start," she agreed.

"That must have been hard for you to accept."

"It was, at first," she nodded, impressed that he understood how momentous the realization had been for her—and did not resent it. "I had been raised to think I would marry someone my parents had chosen for me, that I would never have a say in my marriage negotiations. I would marry someone I didn't necessarily like, or even know. I thought I would remain a virgin until my wedding day. Why would someone shatter certainties built over a lifetime in a few days if it wasn't meant to be? Especially if he was only a stable hand."

She had never expected to feel a pull toward someone so unsuitable, so low in rank, and had not welcomed the realization. It had taken courage for her to acknowledge such outrageous feelings for a man she should never have met, and to act on them instead of conforming to what society expected of her. And she had been rewarded a thousand fold.

Beatrice lay on her back and looked at the sky. A few clouds tried to obscure the sun but slid past before they could dim its brilliant light. After a while she felt Edward's hand wrap around hers, the fit between them perfect.

Yes, they did belong to each other, there was no doubting it.

That afternoon Beatrice fell in love with Edward all over again, only this time it felt more real, deeper, even more meaningful, for now she knew him for the man he really was, not just the youth who had captured her imagination.

Between them Bridget gave a funny little yawn, and Edward laughed. Beatrice knew she wanted to hear that sound for the rest of her life. As she watched him lift the baby into his arms, her decision was made. Before the week was out she would surrender to the torturing desire she felt for him. They would have to leave the manor soon, and she didn't want to go before having spent a night of passion in Edward's arms.

Mistress Joan had confirmed that very morning that her childbirth injuries had healed nicely. Beatrice had tried her best not to blush, as her first thought had gone to Edward and what it meant for them. All she needed now was to convince Edward he could make love to her, for she knew he would be very wary of the pain it could cause her. They had gone full circle. They were back to when she was a virgin trying to make him do what he was striving not to do.

"We will need to leave soon," he told her as they made their way back to the manor house. The sun was starting to sink below the horizon, scattering flamboyant ribbons across the sky. "We cannot stay here indefinitely."

"No. Unfortunately."

"Will you travel in the litter with Bridget?"

"No!" Beatrice answered fiercely. Nothing would induce her to go back inside that wretched litter ever again. "I will go on horseback. I will ride next to you."

Edward nodded. He had expected her to say that, and he could not blame her, not after what she had suffered in that litter.

"I will go to the village tomorrow to select a suitable mount for you."

He would make sure to choose a steady mare with a gentle disposition, and they would not trot, not with her recovering from the recent birth of her daughter. They were in no hurry anyway.

"Don't tell Lady Margaret you're going to the village!"

"Why ever not?" Edward lifted an eyebrow at the earnestness of her tone.

A pause. "She might…she will want to accompany you."

"So, what if she does?" Beatrice didn't answer, but the expression on her face was worth a thousand words. "Oh, Beatrice!" Edward laughed, amused by her reaction. She was jealous! The thought warmed him. "She might well want to come with me, but it doesn't mean anything will happen. I'm hardly going to tumble her in the bushes on the way there. Or back," he added with a wink before she could challenge him.

"But…"

"But what?" he coaxed when Beatrice drew to a halt, a look of unease on her face. "You can tell me."

"Aren't you going to take advantage of the fact that she wants you? I mean, you must be getting—"

Edward planted himself in front of her, interrupting the argument. "Stop. I'm not getting impatient. Or rather, if I am, Lady Margaret is not the woman I would choose to put an end to it," he amended in an effort at honesty.

"Is Mistress Joan the one you would choose, perchance?"

"No, not her either. I would never dare," he said wryly, taking a step toward her.

"Why not?" Beatrice asked in a breath, coming even closer. "She would have you in an instant."

"I know, but you would only wring my neck afterward, so it would hardly be worth it!" Her face fell in dismay. He barked a laugh, knowing full well she had expected some kind of declaration instead of a teasing. "Oh, Beatrice, forgive me, I could not resist. You know I'm jesting and I want no other than you. What would I do without you?" he murmured, crushing her in his embrace.

"You need not wonder. I don't want you to ever be without me," she breathed, her mouth against his neck. He closed his eyes, relishing the caress.

"Neither do I, but we must not start being foolish or complacent. And if Lady Margaret thinks I'm interested in her, she might not realize it is in fact her mistress I covet."

It seemed that once again he would use the woman to deflect attention from himself and Beatrice. He should feel a pang of guilt at the thought, but he could not.

Whether he liked it or not, Lady Margaret had taken a shine to him. Behaving as if he had not seen it would not change the fact, so he might as well use it to protect the woman he secretly loved. He would do much worse for her.

"You covet me, then?" Beatrice's voice caused shivers to skittle all the way down his spine.

"Most definitely," he confirmed with a purr. "So I will go to the village with your lady tomorrow, and you will send us on our way graciously, all the while knowing that I won't behave in a manner that would displease you."

For good measure he placed a kiss on her jaw, just below the ear, confident that the very public setting would help keep his worst urges in check. They had spent an idyllic day, and now he was holding Bridget and Beatrice, the child he'd never had and the woman he should never have had.

Despite all the past hurts, he felt blessed indeed.

Beatrice melted into Edward's embrace, relishing the fact that he had grown so comfortable with her that he was able to take her into his arms as naturally as if they had always been together and tease her. Finally he had stopped seeing her as a lady above himself and more as a companion, if not quite yet as a lover.

"What if *she* behaves inappropriately when you're alone?" she challenged, determined to enjoy their new relationship to the full. He might not be interested in Lady Margaret, but there was no denying that her lady was smitten. "What will you do then?"

Edward shook his head. "She won't, not your Lady Margaret. She's too proper. She's not going to drop to her knees and beg me to make love to her. Not everyone is as brazen as you, my lady."

The comment and the scorching look he threw her made her flush so furiously that she placed her cheek against his chest to hide her embarrassment. "You're impossible," she murmured. "And stop calling me 'my lady'!"

"I will, if you let me go with Lady Margaret tomorrow."

"I see that you are the one ordering me around now," Beatrice said in surprise, raising her eyes to him.

He stared at her a moment before a smile bloomed on his lips. "Yes, I suppose I am."

Chapter 12

"What's wrong?"

Edward received Beatrice in his arms as soon as he opened the door to her bedroom. As they were alone, he didn't fight the urge to wrap his arms around her and to his horror he felt her go limp against him. That afternoon he had gone to the village with Lady Margaret as planned, in search for horses for the women. Had something happened during his absence? Thinking back to Sir William's messenger's lecherous intent the other day, he cursed his initiative to leave her at the manor house. He had not wanted to tire her with the unnecessary journey, but he should never have left her on her own.

"What happened?" he asked urgently, lifting her chin up so he could meet her gaze. "Tell me."

"Nothing, it's nothing. I got scared stupidly. I heard two men cantering into the courtyard a while ago and, remembering all the warnings about the soldiers, I panicked. You were gone, and I just ran to lock myself in the bedroom with Bridget."

Fury washed over him. "Who were these men, and what did they do to you?"

"Nothing! They were just two travelers asking for a drink. They stayed for only a moment. The maid told me so afterward. I overreacted, that's all. They didn't do anything wrong, but it made me think that I wouldn't know how to defend myself if they had meant trouble. I have always relied on others to ensure my safety, and I have no idea what to do if someone attacks me or my baby."

Edward mused on this for a while. "You're right. I will show you how to take care of yourself," he said with decision, walking to the other side of the room.

"What?"

"I agree with you—you should be able to defend yourself. The country has been unstable for a while, and though God knows I don't wish it, it might be that you find yourself exposed to danger sooner or later." Edward didn't add that her husband could not be relied upon to ensure her safety. He had thought nothing of leaving her and her baby alone in an unknown house with only one man in attendance.

"I couldn't...I wouldn't know where to start. I don't even have a sword or anything," she stammered.

He smiled at the image of Beatrice with a sword in hand. It didn't seem as ridiculous as it would with a less spirited lady. "I have no doubt you could handle a sword, if properly taught," he said, his voice warm with approval. "I might teach you one day. But no, for this purpose you need something you could easily find when the need arose. A knife, for example. There are knives everywhere."

He turned to the table where the remnants of her repast had not been cleared and saw a small knife lying there. He picked it up by the blade and handed it to her.

"No, I don't want to," Beatrice recoiled in horror. "I cannot plunge a weapon into a man's body!"

"I know you don't want to," Edward said in a gentle voice, knowing full well that the idea was abhorrent to her. He reached behind her back where she had hidden her hands and wrapped her fingers around the handle. "And it might be that you do not need to use it. If an attacker sees you holding a knife confidently, as if you would have no hesitation in using it, he will think twice about bothering you. In any case, your rank is your best protection. It would take a singularly dishonorable man to attack a lady such as you, one who means to defend herself."

"I don't know…" She let go of the knife and shook her head.

"I do. Show me you are not a victim. Show me you could defend yourself, Beatrice. Take the knife." He saw her bite her bottom lip in hesitation. "Don't worry, you are not going to hurt me," he reassured her, guessing she was afraid that her inexperience could inadvertently cause him harm.

Slowly Beatrice extended her hand and took hold of the knife, but she knew there was nothing confident or threatening in her attitude. Her hand was trembling. It was truly an awful feeling to be pointing a knife at another person, to know that you could end that person's life with one thrust of your arm.

"I can't. I'm sure I could not strike anyone with it." She thought back to Ralph spitting up blood and dying. "I'm not a soldier. I don't think I could live with myself afterward if I killed a man."

"I am not asking you to stab someone in cold blood, only to defend yourself or your children if need be. You will not think about all this the day you see someone you love being threatened, I can promise you. It will be instinctive."

He was right. Beatrice imagined someone coming to

take her baby or hurt Alys, and she knew that in such a situation she would pick up a knife, a sword, anything, and defend them to the death. There would be no hesitation, no remorse. If someone dared to endanger what she held most precious in the world, they would have to pay the price for it. She looked straight into Edward's eyes, her resolve stiffening.

"Yes. I will do it if I have to."

He nodded, trusting her absolutely. "Good."

Edward placed his fingers on top of hers and guided the knife to his neck until the point of the blade was resting against his flesh. She swallowed hard but kept her hand steady when he released his hold, letting her get used to the unsettling sensation of having someone's life in her hands.

"Strike as soon as you get the chance," he instructed her. "Do not hesitate. Do it once but do it properly. No half-hearted attempts that will only anger your aggressor further."

"Yes. I understand." She looked at the knife pressing against Edward's throat and gave a shudder. "There will be only one chance."

"Exactly. You are not trained. You could not recover from a mistake." His eyes were glittering with intent. "I need to know you can do it, because you could easily be overcome, even if you are armed. See?"

It happened in the blink of an eye.

Before Beatrice had time to move, Edward had taken the knife out of her hand and tumbled her onto the bed behind them. He was pinning her under him with his weight, holding her wrists above her head, keeping her still. She could not move an inch—he was too strong and he had been too fast. He nudged her legs open with one knee and placed his hips between her thighs. The movement was not rough but there was no mistaking what he wanted to illustrate. She was utterly at his mercy. All she could do was scream, but even then she was sure he could have silenced her without weakening his hold.

And he had not even taken the knife to her throat. An attacker would not hesitate to use weapons as a further deterrent.

She gulped at the force of his demonstration.

"Yes, I see," she breathed. There would be no second chance.

"I need to know that you will never find yourself like this, pinned under a man you don't want, a man who will force you if given the chance," Edward told her, placing his forehead against hers. The tender gesture and the soft voice were at odds with the position he was holding her in. He looked like a man assaulting her, but he sounded and acted like a lover.

Beatrice wanted to speak but no sound came. Tears welled in her eyes. She turned her head sideways and felt him release his hold on her wrists.

"But it will happen soon enough," she said in a sob. "Sir Robert warned me before he left that he wants an heir. He is my husband, so I cannot take a knife to him. He is the only man I would need defending against, the only one I have to endure."

Every word was a stab to Edward's guts because Beatrice was right. There would be no chance to defend herself against her husband. He might teach her how to fend off an attack from a stranger, but nothing he showed her would protect her from a man who owned her and was entitled by law to possess, strike, or humiliate her whenever he wanted.

He lifted his weight from her and buried his head in the crook of her neck, lost in a sea of despair. He took her into his arms and held her tight whilst sobs racked through her.

"Beatrice," he breathed, lost for words.

There was nothing he could say, nothing that would make any difference.

He was feeling murderous, but tried his best to control the surge of hatred threatening to engulf him. Before today he had not allowed himself to dwell on the thought of Sir Robert bedding Beatrice, for fear he would not be able to restrain himself in his presence otherwise. Now that he knew for certain that her husband, not content with being condescending and thoughtless toward her, was also in effect raping her on a regular basis, he could not bear the idea of Beatrice ever going back to him.

But what could he do? How could he ask her to leave the life of a lady to run away with him? They would have to live as outcasts, condemned by all. He had asked her to do just that when she was an unmarried, free girl, and she had hesitated, as well she might. Now she had two children to think of, and possible retaliation from a husband everyone would side with. The decision was even more momentous, with the danger to her safety very real.

But how could he ever countenance handing her back to Sir Robert?

Never had he felt more powerless.

After a long while, Beatrice stopped crying. Having expelled years of misery in her outpouring of grief, she felt better, stronger. Her tears seemed to have cleared the fog in her mind, and for the first time she could see her future clearly.

Lying against Edward's hard body, bathing in his wonderful smell, she knew she could never bear to go back to Sir Robert, not now. All these years she had thought Edward had abandoned her, but now that she knew he hadn't, and that he was free to be with her, she could not envisage any other life that one by his side.

She lifted her eyes to him.

He had once asked her to run away with him, and now she would be the one asking the same thing of him.

"Take me away, Edward," she breathed, feeling as if she was sealing her fate.

He didn't move. It was as if he had been waiting for the demand, as if he had been thinking the same thing himself without daring to voice it out loud.

"I can't," he said slowly. "You know I can't."

"You asked me once. I hesitated, and look where it got me!" she cried out, sitting up in anger. "It is the only solution. I can't go back to my husband, and I can't let you go. So take me with you."

"Beatrice..." he started, but she cut his protests short.

"I'm serious. Without you, I will never have the courage to leave, but I will die if I have to return to Devance Castle and to Sir Robert's bed. I would not mind dying if I was on my own, but my girls need me. Take me, take *them*, away from him... Please, save us."

Edward sat up in turn. "You will be mocked and spurned by everyone if you run away with a squire, you do know that! We will never have the life you are accustomed to."

"I care not about that! I will be with you. It's all that matters." She made a cutting gesture. "I have never been so happy as I have been here alone with you. Surely you must have seen that?"

He sighed. "You say this because it has been only a few days. But when it is every day, when you have lost all the respect of the people who knew you, who will think you sank below your dignity for—"

She interrupted him once more, because each of his argument only reinforced her determination. "Will I lose your respect?"

"No, never!" he flared. "How can you even ask this?"

"Then it's all I want to know. Edward, we have lost seven years, seven long years we will never get back. I do not want to lose another day, because whether it is now or in twenty years' time, I know we are meant to be together. And I cannot afford to wait to become a widow. Sir Robert is older than I am, but not quite in his old age yet. I cannot wait until he dies—I don't want to!" she cried out, the idea of spending another thirty years as his wife making her stiff with horror. "I cannot go back to him! I cannot let him father another child onto me. I don't want him to touch me ever again!"

The argument struck home, as she knew it would. The blue in Edward's eyes became a dark pool of anguish. He could not countenance the idea of her in her husband's bed any more than she could.

"All right," he said eventually. "We will go back to Devance Castle while he is still away and take your daughter with us."

That he would think about Alys in such a moment brought fresh tears to Beatrice's eyes.

"I love you." In the end, the words that had threatened to escape her mouth so often came out simply, the declaration all the more poignant for it.

There was a pause, then Edward shook his head. "I love you too. I would not attempt this otherwise, for 'tis pure folly."

The words Beatrice had so often desired to hear were said in a bleak tone, as if he regretted his feelings for her. Nonetheless they made her heart beat faster.

"If you do love me, then we will be all right."

"I am not so sure. I have nothing to offer you."

Edward ran his hand through his hair in an angry gesture. Never had he felt more inadequate. What good was all his training now? He had gone from being a peasant's son to being the squire of a respected knight, a dizzying, unthinkable ascension for the poor boy he had been. And yet it still wasn't enough! It meant nothing if it did not earn him the woman he wanted.

In that moment, he felt as powerless as if he had still been a stable hand.

Beatrice smiled at him, a smile that knifed through him because he knew himself for an impostor, even if she did not see it.

"You mean you cannot give me a prestigious title, wealth, status, a castle and domains, servants, and precious gowns?" she asked, stroking his cheek tenderly.

"Yes," he said, his voice vibrating with frustration. "None of these things you deserve!"

"I've had all these all my life, and not once did they make me happy, not once did it make me grateful to be a lady. I want *you*, Edward, I always have, from the moment I met you."

"Why?"

She rubbed her cheek against his shoulder like a contented cat. "Because I want a man I can wake up next to in the morning, a man who respects me and loves me. I want to be able to care for my children as I see fit and make them happy in turn, I want for them a father who doesn't consider them unimportant because they are girls. I want to smile every day, I want pleasure. All this you can offer me."

"Is it enough?"

"Enough?" She let out a small laugh. "It is more than I could have dreamt of. I am not seventeen anymore, untried and untested. I have seen enough of life to know what I really want. I am not throwing away my chance of a future with you a second time. I want a man who wants me, not one who owns me. I want a man I don't hate, who doesn't frighten me, who doesn't hurt me when he beds me." Her voice broke.

Edward's blood started to boil with unrepressed hatred. "I swear I'll kill him for that," he said through clenched teeth.

Beatrice shook her head. "I don't care about Sir Robert enough to want him dead. I just want to leave him. I just want to be with you. The rest doesn't matter."

"Then we will set off as soon as you are fit to travel," Edward declared, taking her hand in his. The image of Sir Robert forcing himself on her had erased all the remaining doubts in his mind.

He would do the unthinkable and claim Beatrice for himself if it was the only way to protect her from the husband she had never wanted,

It was undoubtedly folly, but the alternative would be worse than death. He had no choice. Sir Robert would never get to hurt her again. To know that his cowardice had condemned her to go back to a tyrant would poison every moment of the rest of his life and place her and her daughters in danger. He could not allow it.

What they would do or where they would go if Sir William threw him out in outrage, he did not know. Beyond taking her away from her husband, he could not think.

"I am ready to travel. In truth, I have been ready for days, only I didn't want to put an end to this."

Beatrice stared at him, eyes heavy with desire. Then she placed a hand on his chest. His whole body leapt. Damnation, in the blink of an eye he was ready to burst! Weeks of restraint had tested his self-control to the limit. After days of sleeping next to her, of holding her soft body against his, of watching her laugh, eat, talk, walk, he was desperately, hopelessly hungry for her. Lying on top of her before had almost pushed him over the edge. With her breasts pressed against his chest and her legs parted in such a way, he had almost gone mad with the need to drive into her.

But he could not. Not only was she not recovered from the birth, but she was a married woman. Honor demanded he did not give in to his desire, even if she shared it.

"Please don't," he said through gritted teeth. "It's all I've been able to do to keep away from you these last few weeks. If you touch me, I don't think I will be able to stop myself. I want you too much."

"I know. And I am grateful for your restraint. But I've just told you, I am healed. I have never felt better, and I'm desperate for you."

Feeling like a seventeen-year-old virgin again, Beatrice leaned in to speak into Edward's ear. She knew why he was resisting his desire for her, and she knew everyone would agree they should not surrender to passion, but she could not stop herself. As she saw it, Edward, not Sir Robert, had the prior claim to her, and even if he did not, after the way Sir Robert had treated her and Alys all these years, he did not deserve her faithfulness.

"Make love to me, Edward."

"I cannot. Your husband—"

She stopped him with a swift kiss on the lips. "The normal rules don't apply here, and we both know it. My husband was forced on me by my parents. Still, I might have accepted my lot and sacrificed myself to preserve his *honor*, but Sir Robert doesn't know the meaning of the word. He's forfeited the loyalty I owe him with the way he's treated me year after year, bedding all the women he could find and never once offering a kind word to me."

Before Edward could protest further, she stood and started to remove her clothes, overcome by an irrepressible desire. After years of longing for him, after weeks of his company, after nights spent in his arms, she could not wait a moment longer for his touch. Feeling his body on top of hers earlier in a grim parody of lovemaking had inflamed her senses, and she longed to feel the real thing.

The plain clothes she had taken to wearing made the task of undressing easy. When the undershirt fell onto the floor, Edward let out a growl, almost the sound of a man in pain, and he averted his gaze.

The reaction was a stab in Beatrice's heart. Of course, she was no longer the lithe young maid he had held in his arms all those years ago.

"I…I'm sorry," she stammered. "I know what you must be thinking. I am not as young as I once was. I've had two children since we…"

She flushed and hid her face in her hands. For a moment, she had been so lost in her own desire that she had not paused to reflect how she would appear to Edward. She had not thought for a moment how she would not be as desirable to him if he saw her naked. He was a man at the height of his virility. The years had only made him stronger, even more attractive. Honed by years of training, his body was more athletic than ever, his eyes had lost none of their sparkle, and his beauty was even more obvious than before.

How could a man like him still want her seven years later, when the flush of youth had faded from her cheeks and years of misery had taken their toll? Maternities had altered her once-supple body, lines of worry and pain now marked her face. Time had been less kind to her than it had been to him.

He could have all the women he wanted. Why would he want her as she was now?

She bent to retrieve her clothes, intent on covering herself. It had been a mistake to bare herself to him. Before she could lift the undershirt above her head, Edward had knelt at her feet. The clothes were snatched away from her hand and thrown to the other side of the room in an angry gesture.

"Beatrice, no, please, don't cover yourself," he all but snarled. "Look at me! I'm sorry, I should never have averted my eyes, but…"

"But…" Her breath caught in her throat. His eyes were burning with intent.

"I don't want to hurt you. I cannot bear the idea that I will, even if I don't mean to. And I want you so much that I know if I look at you, if you touch me, I will not be able to stop myself." He spoke with a strained voice, every word a struggle. "I have stopped myself for weeks, and I know we cannot lie together, but I can't help myself…I want you too much."

"You cannot possibly, not now you have seen me naked," she said in a small voice. "Look at me!"

"Oh, I am looking at you, never fear! I look at you every moment of every day, my sweet, and ache for you. Surely you know that?" Still at her feet, he poured his gaze into hers, then let it wander over her figure. Despite Beatrice's initial doubts, she could see he was telling the truth. If she was dissatisfied with her body, he at least could find no fault with it. Quite the opposite. "Shall I tell you what I see?" he whispered, sounding positively entranced.

She nodded, unable to deal with the intensity of his voice.

"I see the love of my life," he said simply. "A woman at the height of her beauty, not a girl anymore but a real woman. A woman I have not stopped thinking about from the moment I laid eyes on her all those years ago, even though I had no right to her. I see a brave woman I should have protected, a woman who jeopardized everything to be with me, several times, who makes me laugh and makes me ache with the need of her at the same time…a beautiful woman I want now more than ever."

"You still desire me?" she breathed, driven to the edge of sanity by his words.

"Desperately," he growled, throwing her a dark, sultry look.

"Then take me, Edward, for I am yours," she said, echoing the very words she had told him the day he had

Virginie Marconato

taken her maidenhead.

"Oh, Beatrice," he said from deep within. "I won't take you, but I will give you the pleasure you deserve." Before she could blink, he swept her off her feet and carried her to the bed behind them.

Beatrice felt deliciously exposed. Being naked under a fully dressed man, the very man she had fantasized about every moment of every day, was highly erotic, sending her blood racing in anticipation.

"Kiss me, Edward," she breathed.

He dipped his head. She had expected a fiery kiss, full of unbridled passion, but this was the kiss between kindred spirits, a kiss only soulmates could share, and all the more precious for it.

She moaned when his mouth left her lips and his hands started exploring her body. Everywhere he touched, tiny bursts of pleasure skittered over her heated skin. Her neck, her breasts, her hips, he explored every inch of her body, even the most surprising ones…her armpit, her navel, the back of her knee. She almost screamed when he let his tongue slide in between her toes.

Finally Edward straightened up to look at her, magnificent in his virility.

"I have wanted to have you in my bed every day and every night for the last seven years. I cannot believe I let you go when I had you in my arms at your father's castle. If I'd known that day that it was to be the last time I ever saw you, I would have abducted you," he said darkly.

"Well, now I am in your bed, so do what you want with me."

"There is one thing," he said in a low rumble, letting his fingers dance on her skin once more.

"What is that?" she asked, breathless with anticipation.

He surprised her by lifting her buttocks and placing a cushion under her, so that she was slightly elevated. Then slowly, he pushed her thighs apart until she was fully exposed. Beatrice resisted the reflex to close her legs as, despite her confusion, the daring of having Edward look at that part of her made her insides dissolve in need.

She opened her mouth.

"No. Say what you will, I cannot take you. I want you to be able to say in all honesty that no other man than your husband has entered your body since he married you. But I cannot deny you the pleasure you've been missing all these years. I am going to do what I never dared to do when we met," he said, eyes fastened on the place he had so boldly exposed.

"But you already kissed me once there," Beatrice mumbled. If he didn't remember doing it, she certainly hadn't forgotten the incredible sensation.

A finger trailed a lazy path on her inner thigh as a smile bloomed on Edward's lips. "Oh, I do remember. I *kissed* you there once, yes. But I stopped before I could give you all the pleasure you could have. I was too intimidated by you, too afraid of being presumptuous. I have regretted it ever since." The words were just a low rumble. "The last time I had you, I didn't dare behave as I would with another woman. You said you wanted me to behave with you like I would with a woman who wasn't so far above myself?"

"Yes." The word was little more than a croak.

"Well, then, I will, and this time I will give you all the pleasure I can."

"I doubt you can do more than you did then."
Beatrice was now breathing with some difficulty.

His smile widened further. "A challenge, sweeting?
You know how I respond to those…" Her insides melted
like candle wax, and she knew she was not far off from
the explosion of pleasure he was the only person to have
provoked in her. "I'm going to make you forget anyone
else ever touched you," he said in a voice heavy with
longing.

She had already forgotten. In Edward's arms she
was seventeen again, pure and untouched.

"Please," she pleaded, unable to wait any longer.

"My love," he said before dipping his head.

First he kissed the flesh on her inner thighs, little
teasing touches that made her squirm. The caresses soon
grew bolder, and she started panting with need. When his
tongue followed a path from her knee down toward her
most secret part Beatrice closed her eyes and lay back on
the bed, knowing she would never dare watch him while
he gave her such intimate pleasure.

Finally, there was the delicious kiss she
remembered, only this time it didn't stop after that brief
touch. Her mind dissolved in an array of sensations each
more exquisite than the last when that one kiss became a
caress and then a feast. Beatrice could not think, she
could only feel. With his mouth on her, Edward was
creating a new world. She tried to picture what he was
doing, tried to understand how it could feel so good, but
when he slipped a finger inside her, she lost track of
everything and just let herself go.

The more she moaned, the more he groaned in
response, the vibration of his deep rumbles traveling up
her flesh. It was indeed nothing like the kiss he had given

her when they were younger, or even what she experienced when he filled her pulsing flesh.

It was something different again, and just as wonderful.

Just when she was thinking she would not be able to withstand more of the exquisite pleasure, one hand closed on her breast and tugged at her nipple. It was enough to make her body explode in violent spasms.

The world tilted on its axis, and then everything quietened down, like the ripples on a lake easing after a stone had been thrown in, like the rumble of thunder receding into the distance after a storm. There was a moment of peace.

And then...and then Beatrice burst out in tears.

Appalled, Edward took her in his arms and held her tight against him. "I'm sorry, I'm so sorry, did I hurt you?" he asked, his mouth in her hair. He had been too rough, too lost to his need for her to see her distress! How would he forgive himself? "I knew it was too soon, forgive me. Oh, Beatrice, please!"

"No, no, it's not that," she said between two heart-rending sobs. "You know you could never hurt me. But it was just..." She shook her head, as if unable to explain herself adequately. "Experiencing so much pleasure after years of being wary of a man's touch was...well, it nearly killed me. What I feel for you is so intense it's almost painful."

Edward rewarded this answer with a kiss on the temple and allowed himself to breathe again. He had not hurt her, that was the main thing. She had been overwhelmed by the long overdue release, that was all.

"I know, sweetheart," he said, rocking her back and forth against him. "Cry all you want. I'm here."

Her felt her smile against his neck and he closed his eyes, happier than he had been in years. His body was throbbing with unfulfilled need, but his mind was at peace. As he saw, he had not dishonored himself—or her. He had simply done what needed to be done. They would both be able to walk away with the knowledge that they had not lain together.

After a while, Beatrice drew away from him. "But you…"

"What about me, sweet?"

"Well. You know…" She reddened. "I got my release, but you—"

He stopped her with another kiss to the temple and brushed her cheek. "Hush. I've never felt more satisfied in my life."

And oddly, that was the truth.

Chapter 13

No answer. Now was a good time to go and see about the window Beatrice had asked him to check. Edward walked into the darkened room but, contrary to what he had first thought, he did not find it empty.

Lying on the bed was Beatrice, fast asleep. He walked closer. Next to her was baby Bridget, suckling on her breast. A smile stretched his lips. He knew Beatrice was feeding her child herself, but he had never seen it that clearly. Then all of a sudden the baby lost its grip on the nipple and creased her face in protest. Soon she started to wail. Immediately Beatrice opened her eyes and settled her back on her nipple as naturally as if she had been doing it all her life.

Their eyes met briefly. She was still half asleep but she smiled at him.

"Edward," she mumbled before closing her eyes again.

The intimacy of the moment squeezed his chest. It was as if she thought he had every right to watch her feed her baby. Then her eyes flew open. She was properly awake this time, fully conscious of his presence—and of her bared breast—but she did not even try to cover herself up. He loved her for this proof of ease between them.

"Edward," she repeated in a different voice. No longer lazy, it was hoarse with longing.

"I came in to see to that window," he explained before it started to affect him. "But I didn't want to wake you up."

"Do you disapprove?" she asked, nodding toward the baby by her side. "Grand ladies are not supposed to breastfeed their own children. It is not what we are here for."

"No, I don't disapprove," he said in a growl. "It only makes me realize you weren't lying when you said you wanted a different life."

Beatrice raised her head slightly. "One with you, a mere squire, you mean? Well I do, and I meant every word of it. Did you doubt me?" she asked, temper flaring.

"No, only I thought you were trying to alleviate my doubts. I for one cannot wish you to be married to a squire, much less living in sin with him, even if that squire is me."

"Would you wish me married to a man like Sir Robert? No. I thought not," she said when his face became thundery. "And why wouldn't I want this? Feeding a baby feels so incredible. I have a child already, and yet I never knew." She stroked little Bridget's cheek. "I want to do it again, with your children."

Edward felt as if she had winded him with a well-placed kick. "My children…" he said in a breath. The thought of her body rounding with his child was enough to make his head spin.

"I know," she soothed, taking his hand in hers, as if she knew she had gone too far too soon. "First we need to find a way of being together. But I will give you children one day, Edward, I know it, just as I knew I would have you."

She spoke with absolute serenity, as if there was no doubt in her mind that it would happen. Edward was humbled. Seeing that she wanted him so unequivocally helped alleviate some of his doubts. Maybe there could be a way for them to be together after all.

Then his eyes landed on the hand he was holding.

"You have taken your wedding band off." He was aghast.

"Yes. I could not bear wearing it, or even seeing it, after what you…after what happened."

Beatrice met Edward's eyes boldly and thought back to the previous afternoon. She had gone to the fountain once he had left her bed to go and see to the new horses. Her body had been warm and tingling from the pleasure he had given her. She had felt reborn, stronger than ever. As she had reached out to the hawthorn bush to pick one of the snowy buds she had seen her wedding band around her finger.

Without the slightest hesitation she had taken it off and thrown it into the water. This time she would follow her heart and forget conventions. She would make her grandmother—and herself—proud.

"What did you do with it? Where is it?"

"It's gone. I threw it in the fountain."

"My God, Beatrice!" Edward cried out. "I have to go and retrieve it."

"You needn't do any such thing," she countered calmly, stopping him with a look. "I will never wear it ever again. I do not want to set eyes on it again." The feeling of freedom she had experienced as she finally disposed of it had been exhilarating. A prisoner being freed from his shackles after years of captivity would surely experience the same relief. "If I ever wear a wedding band again, it will be the one you place on my finger."

In that moment Edward saw there would be no going back. In her mind, Beatrice had already left Sir Robert and her old life behind. All he would be able to do was to follow her in her new life, and learn to accept her sacrifice.

****

Beatrice trailed her finger on Edward's thigh and brushed the pale circle above his knee. He groaned at the sensation.

"So this is your wound..." she observed, before throwing him an impish grin. "You refused to show it to me, but I got to see it after all."

"Yes, unsurprisingly you did." He smiled back and covered her hand with his. "Are you ever thwarted in your desires, my lady?"

Her brow darkened. "No, never. Only when it truly matters. I can have all the food I want or order dozens of gowns at a time if I so wish, but there is one thing I have always wanted and it has been denied to me."

"Isn't this what you wanted?" Edward asked, glancing at their two naked bodies entwined on the crumpled sheets.

"No, I want more, and you know it. I want more than a few days in your arms and a lifetime of regrets at the memory. I told you, I want all of you, not just a few weeks of stolen kisses. I mean it. I want you to stop worrying about who I am married to and make love to me at last. I want to feel you inside me."

She sat up on the bed, indignation flashing in her eyes. Edward knew she was furious, but all he could think was how magnificent she looked in her anger. Who else would dare to defy him thus whilst naked?

Only his Beatrice.

"Don't tell me you are having a change of heart? I thought you had agreed!" she cried out.

He caressed her hip in an appeasing gesture. "So I have, fool that I am."

The flare of anger in her eyes was instantly doused. With a smile she nestled back into his embrace. Her hand wormed its way up his arm to settle on his chest. The gesture had become familiar over the last few days, and he knew he would never be able to be parted from her now, however mad it was to even think such a thing.

This was true happiness, Edward thought as he kissed Beatrice on the forehead. He didn't need anything more. Well...perhaps he wouldn't say no to a proper night of passion in her arms. It was becoming increasingly difficult to resist the urge to plunge inside her soft warmth. Worse, he had not allowed himself to pleasure her since the day he had shown her how to use a dagger, fearing that he would not be able to stop himself from possessing her if he did.

But he could not, for both their sakes. Not yet.

"Sir William told me one day that you had contrived his meeting with Lady Margery?" Beatrice asked him suddenly. "How on earth did you do that?"

He gave a laugh. "The way your mind works will always be a mystery to me. Why are you asking me this now?"

"Because without this we might never have found each other again."

"We wouldn't," he confirmed. "I only introduced them so we would have a reason to meet one day. As soon as I heard Lady Margery was Sir Robert's cousin's daughter, I made sure her path crossed that of my master."

"So you kept track of my whereabouts all this time?"

"Of course. I always tried to have some news of you and Sir Robert over the years and, sporadically, I did." He paused. "The day I learnt about the birth of your daughter I drank myself to a stupor."

Edward didn't add that the following morning he had woken up in the arms of a naked woman he had no memory of meeting. As soon as he had felt her stir he had taken her in a blaze of fury and bitterness, imagining Beatrice's pain if she saw him making love to another woman, just like the idea of another man bedding her and giving her children was tearing him apart. The fierceness of his thrusts had frightened him but the woman under him had not complained, rather the opposite. When she had cried out her pleasure, he had almost howled in despair.

That was when he had decided he would have to find a way of seeing Beatrice again. Her absence was eating at his soul, giving his every action a nasty aftertaste, slowly transforming him into a monster.

It had taken a while, but finally he had landed on the perfect way of ensuring he could meet with her.

One day at a jousting tournament he had heard a certain Lady Margery Raglan mention that her father was none other than Lord Devance's cousin. Immediately he had contrived a meeting between her and his new master with the aim of learning more about Sir Robert's or, more pointedly, Beatrice's whereabouts. The meeting had been a resounding success, more than he could have hoped for.

"I managed to get the two of them to talk. By the

end of the day, Sir William declared himself smitten, and a month later he and Lady Margery were married."

Edward had been quick to find a way of exploiting this union to his advantage. The opportunity for a visit to Devance Castle had come at the right time, for he could not have gone much longer without seeing Beatrice again.

"You are quite manipulative. Who would have thought it?"

Beatrice was humbled that Edward would have gone to such lengths to ensure they could meet again.

"I am when I want to be. If I want something, I will make sure I take it." He closed his hand on her breast. Beatrice smiled at the possessiveness of the gesture. "The irony, of course, is that we might have stopped at Devance Castle anyway after the battle of Barnet. The men needed to rest, and it was one of the closest places at hand. I needn't have plotted so much."

"I'm glad you did. Some things are too important to be left to chance." Beatrice stroked his chest lovingly.

"Quite."

They carried on talking and only fell asleep as dawn was graying the horizon. Beatrice woke first, feeling happier than ever. Today they would leave to get Alys and finally be together.

She ran a finger along Edward's jaw, watching the blond prickles on his skin, feeling their roughness tease the tip of her finger. A smile creased her face.

"Edward?" she whispered when she could not wait any longer for him to waken.

"Mm?" he mumbled, still half asleep.

"Can I ask you something?"

He gave a theatrical sigh, but when he opened his

eyes the look in them was one of amusement, not irritation. "I think you are going to ask, whether I want it or not." He gave just the hint of a smile. "You always do. And what's more, whatever it is you are about to ask, you will expect me to do it."

She laughed, not in the least chastened. "How well you know me!"

The blue eyes twinkled. "I do, for my sins. So tell me, what it is you want to me do?"

"Could you not shave today?" Beatrice said, feeling suddenly very absurd.

With a snort, Edward lifted himself onto one elbow. "You want me not to *shave*?" he asked with a slanted smile. "Why on earth would you want this?"

"It's just... It makes you so handsome," she answered shyly.

This time he laughed outright. "If that is the case, I had better comply." He rubbed his rough chin with a hand. "Who knew beauty was so easily achievable? Although I don't see any beard on your chin, and yet you are undoubtedly beautiful."

He stroked her cheek with his hand and she leaned into the caress, like a cat would rub its head into its master's palm.

"I never said you weren't handsome without a beard," she clarified. "Far from it. Only it reminds me of before. You were rarely clean shaven in those days, and I loved it. I still do."

"Yes, you always liked anything that made me different from a nobleman," he said wistfully. "Why, one day you made me catch and cook a rabbit on a wooden spit in the meadow!" He let out a small laugh at the memory.

"Yes, and it was delicious, too," Beatrice replied, unabashed. "But I seem to remember you liked everything that made me a lady, so I think we're even, wouldn't you say?"

"Ah, but that's where you're wrong. I never liked anything that wasn't a part of you. I never cared about your rank. If anything, it only got in the way."

"You liked my smell…" He had told her so many times, burying his nose into the crook of her neck to inhale it.

"I still do," he said, nuzzling at her throat in the same delicious way.

"Well, let me tell you that rosewater is expensive. Only a lady could afford to use it. I doubt you have smelt it on every one of your…" She stopped before she could finish the sentence. She didn't want to think about Edward's many conquests right now. Then a thought struck her. "Wait. I am not wearing it today. In fact, I didn't take any with me when we left Devance Castle." Her eyes arrowed in suspicion. "How can you say you still like it? You are a shameful liar!"

Edward looked at her with the same expression you would give someone accusing you of stealing the purse they were holding in their very hands. "It's not the rosewater I like, Beatrice, it's the smell of your own skin. Hadn't you realized it by now?" He kissed her neck again, then licked the hollow at the base of her throat.

"What about when I spoke French to the Comte de Baylac's envoys?" she insisted, doing her best to ignore the maddening way he was nipping at her flesh. He'd heard her welcome the men in the courtyard. Afterward, in bed, he had told her how alluring he had found it. "You cannot pretend I would have learnt how to speak French

241

if I weren't a lady."

But once again Edward dismissed her claim with a wave of the hand. "It's the confidence it gave you I loved, not the language itself. It was as if you were finally free from constraints. Whenever you spoke to your parents, you always sounded different from when you spoke to me—guarded somewhat, restrained, unnatural. When you spoke in a foreign tongue, it seemed to allow you to be yourself, to be the woman I love."

The declaration, as sweet as it was sincere, left Beatrice speechless.

"Then I guess you do love the real me, not the lady," she murmured, stunned.

Instead of answering, he gave her a scorching kiss that left her in no doubt about his feelings. "I guess I do, for I love you best when you are naked and in my arms. There is no frippery, no artifice. In that moment you are not Lady Devance or anyone else. You are only Beatrice, and you are all mine."

"Yes. All yours."

And soon, she would be in deed as well as in principle. Once she had left her husband, she would find a way to make Edward agree to finally make love to her.

While she nestled herself in his arms, Beatrice's mind took her back to the time he had taken her maidenhead.

That day she had gone to find him in his room for the first time, thinking the private setting would encourage him to be bolder. It hadn't. As usual, he had merely kissed her until it was all she could do not to collapse in a heap at the strength of her desire for him.

So Beatrice had done the only thing she could think

of to persuade him. She had dropped to her knees and undone his hose to pleasure him. The lewdness of this act, which she had only ever heard mentioned in scandalized whispers, had set her body on fire, and at first Edward had been too shocked by her daring to say anything. The feel of his hardness under her tongue had been a totally unexpected sensation.

It was both powerful and delicate, hard yet smooth.

Beatrice whimpered out loud in longing. If he felt so good in her mouth, how much better would it be when he took her as he should? Having no idea how exactly to proceed, she did what felt comfortable to her and smiled inwardly. Judging from the grunts escaping Edward's lips, she was doing something right. At last she had found the ultimate weapon! Whatever his reservations about bedding her, he would not be able to resist her any much longer.

She moaned in anticipation.

"Please, my lady," Edward said in a rasp, and although her mind told her he was begging her to stop and give him a chance, she chose to behave as if it was a plea for more and carried on.

He did not draw back. His fingers came to weave themselves into her hair, anchoring her in place. For a while Beatrice tasted victory, but a moment later he forced her back onto her feet. At first she thought she had not managed to tempt him after all, but then he planted his gaze into hers and she saw she had succeeded only too well in her seduction. He was panting hard, and his eyes had gone wild with need.

He had never been more handsome—and she more desperate.

"Make love to me, Edward."

"Tell me you really want me to," he asked urgently, on the edge of control.

"I do. Can't you tell?"

A groan had escaped his lips, and a heartbeat later she had been on his pallet, pinned under him.

"Do you remember the day you made love to me for the first time?" Beatrice now asked lazily, trailing a finger over his chest.

"How could I forget it?" Edward murmured. "After what you did to me?"

"You would never have relented otherwise," she argued, blushing.

Edward gazed at her. "I might not. We will never know. In any case, I cannot regret any of it, even if I wish you hadn't been forced to resort to such measures."

Something in his voice alerted her. "You think I…found it distasteful?"

He made a grimace. "Did you not?"

"No! I know that I should not admit to it, but I…I liked it. It aroused me." She hid her face in the pillow, not daring to meet his eye after she had confessed to such a shocking thing.

There was a silence. Then he leaned in to whisper in her ear.

"I always thought you had only done what you could to entice me. Not for a moment did I imagine you had actually liked it! Thank you for setting my mind at rest."

She risked a glance at him when she understood that, far from being disgusted by her admission, he was relieved to hear she had not felt obliged to do something she found degrading. Well, she could reassure him on that score.

"Yes, I did like it and it did arouse me. Why should

it not? Didn't it please you to love me with your mouth?"

He gave a growl at the very intimate question. "Yes, it did."

"Well, then, it was the same for me."

Giving pleasure to your lover, hearing their moans and knowing you were the one making them shatter in release, was highly erotic. Why would it be different for her?

Edward let out a sigh. "All these years I felt guilty over it. I never thought you'd actually enjoyed it."

Beatrice lifted her head and met his eyes squarely, all shyness suddenly gone. "It was the most wickedly satisfying thing I had ever done—and I cannot wait to do it again."

****

Dressed in all her finery, Beatrice felt heavy and encumbered, a far cry from the carefree woman she had been since the birth of her daughter. In the past month she had got used to the comfort afforded by simpler clothes. Her truncated hennin was digging into her scalp, and the elaborate gown would make breastfeeding a hundred times more complicated, but of course she could not set out for Devance Castle looking anything less than a lady.

No matter. In just a few days' time, she would not be accountable to anyone for her decisions, and what she wore would be the least of anyone's problems.

"I thank you for everything you did for my daughter and me," Beatrice told Mistress Joan, who had come for a last visit before their departure.

Her reluctance at leaving this haven of tranquility was mingled with a sense of excitement. Soon she would be free from her husband, free to begin a new life with the man she loved.

She and Edward still hadn't thought beyond getting Alys from Devance Castle and fleeing, but even the uncertainty ahead was not enough to dampen her ardor. She would take all her jewelry with her, and that alone would ensure them a few years' subsistence. There was little cause for concern in her mind, even if she knew Edward still harbored doubt and a sense of guilt at denying her birthright and making her the object of gossip and censure.

Beatrice didn't share that worry. As long as she could have Edward and her children by her side, she would be happy.

"It was my pleasure to help you. Do you still breastfeed your child regularly?" Mistress Joan asked her with a side glance, tickling Bridget's toes.

"Yes. It is exhausting, especially at night, but I love it. Don't tell me you are going to ask me to stop now that I am leaving?" Beatrice said with a smile. "I have no intention of finding a wet nurse."

"No, rather the opposite. I am going to encourage you to carry on as long as possible, at least until you are reunited with your husband and can resume your marital duty, for while you breastfeed your baby regularly you cannot get pregnant." She averted her eyes and focused her attention on the little girl. "I am sure you will agree it would not do for Sir Robert to be told that his wife fell with child while she was away from him."

Beatrice opened her mouth to protest but there was nothing to be said. It seemed that Mistress Joan had been more observant than Lady Margaret.

"Thank you," she told the midwife with a small smile. For the first time since Edward had pleasured her she was actually grateful for his restraint because it meant she could face the woman with her head held high. Indeed there was no chance she could be with child. "But I can assure you that my husband will never be told such a thing."

Chapter 14

The chaos in the courtyard could only mean one thing.

Sir Robert and his retinue were back.

Beatrice glanced at Edward in dismay, knowing he would be thinking the same thing as her. Now they would have to confront him. This had never been part of the plan. They had thought to fetch Alys and disappear while he was still away.

They stayed hidden in the woods while they debated on the best course of action. Lady Margaret was a few miles behind with the baby and the rest of their escort. They hadn't been able to resist the appeal of a gallop together on the last stretch of the journey.

"We need to change our plans. I will have to see Sir Robert now," Beatrice said, aghast at this new development.

"Out of the question."

"There is no other way. Remember that I will have to act as if I barely know you," she reminded Edward, knowing he would hate it.

"As if I'm not fit to kiss the ground you walk on, you mean. Don't worry, I should be able to cope with it. I've had a lifetime of practice," he answered bitterly.

"Please, Edward, don't be angry with me."

"I am not angry with you." His jaw clenched. "At least this contretemps has shown me without a doubt that

I could not bear to let you go back to him. It is bad enough imagining you facing him for a day. I see now that I have no other option than to take you away or lose my mind at the idea of you in his bed." He bunched his fists.

"I will not be long. I only need to go and get Alys and allay his suspicions. I doubt he will want to spend much time with me anyway. He will be too busy overseeing the arrival of his men."

Edward turned to her. "If he tries to touch you…"

Beatrice shook her head. "He won't, not in that way, not when I have not yet been churched," she said with more certainty than she felt. Her husband was unpredictable—it was one of his many foibles. Although she knew he found the idea of her giving birth repugnant, he might just choose to forget she hadn't been properly cleansed if the mood took him to start making his heir.

"He is just back from a deadly battle, so his blood might be up. I've seen men go crazy with lust after having narrowly escaped death." Edward looked nothing short of murderous at the notion.

"He won't come near me," Beatrice repeated, partly to convince herself. "I still remember his disgust at my body after I had Alys. And I daresay he will have met up with more than one woman on the way back here, so his most pressing urges will have been satisfied."

Far from displeasing her, the notion that Sir Robert bedded as many women as he could had always found favor with her. She was grateful to her husband's many conquests for relieving her of some of her marital duties. The more time he spent in other ladies' arms, the fewer his visits to her bedchamber were. In fact, she suspected that if she had given him a brace of heirs he would have been content to leave her alone.

Edward seemed unmoved by her arguments. "Let me go and talk to him. If we are really doing this, then I should be the one facing his anger."

She recoiled in horror at the suggestion. They could not risk him being recognized, not when they were so near their goal!

"No! He will kill you if he so much as suspects what we did or who you are. I have to do this alone. Tonight it will be all over. Please, one more day is all I ask. There is little risk. He will not get angry, as I am not going to let him suspect what we are planning."

Edward was sitting ramrod straight in his saddle, obviously fighting the urge to draw her into a kiss. Beatrice was grateful for his restraint, for she was finding it nearly impossible not to give in to the temptation herself. Although they were hidden by bushes, it would not be safe to get too close. Not now, not when it could put all their plans in jeopardy.

"Tonight, Edward," she said in a low voice, bunching her fists on the reins to stop herself from reaching out to him. One thing was for sure—she could not risk him seeing Sir Robert while he was seething with resentment. He would only betray his innermost feelings. "You might go to the stables to ready the horses and wait for Alys and me. I will come as soon as I can."

"The stables, where I belong."

She could not repress a movement of irritation. Why did it have to be so complicated all the time? "Please don't be like this. You don't belong anywhere but by my side. You just need a little more patience."

"I know, I'm sorry. It's just…the thought of you and him together is enough to send me mad."

"It is the last time, and nothing is going to happen. It will all be over by tonight."

She kicked her horse onward before he could argue further. A moment later, they entered the courtyard. The first person to see her was Sir William. While Edward helped her dismount, Sir William walked over to join them and, despite the welcoming smile, Beatrice detected a glint of uncertainty in his eyes.

Of course, he would be looking at her differently now, the first person to disown her for her decision to leave her husband and live with a squire. Her heart squeezed in dismay. In truth, she was not worried for herself, even if she would miss Sir William's easy friendship, but this was Edward's master. Would he unleash his displeasure on him?

The idea had not entered her head before, but the man might consider himself betrayed. He had taken as his squire a man who in normal circumstances could not have aspired to such an honor, had given him his trust, and now because of him his household would become the focus of gossip and ridicule. He might well consider himself ill repaid for his generosity.

No. Surely Sir William was more kind-hearted than that. From the start she had considered him one of the most personable men she had ever met. His attitude toward his wife was enough to tell her he was a good man, a man who knew what love was and valued it above all things. Hadn't he agreed to leave Edward behind, all the while knowing about them? It had to be a good sign.

"My lady, you are safely returned." She held out her hand for him to kiss. "I trust my man took care of you."

"He did." Beatrice tried to stay composed, but she wasn't entirely successful as an image of a blond head buried between her legs flashed through her mind. Indeed Edward had taken good care of her, in all senses of the words. "I thank you for your thoughtfulness in allowing him to stay behind," she added, a smile of pure happiness blooming on her lips.

Sir William's eyes flicked to Edward. "I think we both know I had no choice in the matter. But I—"

The sentence was cut short by a voice she had hoped never to hear again.

"There you are." Sir Robert walked over to them in his usual swagger. Beatrice gasped at the sight of her husband. In one month he seemed to have aged ten years. His features, which would never have been described as anything other than rough, were now even more harshly defined. "I confess I was surprised not to see you at Devance Castle when we arrived, my lady."

He didn't make any move to take her hand, nor did Beatrice hold it out for him to kiss. The idea of even such simple contact made her flesh crawl.

"I had to delay my travel, on the midwife's advice. She didn't think it advisable for me to ride so near the birth if I wanted to bear other children," she lied, knowing Sir Robert would be too disgusted by her women's troubles to ask for any more details.

"Indeed, I will want an heir," he confirmed bluntly. "Two girls are of no use to me, as you well know."

"That is why I saw no reason to go against her advice. You had, after all, informed me of your intention of staying away from Devance Castle a while, so there was little incentive for a hasty return." Beatrice was surprised by the ease with which she answered. "You will be pleased to know that Bridget is thriving," she added, knowing he could not care less about his daughter.

"Yes. I suppose at least you produce healthy babies." He grunted. "That is small consolation, though, since they always seem to be girls."

There was a rustle of fabric behind her, and Beatrice guessed Edward had moved in anger. She knew he would be struggling to master his temper, but she didn't dare turn her head to reassure him, as at that moment her husband started to look at him with a sudden intensity. Her heart almost stopped beating when he frowned. There was no mistaking the meaning behind the grimace.

He was trying to remember where he had seen him before.

"I am safely returned. Your man can go to his duties. His services are no longer required," she told Sir William, striving to keep her voice steady. Edward had to leave.

Now.

"You heard Lady Beatrice, you can go," Sir William told Edward at once, clearly aware of her fear of seeing the two men come to blows. Indeed he seemed to fear the same thing himself. "Go, Edward," he repeated more firmly when he didn't move.

"Your name is Edward?" Sir Robert asked, stalling his retreat with a raised hand.

"Yes, my lord, it is very common, I know." In the circumstances, Edward's efforts at detachment were commendable. Beatrice was sure she was the only one detecting the strain in his voice. "Sir William has another man called Edward. Perhaps I should change mine, to facilitate matters."

A silence followed. Though she kept her eyes firmly ahead of her, Beatrice could easily feel the tension between the men.

"My lord, I would like to go and see Alys, if I may. I have missed her," she interrupted. "Then I shall go and rest. The travel has wearied me somewhat."

"You were only a couple of days' ride away. Try coming all the way from mid Wales," Sir Robert replied in irritation. "If you're tired, think how I must feel!"

For once Beatrice didn't mind the outburst. As long as his attention was diverted from Edward, he could speak to her as sharply as he wanted. For a moment she had truly feared he had recognized him. She cursed the impulse that had made her ask him to keep a short beard. With it he looked exactly as he had seven years ago, different from the squire who had walked into Devance Castle over a month ago. His hair had grown in the interval, too, and the reckless ride had ruffled the usually smooth arrangement of his locks. Apart from the rich velvet tunic, he was the very image of the stable hand he had been at her father's castle, so much so that Sir Robert had noticed him for the first time.

Sir William dismissed Edward surreptitiously while she talked to her husband. She gave him a grateful smile and knew that her instinct had been right. The man would not disown them for their decision to be together.

Before she could take her leave of Sir Robert, a commotion was heard in the background and he disappeared without another word, already bored of her company.

"You look different, my lady," Sir William said once they were alone. "Rested."

"Thank you. I am not rested so much as happy." Beatrice voiced out loud what he had not dared to say.

"Be careful. I am not sure what you hope will

happen now," he warned, speaking for her ears only. "Edward is a good man, but he cannot pretend to make a woman like you happy."

"On the contrary," she disagreed. "He can. He can and he has."

Sir William regarded her appraisingly for a long time, then seemed to conclude that she meant it. "Society will condemn him strongly for this, and you to a certain extent. I'm afraid there can be no future for you two, however regrettable that is."

She placed a hand on his arm. "I know you mean well, and I am sure you are right, but you must see that I cannot choose to stay with my husband when a man like Edward wants me," she whispered conspiratorially. "You have seen Sir Robert's behavior toward me. I will not offend your judgment by suggesting you have not noticed how despised and frightened he makes me feel."

"No," Beatrice had the satisfaction of hearing Sir William say. "But I will not offend your intelligence by pointing out that not many people will be as understanding. Besides, Sir Robert is never going to let you go."

"He won't if he is consulted," she agreed with a smile. "But as he will not be given any choice, there is little he will be able to do."

Sir William took her hand. "I wish to God I had not agreed to Edward's suggestion to stop at Devance Castle after the battle of Barnet," he said kissing the fingers lightly.

"And I will forever be grateful that you did," Beatrice said, squeezing his hand in return. "Please do not be too disappointed in Edward. He would never have behaved any other way than with perfect courtesy toward me, but I am afraid I left him no choice. I forced his hand most shamelessly." Beatrice blushed when she recalled just how she had achieved this, and though obviously she didn't give Sir William any more details, he cocked his head in understanding.

"If that is the case, then I can only sympathize with him. Although I doubt very much anyone could force Edward to do something he did not want to do. He is as stubborn and proud as they come."

A gurgle of laughter escaped Beatrice's lips at this very accurate description of Edward, the sound of a woman in love. "Yes, he is, isn't he?" she said as if these were two of his most enviable qualities. "Now, if you'll excuse me, I have to go and speak to my daughter."

Alys needed to be told what was going to happen. She had a feeling the little girl would not raise any protest at the idea of going on a trip with Edward. It had been obvious her daughter was as taken with him as she was. At the thought of the happiness to come, her heart leapt with joy. On the way to the nursery, her feet fairly danced on the stone floor. This time she *could* taste freedom on the tip of her tongue.

Tonight she would be out of Sir Robert's clutches forever.

****

"Lady Margaret tells me Sir William's man slept in the antechamber to your room during your stay at the manor."

Beatrice's heart skipped a beat at the abrupt announcement. Her husband sounded none too pleased by the arrangement. Really, what business did her lady have revealing such a thing? Was she jealous? It was possible. It would not have taken her long to see that

Edward did not reciprocate her feelings and start wondering why... Still, did she have to betray her mistress thus?

"He did, for my safety and that of our daughter," she confirmed mildly. "We thought it best, considering the number of soldiers we saw riding past, day and night, looking for trouble."

"And did any of them get between your legs? Is there a chance my next child might not be of my loins?"

"What? No!" Shock made her cry out. He wasn't worried she might have been raped, he merely wanted to ensure his honor was safe. As if *he* would be the injured party if she had been assaulted! Hatred surged through her. The man really was a monster.

"And the squire did not try anything either, while he slept so close to you? A man is a man, after all, and he might well have chosen to overlook your bloated figure for a chance at release. In the dark, it would have made little difference."

Another gasp escaped Beatrice's lips. How dare he! Edward who, according to society, had no right to even look at her, had called her a woman at the height of her beauty when he'd seen her naked, and yet the man who had married her was telling her she was only fit to rut with in the dark because then the few pounds pregnancy had added to her body wouldn't be seen.

It was unbearable.

"No. He did not do anything to compromise my honor."

It was true but she could not help but flush when she remembered it was only because of Edward's scruples that she was able to make such a claim in conscience. To her horror, Sir Robert bared his teeth in a parody of a smile.

"I see. He did not bed you, but you wanted him to. You wanted him to take you, like the wanton you are," he asserted, eyes narrowing. "A squire, upon my word! Were you so desperate after months without a man between your legs?" Beatrice winced at the crude words but stayed silent. "Your tastes do run to the unrefined, my lady. A stable lad first, and then a sq…" Sir Robert stopped as understanding dawned. "*Edward.* That's the same man, isn't it? I *knew* his face was familiar."

And just like that it was as if a dam had burst. Beatrice could contain her loathing for her husband no longer. He had called her bloated, wanton, unrefined. He'd reprimanded her for not being here to meet him when he did not care a fig about her, he had not asked to see his daughter, he had not thanked Edward for looking after her and he was talking to her as if she was his dog.

Straightening her spine, she looked at him with all the scorn she could muster.

"Yes," she answered boldly. "He is the same man. He did not have me during our stay at the manor, but he did all those years ago, before our wedding. I was no virgin for you, I was already his. I still am."

"He took your maidenhead?" Sir Robert asked through gritted teeth.

"Yes, and he had me every time I went to him." Though she knew he would make her pay for it, she said each word with relish and loved to see the humiliation darkening Sir Robert's face. He leaned in toward her, an evil glint dancing in his eyes.

"You outdid yourself on our wedding night, my lady, sobbing that I hurt you when you were already the worst kind of slut!"

"That wasn't a lie. You *did* hurt me that day. You always do," she spat out.

"Oh, I do, do I? Believe me, you've seen nothing. And I imagine your precious Edward never did, even when he broke you in?"

She did not let the crudeness get to her. There had been nothing degrading or painful about that day. "No, he never hurt me."

"I told you I would kill him if I ever saw him again, and that was before I knew he had stolen your maidenhead from me," he hissed, his face distorted by anger.

"My maidenhead belonged to no one, least of all to you," Beatrice challenged haughtily, wondering where this new confidence had come from. Sir Robert seemed to understand it better than she did and attributed this change of attitude to Edward's influence.

"You think you can defy me now that the fool is back?" he shouted, standing up at last. "We'll see about that! You won't get to enjoy him for much longer, that much I can guarantee. By tonight he will be a rotting corpse, but before that…"

He took her wrist and dragged her out of the room, marching her toward his bedchamber with a steely determination.

"No," she protested, trying to stop his progress. In vain. Fueled by his anger, he was far too strong for her. They hurried past the few people assembled in the great hall. In the corner of her eye she saw Lady Margaret, her mouth open in shock at her husband's rough treatment, and Sir William, whose hand automatically went to the hilt of his sword. They all knew what was happening, they all had guessed where he was taking her and why, but they could not stop Sir Robert.

She was going to be raped, but because she was his wife no one would lift a finger to help her. Only one person would have dared come to her aid, and he wasn't here.

"No!" she screamed in anguish. "Ed—"

Sir Robert placed a hand on her mouth to silence her, squeezing her jaw viciously hard. The pressure was so strong Beatrice knew it would leave a bruise. She whimpered in pain. "Hush. I don't mean to kill the whelp just yet. First there is something I have to do."

Not waiting for her response, he hoisted her onto his shoulder. Beatrice tried to hit him, but none of her blows seemed to register. Once in his room, he dropped her onto the floor so carelessly that she fell flat on her back.

He closed the door with a kick and then stayed stock still for a moment, watching her scramble backward in dread. The glint of fury in his eyes became even darker, a glint of lust. He took a step toward her, and Beatrice's blood ran cold.

"I haven't been churched," she said hurriedly, knowing this would make him pause. Using the bedpost to steady herself, she stood up onto her feet.

"I know. Don't worry, I have no intention of sullying myself." Beatrice would have sighed in relief if a grimace had not transformed his face into an ugly mask. He was not finished with her. She took another step backward along the edge of the bed. "There are other ways to teach you who is master. Drop to your knees," he barked.

Beatrice froze in horror when she understood what he meant to make her do. Sir Robert walked over to her and pushed her down when he saw she wasn't obeying his orders. Her knees hit the stone floor and she cried out in pain.

"There. Let us see how we can silence that foul mouth of yours."

He unbuckled his scabbard and dropped it on the nearby table.

"I would keep that sword if I were you. You're going to need it."

Beatrice gave a cry. Silent as a cat, Edward had slipped into the room. He was standing by the door, sword in hand and an expression of such hatred on his face that although she knew it wasn't aimed at her, she recoiled.

Like a wolf about to pounce on his prey, Edward entered the room. If only he'd had fangs and claws to rip the man in front of him to shreds! He would have relished the task. When he'd been forced to leave Beatrice's side earlier, it had felt as if a part of himself had been torn away. Why had he allowed her to convince him she would be fine? He should never have left her alone with her bastard of a husband!

And now he was face to face with her tormentor, he felt such fury that for a moment he feared it would render him quite incapable of fighting. He forced himself to take a few deep, steadying breaths. He could not falter, not now. God knew he was capable of taking the man down, he had faced his share of opponents in his time.

Still, never had he been possessed with the need to kill before.

"You! I swore I would kill you the next time I saw you, boy!" Sir Robert snarled, rounding up on him.

"And I swore the same thing when I saw you treat your wife like a whore in a stew house," Edward answered, his cold voice more lethal than Sir Robert's strident threat. "Why don't you come over here and prove to yourself you're a man with me instead of taking out your frustration on her like a coward? I'm ready."

Now that the moment to fight had actually come, calm descended over him, easing all traces of the distracting fury. Yes. He could do this.

He had to, for Beatrice and her daughters. This was not about him.

"I see that you have taken your master's sword. Do you enjoy taking other men's possessions?" Sir Robert hissed. "You took my wife, isn't that enough?"

Edward's eyes narrowed. "Beatrice was never a possession, but I will certainly enjoy taking her away from a man who mistakes her for one." He glanced at Beatrice in the far corner of the room, and his heart missed a beat when he saw the angry red marks around her mouth. "He hurt you," he said to himself, his voice raw.

That was exactly what he had feared. The bastard had hurt her and would have raped her if he had not intervened! Hate boiled in his veins. How would he ever forgive himself for placing her in danger!

Beatrice shook her head quickly, her eyes huge. "It's nothing. Please don't fight, Edward," she whispered.

Please don't get yourself killed for me. He could see the plea in her eyes.

"Oh, he is going to fight," Sir Robert said before he could answer. "I am not letting him get away with this."

Edward raised his sword. He had no intention of letting the bastard get away with what he had done either. "I await your pleasure."

"Put this away," Sir Robert said contemptuously. "I

only use swords with noblemen. For peasants like you, a dagger will suffice."

He took one that was hanging on the wall for himself and threw another one at him. Edward caught it in midair. For a moment, they eyed each other, both bristling with raw hatred.

Then began the most terrible exchange of blows.

Beatrice had witnessed many a sword fight during tournaments, but this was completely different—brutal, almost primal. The men lunged at each other in desperation, resembling more snarling dogs than well-trained soldiers.

Her husband had been foolish to discard the sword on grounds of snobbery, she thought with some hope. It grated on her to admit it, but he was well versed in the art. However brave, Edward did not possess the wealth of experience Sir Robert had acquired. With the dagger, however, Edward had the advantage. He was younger, fitter. She imagined he had been involved in many a scrap with the village boys growing up. His movements were fluid, graceful, despite the intensity of the exchange. Tiring faster, unused to this type of fighting, Sir Robert was quickly left panting. In one smooth motion, Edward sent his dagger flying out of his hand. It slid on the floor, coming to a halt at Beatrice's feet.

For a moment everything froze. Then she bent to pick up the dagger.

Both men faced her, locked in a deadly embrace.

Edward, his blue eyes ablaze with loathing, was holding the point of his blade to Sir Robert's throat whilst pinning him tightly against his chest. His arm twisted in an iron grip, her husband was grimacing in pain.

He gritted his teeth. "Go on then, boy, kill me. You know you want to. Or have you not got it in you to kill a gentleman, coward that you are?"

"You might be a nobleman, but a gentleman you are not. In any case, I am no coward," Edward said, yanking at the arm sharply. Sir Robert grunted and swore. "You might get to see that sooner than you wish."

"Edward, no!" Beatrice screamed and ran up to them.

"Well, look at that. My dear wife is coming to my rescue," Sir Robert commented drily. "It seems she doesn't want me to die after all. How touching. She must be fonder of me than I thought. All this time in bed together must have had an effect on her and she wants more." He gave a horrible laugh.

"Silence," Edward growled, unable to hear another word on the subject. In front of him, Beatrice had blanched so much he feared she would faint. Then she lowered her eyes and bit her bottom lip. He hated that her husband could make her feel so soiled. Had he not been restraining Sir Robert, he would have scooped her into his arms.

"Or perhaps she wants to kill me herself," Sir Robert said, nodding toward the dagger she held. "The spineless little thing thinks she can make me pay for what I supposedly made her endure in bed. Well, what about what *I* had to endure? Rutting with her was about as pleasurable as rutting with a corpse, and it was all for nothing! She only bore me useless daughters who will no doubt grow up to be as wayward as she is! Little sluts who will open their legs for the first—"

Edward cut the litany of insults short with another yank of his arm. By rights he should cut the man's throat for what he'd just said, but Beatrice didn't even look at her husband.

Instead she lifted her eyes to him.

"Don't listen to him, Edward," she told him softly. "He wants you to kill him because if you do then his men will make you pay for it. It's his revenge against me. He wants me to have to live without you. Don't do it. You will never get out of this alive if you kill him now. Please, think of me. Think of us."

As much as it pained him not to gut the man, Edward knew Beatrice was telling the truth. He released his hold on Sir Robert fractionally, indicating he would not hurt him further. If he was killed now, all their plans would go to waste. He could not give them up so foolishly for a man who was nothing but a despicable tyrant.

He watched Beatrice turn to her husband and finally look at him without hiding the loathing she felt for him. Hatred and misery made her eyes glitter dangerously. His chest squeezed for her.

"I am running away with him, as I should have done seven years ago," she told him, panting with disgust. "There is nothing you can do to stop me."

Sir Robert snorted. "Ha! So you'll be his wh—"

The word was cut short by the point of the dagger pressing into his neck, but once again Beatrice was unimpressed. She carried on as calmly as if they were exchanging pleasantries at a banquet.

God, how he admired her!

"Yes, I'll be his whore. I will find it less degrading than being your wife."

"You might go to live in filth with your stable lad, but I will keep Alys and..." He stopped, unable to remember the name of his own daughter.

"Her name is Bridget," Beatrice spat in contempt. "And we'll see about that. They are *my* daughters, and you have never betrayed any interest in them. You don't even remember their names."

Edward could only smile. If she decided to take them away, the man would not realize their disappearance until a good month after their abduction.

Sir Robert tried to look over his shoulder to catch his eye. "Well, boy, you heard her. Release me."

It was over. Beatrice looked at Edward and nodded slowly. He took the blade away from Sir Robert's throat and took a step back, keeping his dagger up and pointed toward him. It was clear he didn't trust him in the least. She held her breath. What now?

Sir Robert stayed still for a moment, then winced and rubbed his arm. "So you want him, do you?" he asked her in a bark. "Well, I'm afraid I can't allow it."

Taking them both by surprise, he lunged forward and grabbed his sword, turning in a great sweeping arc as he did so, aiming at Edward's throat. With the length of the blade he would be able to slice it open whilst being out of range from the much shorter dagger.

In the blink of an eye, before she knew what she was doing, Beatrice plunged the dagger she was still holding into Sir Robert's back, burying it to the hilt under the shoulder blade. His sword arm faltered at the last moment and, instead of cutting Edward's throat as he'd intended, he merely grazed the flesh. A few drops of blood spluttered onto Edward's tunic, falling like rubies on the ivory fabric, but he was otherwise unharmed.

Sir Robert staggered and fell to his knees. He tried to turn and look at Beatrice, but he never made it. He let go of his sword and toppled forward, the dagger still embedded in his flesh. After giving a groan, he lay utterly still.

Beatrice floundered and fell onto the bed behind her. In two quick strides Edward had joined her.

"My God, Edward, what have I done, what have I done?" she whispered in shock, looking at her hands, rubbing them frantically. There was no blood on them, but she knew they had killed a man, and the terrible notion would stay with her forever. "What have I done?"

"Listen to me, Beatrice. You saved my life, that's what you did," Edward said firmly, holding her face in his hands, forcing her to meet his eye. "He would have killed me. You saved me. He would have taken your children. You saved them. More importantly, he would have made you pay for your defiance, and you saved yourself. Look at what he did to you already." He cradled her face, brushing at the red traces with his fingers, as if to show her what kind of man her husband had been. "You had no other choice, do you hear? You did what you had to do."

He didn't speak any more but just gazed into her eyes, willing her to calm down and find a way of accepting the events.

After a while she did.

"You told me I would manage to use the knife if someone I love was threatened."

"And so you did," he agreed with a nod. "I'm proud of you. You did not hesitate."

No, thank God she had not.

She followed the red welt on Edward's throat with a trembling finger. Oh, how close she had come to losing him! Another heartbeat, a moment's hesitation, and Edward would be lying in a pool of blood right now, not

Sir Robert. As horrified as she was at having killed someone, she knew she could not regret her gesture. If one of the two men had to die, there was no doubt in her mind which one it should be.

"No, no, no," she said in anguish. "Edward!"

"I'm here, I'm not dead, it's all over," he soothed, engulfing her into his arms. "You saved me, remember? You saved me."

They stayed in each other's arms for a long moment until Beatrice drew away from the embrace, eyes blazing.

"Don't ever leave me now, do you hear? Don't you dare tell me you are not worthy of me, that you have nothing to offer me! Don't you dare call me 'my lady' ever again, do you hear?" she almost screamed, pummeling at his chest. "Don't you dare!"

"No, I wouldn't dare," Edward murmured in her hair, smiling. "I'm yours to command, my Beatrice. Always."

Chapter 15

"I'm sorry to announce that Sir Robert has succumbed to a stroke whilst attempting to bed his wife with what I can only qualify as regrettable force," Sir William declared to the people assembled in the hall.

All around them they heard a chorus of gasps, but the embarrassing nature of the claim, added to the dislike most people obviously felt for the man, prevented any questions from being asked. Besides, everyone had seen the way he had dragged Beatrice to the bedchamber with the obvious intention of bedding her.

Of *raping* her, he should say.

Edward could not help a surge of hatred from bursting through him. None of these people had thought to come to her aid even though they had seen what was happening. Miserable gutless cowards, the lot of them! When Sir William had come to find him at the stables and handed him his sword with the tacit agreement to use it as he saw fit, he had barely restrained the urge to slice his way through the throng of onlookers and make them pay for their cowardice. Then he had decided it would be preferable if he stole up to the chamber without being seen.

And a good thing he had. Because now they were able to claim Sir Robert's death had been natural.

"I will make all the necessary arrangements for the funeral," Sir William added, looking every inch the man in control. "The sooner it can be arranged, the better."

This time a murmur of agreement followed the declaration. His standing as a relative, albeit distant, placed him in a prime position to deal with the situation, and no one asked for the unenviable task of disposing of a man's body.

Once everyone had dispersed, Edward walked toward his master. "I don't know how to thank you for what you did, my lord."

Thanks to him, he had not only been able to reach Beatrice in time, but no one would know what had really happened in that bedchamber. Sir William had brought a healer from the village and paid her a handsome sum to keep silent about the real cause of death. The woman, a kindhearted soul who had seen the treatment Sir Robert had inflicted on his wife throughout the years, had been all too happy to go along with the pretense. The body was now wrapped in linens, and with four people swearing his heart had given just out, no one would question the manner of Sir Robert's death.

Beatrice was free—and safe from retribution. She would not have to face questions and comments about what she had done.

Sir William shook his head. "You can thank me by promising you will be the man her ladyship hopes you are. She deserves some happiness." Edward could only agree with that. "I will take issue with you if I ever see her unhappy on account of something you've done."

"If it comes to that, I swear I will hold out my arm myself and ask you to cut off my hand for me."

There was a pause while his master considered his words.

"Go to her, then. I think you have both waited long

enough."

****

The door of her bedchamber opened without a creak.

"How dare you present yourself in front of me after what you did?" Beatrice cried out, rounding up to face Lady Margaret, the only person who might come to her chamber at this late hour. After going to Sir Robert behind her back, the lady now had the gall to come to her—and without knocking!

"Forgive me, but I thought you'd be pleased to see me," a deep voice answered.

"Oh, Edward! At last!" She ran into his arms. "I've missed you so!"

After a month in his company day and night, she had found it excruciating to be so long without him. He'd spent the day with Sir William, as was expected of him, overseeing Sir Robert's funeral. For their plan to work, it was vital to maintain the appearance that they were nothing to each other. But never had the pretense weighed on her more, and never had she needed to be with him more! Dozens of times during the day she had almost rushed out of the room in search of comfort…before urging herself to patience.

Now was not the time to put a foot wrong. And so she had remained in her room, biding her time, recovering from the day's ordeal. She was finally free, but her freedom had come at a price. She'd had to kill a man. That the man in question had been a monster did not make it much easier for her to accept.

Early in the afternoon, she had made an appearance in the great hall, on Sir William's arm, to ensure everyone saw her disheveled state and the bruises on her jaw. It was the best way to make people accept their version of events—namely that her husband had succumbed to an excess of passion in her arms. After that, no one had blamed her for retreating to her bedchamber.

But now, finally, Edward had come to her, and everything else vanished from her mind.

"I want you. I need you. Make love to me," she panted, grinding herself against him. Oh, he was already hard, so hard the woman in her melted.

His face was a picture of pained hunger. Nevertheless, he did not move, did not sweep her into his arms. Instead, he brushed her jaw, where he would see the bruises Sir Robert had inflicted on her, and then her cut bottom lip. She shivered under the caress. "You've been hurt, my love. I don't think—"

"No! No more excuses. We've waited long enough. I'm serious, Edward. I can't wait another moment. Bar the door." To her relief, he did as he was asked. When he faced her again, she understood she had won. There would be no more delays. He looked like a man on the edge of surrender. In one flamboyant move, she sent her shift to the floor. She was past shame, past everything. Her whole body was throbbing with need. "So you think I'm beautiful?"

"My God, beautiful doesn't even begin to describe it," he growled, his eyes glued to her breasts. "You're glorious."

"You want me?"

"More than anything I've wanted in my life."

"Then take me. Now. I'm yours. Forever."

With a roar, he swept her into his arms and carried her to the bed. Writhing under him, she spread her legs wide, sighing in relief when his weight settled over her.

For a long moment they simply stared into each other's eyes. Then they spoke at the same time. "I love you."

Beatrice smiled. This time he didn't sound bitter when admitting it. "Prove it."

Edward's eyes seemed to catch fire. Then his mouth fell on her breast. "Like this?" His wicked tongue swirled around her nipple, teasing it to a hard nub.

As delicious as the caress was, she moaned and arched her back, demanding more. "No, not like this."

His hand, warm and strong, cupped her sex. She moaned when he slipped a finger inside her. She was so ready it almost caused her to erupt. But it was not enough, not what she needed right now. "Like this?" the wretched man asked, his mouth still at her breast. What was he doing, teasing her so, when she was on the verge of desperation?

"No! Edward, please, I'm begging you!"

The words seemed to act like a whip to a stallion's rump. He tore at his hose, and in one powerful thrust he was inside her. "Like this?"

"Ah! Yes!" Beatrice bit the back of her hand, but it wasn't enough to muffle her cries of ecstasy. Nothing had ever felt so good. Finally the man she loved was where he belonged. Inside her, making her complete.

"Forgive me, I'm being a boor. I should have undressed and seen to your pleasure first," Edward told her between gritted teeth, retreating and thrusting inside of her anew.

"You are seeing to it now," she replied in a gasp. This was perfect. How could he not see it? "And we have a lifetime for you to see to my pleasure, and me to yours."

A lifetime. Yes.

It didn't take Edward long to realize that this lovemaking would be over sooner than he wanted. He was too far gone already, as was Beatrice. He surged inside of her, knowing he would not last much longer. His whole body was about to burst into flames. It was just like their first time all over again, when he had been floored by a release so acute he had not known whether it was pleasure or pain of the most refined kind. Jesus, but he was a grown man now! He should have more control than that!

Just as he was thinking he would have to make it up to her afterward, he felt her flesh tighten around his shaft, clenching him like a fist.

"Yes, Edward, ah…"

His name in her mouth was enough to push him over the edge. Watching her neck arch in surrender, he emptied himself inside her with a roar and fell into her arms, panting with an excess of sensation.

They stayed thus entwined for a while before Beatrice placed her hand on his abdomen. Desire started to flow back into his veins, slow as a trickle at first, then with the strength of a torrent. Despite the intensity of their lovemaking, he hadn't had anywhere near enough of her. After years of frustrated desire, he needed more. But how could he tell her as much without appearing like the most selfish rogue? He'd just rutted on top of her, without taking the time to undress or build her need first…

"Edward?" she asked, pressing herself against him.

"Mm?"

"Could you take your clothes off now?"

He stilled, doing his best to ignore the stirring in his

groin. If he did as she wanted, he would not be accountable for his actions. "Why do you want me to remove my clothes?"

Forget trying to master his heated blood! Her answer sent him fully hard in an instant. "Because I want you again."

Dear God. This woman would be the death of him. "I'm not sure we—"

"I am. Start undressing or I will do it for you."

Edward gave an inward smile. Just like the first time, it seemed he would not be allowed to let his scruples stand in the way of his lady's desire. Fine by him.

The clothes were ripped from his body as fast as if they were burning his flesh.

Once Edward was naked in front of her, all lean muscles and golden skin, Beatrice forgot to breathe. He was utterly magnificent, and desire exploded in her body when she saw how hard he was for her.

She brought her hand to his chest, unable to resist touching the smooth skin, and moaned. "So soft..."

A growl escaped Edward's lips. "I think you'll find some parts of me are anything but soft right now." Then he frowned. "What's this?" He lifted her hand up for inspection, and she saw the unmistakable trace of her teeth where she had bitten herself.

She gave a breathless laugh. "I'm afraid you made me lose my mind like never before."

"As I feared I was behaving like a thoughtless brute, I am glad to hear you liked what I did. But please, my love, no more injuring yourself." He kissed the angry red marks gently, lingering over the gesture. "That must have hurt."

"Do you know... I have absolutely no idea." Beatrice smiled. In truth, she could have drawn blood and not felt a thing. Once Edward had taken his rightful place between her legs, she had been oblivious to anything that wasn't him or the pleasure he was wrenching from her.

The need for more swept through her, erasing everything else.

She stole a glance at Edward and knew he was thinking exactly the same thing. It would be a while before they had sated their hunger for each other.

"Don't look at me like this, Beatrice," he warned with a dark look.

"Why not?" she challenged. "You once told me you could not lie next to me naked and not want to have me."

"Yes, I do remember," he answered, wrapping an arm around her waist and drawing her closer. The feel of his naked skin against hers was enough to make her close her eyes.

"So what are you waiting for? If you have sated your hunger for me, I certainly haven't sated mine for you."

A heartbeat later, he had rolled on top of her. "You might regret saying that."

"I doubt it. But I could always beg for mercy, I suppose." She smiled as he entered her with a long, luscious thrust that made her whimper out loud.

"Is that you begging for mercy?" Edward asked in a seductive purr. "I cannot tell."

"No, it most definitely isn't." Beatrice gasped when he nipped at her throat. "It's me begging for more."

"My love, you don't need to beg." Edward brought his shoulder next to her mouth. "This time bite me instead of yourself, if you need to. Or better still, let me hear the full glory of your pleasure," he murmured in her ear, easing out of her flesh before plunging back in again.

A moment later, Beatrice did just that.

Epilogue

"Three girls." Beatrice sighed, bouncing her blue-eyed daughter on her knee. "Girls are all I seem to be able to make."

Edward laughed. "Yes, and you make them remarkably well, my love. Just look at her! I've never seen a more beautiful child." He smoothed his daughter's hair tenderly.

"Yes, she is a beauty." Beatrice beamed. "She looks just like you, so I suppose it is little wonder. But do you never wish for a boy?"

He gave her a side smile that dissolved something inside of her. "I could easily be persuaded to get you into bed and try for another child, if that's what you mean." He burned her with his gaze. "Is that what you want, vixen? You could have just said. I'm always available for you." He nuzzled at her neck. "How many times have I told you? You will never need to beg for attention."

"Edward! Be serious for a moment," she chided, shivering at the sensation of his lips against her skin.

"But I am serious."

"So you don't wish to have a son?" she repeated.

He shook his head. "Why would I? Would it make me happier than I am now, more fulfilled? No. I'm happy with my three girls." The way he spoke of Alys and Bridget as if they were his brought a lump to Beatrice's throat. "My namesake King Edward had three daughters by his wife before his son was born, and now he has two. What is good for the king of England is good enough for me."

"Mm. He is said to be very much in love with his wife."

"Yes. And she is an acclaimed beauty by all accounts. I guess we do have a lot in common, besides sharing a name."

Beatrice leaned against Edward and rested her head on his chest. "What did I do to deserve a man like you?" she asked with a sigh of contentment. Her life was everything she could have wished it to be.

Sir William had proved to be as good a friend as she had hoped and not turned his back on them.

After overseeing the funeral of his distant cousin, he had welcomed Lady Devance and her two orphaned girls under his roof, where she had quickly become friends with his wife, Lady Margery. Shortly after her arrival in their castle, she had fallen for Sir William's handsome squire Edward, and despite their difference in status, she had married him as soon as her mourning period was over, raising a few eyebrows and many comments, comments she had ignored with superb indifference.

Eight months after the wedding, their daughter was born, officially premature like her stepsister Bridget.

Beatrice looked at the silver ring on her finger and smiled. Both her predictions had come true. She was married to Edward and she had borne him a child. Others would come—she wanted a big family with him. She had never looked back, but she knew her husband was still prey to doubt from time to time. Like now.

His handsome face was clouded with concern.

"Oh, Edward, please, there is nothing to regret. You

need to believe me. I cannot spend the rest of my life trying to convince you that I made the right choice."

"You left the world you belonged to because of me."

"I would argue that it was *thanks to you*. And since I married you, I have found a world I actually want to be part of. I'm happy here, and our children are as well."

He paused and planted a dark stare into her eyes. Beatrice knew what he would tell her next. "You killed a man for me. The thought still plagues you."

"Yes. God knows I wish I hadn't been forced to do such a thing, but that man would have taken you away from me. He would have killed you," she whispered. "I cannot regret what I did, for I would have died without you."

The certainty in her tone was final. His brow cleared.

"Beatrice, do you know how much I love you?"

"I do." She smiled. "That is why I know I am right where I belong. In your arms."

A word about the author...

I am passionate about history and romance, which seemed to be the perfect combination to start writing my own stories. Being a stay-at-home mum gave me the incentive to start doing so in earnest.

As far back as I remember I have always loved reading and writing. I fell in love with the Middle Ages when, aged about nine, during a history lesson we were taught about the Hundred Years War. Imagining a beautiful lady atop the castle battlements with her veils fluttering in the breeze, staring into distance at her lord riding away to battle struck my imagination once and for all. I had fallen in love!

As a French native married to a Welsh man I am knowledgeable and passionate about both our country histories and keen to feature them in my stories.

virginiemarconato.com

Thank you for purchasing
this publication of The Wild Rose Press, Inc.

For questions or more information
contact us at
info@thewildrosepress.com.

The Wild Rose Press, Inc.